Love
Unexpected

Books by Jody Hedlund

The Preacher's Bride
The Doctor's Lady
Unending Devotion
A Noble Groom
Rebellious Heart
Captured by Love

BEACONS OF HOPE

Out of the Storm: An ebook novella
Love Unexpected

BEACONS OF HOPE ◦❊◦ BOOK ONE

Love Unexpected

JODY HEDLUND

BETHANYHOUSE
a division of Baker Publishing Group
Minneapolis, Minnesota

Published by Bethany House Publishers
11400 Hampshire Avenue South
Bloomington, Minnesota 55438
www.bethanyhouse.com

Bethany House Publishers is a division of
Baker Publishing Group, Grand Rapids, Michigan

Printed in the United States of America

Library of Congress Cataloging-in-Publication Data
Hedlund, Jody.
    Love unexpected / Hedlund, Jody.
        pages ; cm. — (Beacons of hope ; Book 1)
    Summary: "Shipwrecked and stranded at Presque Isle port, Emma Chambers is in need of a home. Could the widowed Great Lakes lighthouse keeper and his young son be an answer to her prayer?"— Provided by publisher.
    ISBN 978-0-7642-1237-6 (softcover)
    1. Young women—Fiction. 2. Widowers—Fiction. 3. Man-woman relationships—Fiction. 4. Presque Isle County (Mich.)—History—19th century—Fiction. I. Title.
PS3608.E333L69 2014
813'.6—dc23   2014018225

Scripture quotations are from the King James Version of the Bible.

This is a work of historical reconstruction; the appearances of certain historical figures are therefore inevitable. All other characters, however, are products of the author's imagination, and any resemblance to actual persons, living or dead, is coincidental.

Cover design by Jennifer Parker
Cover photography by Mike Habermann Photography, LLC

14 15 16 17 18 19 20   7 6 5 4 3 2 1

For my two sons

I thank God for the godly young men
you're becoming.
He who began a good work in you
will bring it to completion.

Chapter 1

The blast of a gunshot awoke Emma Chambers. But it was the whiz of a musket ball over her head and its ping against a metal beam that brought her out of her sweet dreams.

Her back stiffened against the barrel of salted whitefish that had served as her headrest on the cargo deck of a steamboat.

"Don't move!" came the tight voice of her brother Ryan next to her.

She blinked the sleep from her eyes. In the faint light of dawn she couldn't make out anything but the outlines of the barrels that surrounded her and the unending darkness of Lake Huron beyond.

"Pirates," Ryan whispered. "The steamer's being attacked by pirates."

She shuddered in spite of Ryan's instructions not to move. He placed a steadying hand on her arm.

The normal whirring of the paddle wheel and the hissing of the boiler were silent, as if they were holding their breath with her. The damp chill of the lake permeated the air and slithered under the scratchy wool blanket that covered her outstretched legs. The chill rippled against her skirt and wound its way under her shirtsleeves, making her shiver.

Shouts echoed on the deck above them, followed by the stomping of footsteps.

"You've got to hide." Crouching, Ryan peered over the top of the barrel in front of them at the hulking shadows of the pirates moving about on the cargo deck.

"And you." She crawled to her knees beside him. "You need to hide too."

He shook his head. "I'll be fine, Emma. I'm just another man among many. But you . . ." He brushed a hand over her hair, smoothing down the flyaway wisps that had escaped the plait she'd wound before dozing. "You're the only woman aboard. I don't want to take any chances that they'll see you and decide to steal you, along with everything else."

"They won't want to steal me," she said.

She wasn't ugly or anything like that, but neither did she turn the heads of many men. In fact, at twenty-two she'd yet to garner an offer of marriage. And she'd certainly been surrounded by enough men over the years to gain a proposal if she was going to get one. In short, she wasn't anything special to look at, she didn't have any outstanding talents to speak of, and she certainly wasn't made of money.

"Over there." Ryan nodded to a cubicle next to the boiler room. "Crawl over there and hide in that closet."

She hesitated. She'd always been the one protecting Ryan, watching over him all these years, putting his needs before hers and making sure he was safe.

"Come with me," she insisted. "I won't leave you here by yourself."

Another gunshot echoed as loud as a cannon blast. In the calmness of the summer morning, in the vast openness of the lake and under the wide expanse of sky, everything was noisier—the shouts, the stomping, and the scuffling overhead.

With the recent rumors of pirates roaming Lake Huron, *Lady Mist* had left Mackinac Island armed and her deckhands prepared to fend off any attacks. Even so, there was no telling what might happen.

More footsteps sounded on the metal steps that led down to the main deck that contained the cargo, the steam engine, and the wood-fired boiler that powered the engine. The cramped deck was also the place for carrying poor passengers like her and Ryan, who couldn't afford to pay for a cabin or private berth.

Ryan's fingers bit into her arm as he propelled her forward, steering clear of the pirates who'd already descended. "Go, Emma! There's only room for one of us in the closet. Besides, they won't do anything to me. I'm just another passenger."

She scrambled next to him among the barrels, her skirt tangling in her legs. She knew as well as Ryan that the pirates wanted the barrels of fish and any other valuable cargo the steamer was taking to Detroit, and when the thieves started carting off the goods, she'd be better off hidden.

"Hurry," Ryan urged, opening the closet door, bringing with it the waft of coal oil. The boxlike closet was filled with greasy tools and an assortment of spare belts and screws and gears intended to keep the engine in working condition.

She climbed in and bumped her head against a long-handled wrench hanging from a hook in the wall. She could hardly manage to turn around in the cramped space.

Ryan started to close the door.

"Be careful," she called after him, wedging her foot against the door to keep it from closing all the way.

"I'll be fine," he said through the crack, "so long as I know you're safe."

His shadow fell away and he was gone.

She slid the door open a sliver wider and peered after him. Part of her wanted to grab him and force him to hide next to her as they had so many times in the past when they'd faced other dangers together. She wanted to hold his hand and keep him from any harm. But another part told her that he was a full-grown man now and didn't need her help anymore, that she was in fact slowing him down and keeping him from doing the things he really wanted to do in life.

The truth was, now that Dad was dead, Ryan would be better off without her.

The shouts in the cargo hold grew louder, and she sank back on her heels, resting against a large wooden tool chest, trying to calm her breathing. The rolling and scraping of the barrels told her the pirates were indeed stealing the fish—the same fish that honest men had labored to catch, men like Ryan and, at one time, her dad. Fish she'd spent her days drying and salting alongside a few other women in the fisheries on Mackinac Island.

She ought to be outraged by the lawlessness, by the bandits swooping in on the steamer and taking for free what others had worked so hard to produce. But she could only release a pent-up sigh and rub her dry, cracked hands across her eyes. She'd seen altogether too much stealing in her young life, and now she couldn't muster surprise or even disgust for it. She simply wanted to survive. And to make sure Ryan did too.

"Found another passenger, boss," shouted a pirate near the closet door.

Emma peeked out to see a pistol pointed at Ryan's head. Her throat constricted, capturing a scream deep in her lungs.

"Empty his pockets," ordered a pirate who was limping as he rolled a barrel toward the bow and the landing stage.

Emma fought the urge to swing open the closet door and jump onto Ryan's attacker. She would only get herself hurt or Ryan shot if she attempted something so foolish. Even so, in the darkness of the closet she swept her hand along the floor, searching for a makeshift weapon, a hammer, anything she could use to save Ryan.

Her fingers grasped something solid and cold and cylindrical like a lead pipe. But before she could pick it up, Ryan had deposited the last of their money into the outstretched hand of his attacker. The man shoved Ryan back against the boiler room wall and then stashed the stolen coins into his pocket.

As the pirate strode away, Ryan remained unmoving against the wall. From the stiffness of his outline, Emma could tell he wanted to spring after the pirate and punch him. But he held himself back, just as she had. Like her, he'd witnessed enough injustice over the years to know when to stay silent and when to fight. And now wasn't the time to fight. From the sound of the footfalls and voices, they were outnumbered.

For interminable minutes she sat waiting, just as Ryan stood outside the closet, flattening himself against the wall, doing his best to remain invisible. The only motion was the slight pitching and swaying of the *Lady Mist*, the only sound the scraping of her gunwale against the pirate boat.

Maybe they should have stayed on Mackinac. Yes, the winters were unbearably long. Yes, they were isolated from the rest of the world. And yes, the fishing industry was in decline and there was the chance they'd lose their jobs soon anyway. But it had been safe, at least mostly so. They'd lived on the remote northern island nine months—the longest place they'd stayed since emigrating from Ireland a decade ago. Maybe the tiny dormer rooms they'd rented above Beaver Skin Tavern hadn't been home, but they'd come close.

She leaned her head back and closed her eyes, trying to ward off the growing discontent that came over her all too often lately. She was past ready to settle down, get married, and have children. There were even times when the longing for a stable life and family of her own was so keen that it was almost unbearable.

If only Ryan hadn't wanted to uproot their lives again . . .

Ryan finally slid to the door and peeked inside. "Em? You okay?"

"I'm fine." She gave him the usual answer, the safe one, the words that didn't probe too deeply into the longings of her heart. "Is it all right to come out?"

The shouts had long faded, and an eerie quiet had fallen over the steamer.

"I'll go up and check," he said. "Promise you'll stay here?"

"As long as you're back in a few minutes."

He nodded and bolted across the empty deck.

Most of the barrels were gone, revealing a deck littered with broken staves, sawdust, and rat droppings. She could only pray the pirates would let them go without harm. She'd heard stories where bandits boarded a steamer, stole the goods, and then dumped any witnesses overboard.

The hiss and whir of a boiler and engine clamored to life in the stillness, except it wasn't coming from their steamboat. Instead, it came from the direction of the pirate's boat. A shout was followed by the shattering of glass on the deck not far from her closet.

She pressed against the tool chest and held herself motionless until the slapping water of the paddle wheel drifted off, signaling the danger was finally moving away.

She released a deep breath and sat up. She'd survived another mishap. Maybe she and Ryan were penniless as a result, but at least neither of them had been hurt. Hopefully within a day or two they'd be in Detroit and be able to locate work and a new place to live.

And maybe at last she'd have a home again, a home like the one they'd had in Ireland before the horrible days of famine and starvation had come upon them, a home like the one Mam had made for them before she'd wasted away.

Was it too much to hope that perhaps she'd meet a man who would want to marry her? She wasn't an old maid yet. But she wasn't getting any younger either. With each passing year, her chances of getting married were growing slimmer.

The acridness of smoke tingled Emma's nostrils, overpowering the usual heavy stench of fish. She pushed open the closet door and recoiled.

Bright flames lurched high in the air near the metal staircase that led to the upper decks. Shards of broken glass spilled across the floor, along with the oil and base of a kerosene lamp that had fallen. More likely the pirates had tossed it onto the steamer as they'd chugged away.

For a long moment Emma could only stare at the flames lapping at the deck and beginning to creep along the floor toward the rails. They lit up the starboard, giving her a clear view of the emptiness and the murky water of Lake Huron.

If she didn't put out the fire, it would consume the ship, and she'd soon find herself in that cold abyss. With a start, she grabbed the blanket she'd discarded earlier. She sprinted to the railing, crouched low, and dipped the length into the lake. Dragging the dripping mass of wool, she rushed to the fire and whipped at it with the wet blanket.

Smoke spewed into her face and stung her eyes, and the heat forced her back several steps. She tossed the blanket on the flames again, but to her dismay the fire leaped into the air and began grazing the planks of the ceiling.

How could she reach that high with the blanket? She needed help and fast. "Fire!" she shouted. Once again the heat made her jump back. "There's a fire on the main deck!"

She wasn't sure if her shouts had alerted the men on the deck above or if they finally saw the rising smoke, but within seconds several pairs of boots descended on the stairway. Then a wall of fire stopped them halfway down.

"Emma?" Ryan cried out.

Through the orange and yellow flames she caught sight of his face. "I'm here!" She waved her arms. "Tell everyone to get water and blankets. It's spreading fast."

"You need to come up here!" He reached out a hand but then just as quickly jerked it away from the blasting heat.

The fire was sneaking closer to her, and even though she wanted to jump through the wall of heat to Ryan, to the safety he would provide, she had no choice but to move back.

The deckhands and Ryan worked to contain the fire, throwing down buckets of water and snuffing it out with anything they could lay their hands on. From her side of the wall of flames, Emma fought against it with her blanket, making more trips to the side of the steamer to soak the cloth.

But as they worked, the fire only spread with a growing appetite. It continued to push her toward the stern until she could barely see Ryan, who was still fighting the fire from his spot on the stairway.

Flames shot upward from the leeward side, casting bright flickers across the water. Emma coughed and pressed her face into the singed blanket. It was hot, but at least she didn't have to breathe the smoke and fumes. She leaned against the rail, her body weak, legs trembling. She clung to the grain sack containing all the possessions they owned, which wasn't much.

When she dared to peek again at the main deck through her watering eyes, a sickening weight settled in the bottom of her stomach. They were fighting a losing battle.

The steamer was burning up, and there was nothing they could do about it. How would she and Ryan survive? They *had* to survive. They hadn't come this far and suffered as much as they had, only to die in a steamboat fire.

She glanced behind her at the rolling water of the lake. Even though Dad had taught her and Ryan to swim when they'd been hardly bigger than minnows, she didn't relish the thought of trying to stay afloat. For even in early June, the lake was still frigid. If only they were closer to shore . . .

She peered into the distance and could make out the dark shadows of the eastern Michigan shoreline. A thin beacon of light flashed to the north, one of the strategically placed lighthouses along the coast that warned passing ships of the countless shoals that had been the demise of many vessels.

Were they close enough to swim to shore? If she jumped into the waves, would she have the strength to make it all the way across to land? But if she didn't jump . . .

She spun around to the fire that was pressing nearer. It wouldn't be long before she'd have no choice but to plunge into the water. Either that or be roasted alive by the advancing fire.

From the deck above, she heard Ryan's voice. "Emma?"

She leaned over the rail and craned her neck to search for him. He was dangling from the stern. "Ryan?" Her shoulders sagged with relief—relief that he was still safe and that perhaps he could help her figure out what to do next. "What should I do?"

His face was smeared with soot, making his eyes and the worry in them stand out like twin moons. "The fire has spread to this deck, and it won't be long before the floor caves in. The lifeboat's already on fire."

Emma glanced at the burning ceiling. The fire had already eaten through the boards in many places. She clung to the railing, leaning as far away as possible from the inferno.

"We need to get off this hulk," Ryan shouted, "before the pressure of the ripping beams drags her down and pulls us with her."

He tossed a barrel overboard. It hit the water near the rudder with a splash and disappeared underwater for a moment before bobbing back to the surface.

"I'll go first," he called as he climbed over the rail, "and then I'll be there to help you."

Before she could protest, he launched himself off the steamer. He flailed through the air and hit the water feetfirst.

She gathered her skirt into her fists, hoisted it up, and climbed onto the rail. "Ryan!" she cried, the heat of the fire beginning to burn her back.

A head broke through the water's surface—her brother. Her heart started beating again.

Coughing out a mouthful of lake water, Ryan shook his wet hair out of his eyes, caught sight of the barrel he'd tossed in, and swam toward it.

Once he'd grabbed the barrel, he motioned to her, staring behind her at the fingers of flames that reached out to grasp her. "Throw in the bag first!"

Perched atop the rail, she had a better view of the shore. In the distance she thought she saw the flicker of a lantern. But she couldn't put off the inevitable any longer. She tossed the grain sack toward him, and it landed in the water with a splash.

"Now jump!" he called, lunging for the bag.

"Heaven have mercy," she whispered through trembling lips. She tried not to think about what was going to happen next. Then she jumped.

The wind had only an instant to slap her before the waves sprayed and reached out to swallow her. The icy wetness surrounded her, the shock of the cold on her skin paralyzing her. Instantly she began to sink, her nose filling with water, her arms and legs fighting back the dark surge.

Then suddenly Ryan was grasping her and dragging her to the surface. Her face rose above the waves, and she spluttered, her teeth already chattering and her body shaking violently from the cold.

The lake had only been open for about a month, since May when the winter ice had thawed.

"Here," Ryan shouted, clinging to the barrel with one hand and holding her with the other. "Wrap your arm around the barrel."

Her hands were numb, and she struggled to get her fingers to bend. But somehow she managed to drape an arm across the staves.

"Hang on," Ryan said from behind her. He kicked his legs as he pushed the barrel away from the burning steamer.

Over the crashing of the waves, she heard the Bradley whistle, the seven short blasts and one long one that signaled *abandon ship*. The whistle was accompanied by the shouts and splashes of the deckhands jumping from the heat-blistered steamer. Some had clothing ablaze and screamed as they plunged into the lake.

She had the sudden urge to pray, to petition God for some kind of help, to at least spare the men their lives. But she hesitated. She hadn't done much praying over the years. She'd prayed herself hoarse for Mam but to no avail. After she lost Mam, she'd been too busy trying to survive with Ryan and Dad, running and hiding and facing the long days of starvation. And when they'd finally reached America, she wasn't sure she remembered how to pray anymore.

A stinging wave hit Emma's face, filling her mouth with lake water. She coughed and gasped for air while tightening her hold on the barrel.

"We've got to move farther from the boat," Ryan yelled, kicking and flapping in the water, trying to propel them but making little progress against the waves.

The fire had now spread to the uppermost deck of the steamer and to the pilothouse. The smokestacks were engulfed, one of them leaning at an odd angle. Against the backdrop of the dark lake, the burning ship was like a giant torch.

Emma gritted her teeth and began pumping her legs, working with Ryan to swim away from the deadly steamer. But whenever she looked at how far they'd come, it seemed mere inches.

Then an enormous creak came from the steamer, and she and Ryan paused. Above the chattering of her teeth and wheezing of her labored breathing, the terrified cries of the other passengers and deckhands echoed in the early morning. The ship ripped into two and started to sink. The water surged over the flames, finally dousing them and leaving in its place a silent darkness. Within minutes the ship was completely gone, brought down into the freezing lake.

"We've got to keep going," Ryan said behind her. "We're both strong. We can make it if we don't give up."

She hardly had the strength to nod. The cold lake tugged and clawed at her, trying to dislodge her from the barrel. Her hair had loosened from her braid and plastered her face, and her limbs were fast becoming stiff.

"Let's head for the lighthouse," he said, pointing in the direction of the beam of light she'd noticed earlier.

They fought to paddle forward.

"Don't give up," Ryan told her whenever she stopped moving.

"I can't do this, Ryan," she finally said. Her muscles ached, and she couldn't muster the energy to cling to the barrel. Her body demanded that she let go, stop fighting, and slide down into a watery, peaceful grave.

"Just hang on!" His voice had turned urgent. "I think I see a boat."

She rested her cheek against the barrel and closed her eyes. She wasn't sure how much longer she could keep her hold.

"Hey!" Ryan shouted. "Over here!"

The waves in the growing dawn were beginning to calm down, turning gentle and enticing, making her want to sleep. If she fell asleep and slipped under the water, maybe she'd awaken to heaven in the arms of both her mam and dad. They'd finally be together again with no more pain or unhappiness or guilt. And without her, Ryan would be free to get on with his life.

"Here!" Ryan called again.

The water around her began to fade. The cold seeped away. The struggle lessened. She was going down . . .

Strong arms lifted her, heaving her out of the jaws of death, returning her to the sharpness of dawn. Though the lake clung to her and refused to let her go, the thick arms that surrounded her were stronger and more determined. She found herself hauled upward until she was free of the water, pulled over the side of a rowboat against a solid warm chest.

"There you are, lass." The man spoke gently with the hint of an Irish brogue.

With the utmost care her rescuer lowered her into the stern. His lantern cast a glow upon his face, revealing rugged features. Beneath the brim of a flat-topped cap, he peered down at her. The leathery, weather-bronzed skin crinkled at the corners of his eyes.

"You're safe now."

She could only stare up at him, her body shuddering as the cool morning air swept over her wet clothes and skin. And all she could think was that he had the kindest eyes she'd ever seen.

Chapter 2

*P*atrick Garraty hopped out of his cutter and dragged it the rest of the way to the closest dock. The calm water of the bay lapped against his knee-length rubber boots. The pink of the rising sun across the lake lit up the rocky beach of Presque Isle Harbor, as well as the docks and the Mackinaw fishing boats that were returning with far too few survivors.

Being the closest, he was the first to arrive at the disaster. He'd noticed the burning vessel from the lighthouse tower and then raced down the winding stairway into the darkness. Every wasted second could mean the difference between life and death, so he'd rowed as fast as he could toward the steamer, his arms and back aching with the exertion.

Thankfully many of the fishermen on Burnham's Landing had already been awake and were readying their gill nets and their boats when they'd seen the flames shooting up over Lake Huron. Even so, none of them had been able to reach the steamer before she'd gone under, and they were only able to save a scant number of the crew and passengers.

"I can't thank you enough for coming to our rescue," said

a young man who was standing in the cutter, shivering while wrapped in a wool blanket.

Patrick nodded and turned to the woman he'd pulled out first. She'd hardly moved since he'd deposited her in the stern. His gut cinched again, as it had every time he'd thought about what he'd learned from the young man during those minutes rowing back to shore—about the pirates who'd boarded the steamer, their stealing the barrels of fish bound for market, and their setting the boat on fire.

It had stirred memories that Patrick didn't want stirred, memories of climbing aboard steamers, of looting and destroying . . . and worse. There were some things better off left in the past where they belonged.

Patrick wound the dock line around the cutter's bow cleat and fought back the guilt he thought was long buried. "Take your wife over to Fred Burnham's cabin. She needs warming."

The young man scooped the woman into his arms and cradled her against his chest. "She's my sister."

Her teeth hadn't stopped chattering. Even though she too was enfolded in a blanket, her face was pale and her lips blue. Her eyes were glazed almost as if she didn't know where she was.

Patrick steadied the boat as the young man climbed out with his burden. The ease the young man had with the cutter and the help he'd given with the rowing told Patrick this survivor was no stranger to the Great Lakes.

The oars of a fishing boat nearby slapped the water, bringing to shore several rescued crew. He'd get a total count of the losses and then he had to head back to the lighthouse without delay. He didn't have much time left before Josiah would be awake and calling for him.

He hated leaving Josiah alone for any length of time, even when the boy was sleeping. But what choice did he have?

"The name's Ryan Chambers," said the young man. "This is my sister, Emma. Thank you for your help."

"Patrick Garraty, and you're quite welcome."

Ryan studied the rocky shore that stretched to a grassy clearing where a number of crude log huts sat, along with a fish house and a cooper's shop. Numerous new staves had been piled in front, awaiting use as fish barrels.

"Are you a fisherman?" Ryan asked, turning his attention to the reels spinning and squeaking in the breeze, and the wooden net boxes and floats that cluttered the shoreline.

"No," said Patrick.

Ryan situated the young woman in his arms more comfortably. He glanced from Patrick to his boat, then to the other men who were beginning to arrive, wearing their sou'wester hats, brown linen slops, and long boots.

"These other men are fishermen?"

"Most of them."

"Think any of them are looking for some extra help?"

"Maybe." Patrick climbed out of the water onto the dock and peered at the boats that were mooring. He counted the number of survivors: two in his boat, two in another, four deckhands in a third, none in the last one.

He guessed the steamer had been carrying at least twenty, if not thirty, people in all. Had only eight made it to safety? He tipped his cap back and stared over the brightening water. There wouldn't be any trace of which pirate gang had done the deed, but still he couldn't stop from speculating. And from clenching his teeth.

At the drooping shoulders of the young man he'd rescued, Patrick cleared his throat. "Are you looking for work?"

"Aye." Ryan's voice wavered. "The pirates cleaned my pockets and left me without a cent to my name. Now I've gotta find a way to earn enough money to pay our passage on the next steamer that comes through. And put food in our bellies until then."

"Talk to Fred Burnham." Patrick cocked his head toward the biggest of the log structures along the shore. "He'll have work. And if he doesn't, he'll point you to someone who might."

Ryan looked haggard from the recent ordeal, but he managed a smile. "Thank you again."

The young woman lifted her head from her brother's shoulder. Though her eyes were still dazed, they filled with gratefulness. She didn't say the words, but from the intensity in her brown eyes, he knew she was thanking him too.

Patrick nodded.

She let her head sag against Ryan's chest. Wet strands of her long hair stuck to her cheek and the exposed length of her neck—hair that was likely a shade of blond when dry. Her wet garments twisted awkwardly around her legs. She seemed fragile.

Not many women came to this remote northeastern port. It was a newer fishing village, established a few years before he'd arrived. Beyond the shore to the west lay mostly unsettled wilderness, unsuited to all but the heartiest of men. In fact, except for the two Burnham women, there weren't any other females in the area. At least not anymore, not since his wife had finally succumbed to her injuries and died yesterday morning.

With a sigh, he started slowly up the dock toward shore as weariness slipped once again into his body. He hadn't slept more than a few minutes here and there since Delia had fallen. He knew he couldn't go on this way; he couldn't continue tending the light all night and watching Josiah all day, not without getting some sleep.

The weight of all that had happened over the past week threatened to crush him. His situation had become desperate. He'd either have to give up his job as keeper of Presque Isle Light or he'd have to give up Josiah. He couldn't manage both, not without Delia's help.

The thought of relinquishing either one stabbed his heart so painfully it took his breath away. Though he'd considered sending Josiah to live with his relatives down in Saginaw, his entire being resisted. His sorry excuse for a family was no place for a two-year-old boy.

And yet how could he quit his job? The position had been a godsend, and he doubted anyone else would hire him, not after they learned the truth about his past.

The calls of the fishermen closed about him. The familiar lake breeze brushed against his unshaven cheeks, soothing him. For the briefest of moments, he shut his eyes and turned his face heavenward.

All he could do was pray. Prayer was his lifeline, and the only thing keeping him sane.

Emma wiggled the last of the fresh broomcorn through the cords she'd loosened, then retrieved the pliers discarded in the long grass. With the metal prongs she pinched the cords closed and tightened them around the broomcorn, finishing the repairs.

She held the broom out in front of her and examined the new fullness compared to the meager broken and dirty bristles she'd used when she swept the floor earlier. "Aye," she said to herself. "Much better."

She leaned against the rough logs of Burnham's cabin and looked out over the waterfront. Several long docks extended into the U-shaped harbor. The shoreline was covered with rocks of all shapes, with sea grass, poison ivy, and brush growing in the sand between the rocks. The shore abutted a vast forest of tall pine, spruce, and cedar. Only a small area had been cleared of the trees.

At midmorning the area dubbed Burnham's Landing was quiet, the fishermen having all departed long ago. Except for the distant chopping of an ax and the occasional cry of a gull, the fishing village was peaceful. The waves in the harbor were gentle, and the sun shone down on the water with a blinding brilliance.

Emma didn't see any of the other survivors, but she guessed they were sleeping in the shanties, most likely invited in by the fishermen. It was hard to believe that less than six hours ago she'd been close to dying, that she'd jumped from a blazing steamer and had paddled in the cold lake in a desperate effort to save her and Ryan's lives.

She hadn't stopped shivering for hours. In fact, it had really only been when she'd sat down in the sunshine outside the Burnham cabin that her flesh had finally thawed. And now she was loath to get up and do anything else except soak in the sun's rays. With a sigh, she half closed her eyes, drowsy after the horrors of the night.

A boat rowing along the shore came steadily nearer the docks. She watched it through her drooping lashes until it drew closer. Two heads bobbed with each lap of the waves, one of them a smaller head, that of a child. The other was a man who wore a flat-topped cap on his head.

Emma's eyes flew open, and she straightened. The broad shoulders, the thick arms stuffed into a too-tight jacket, and the trim cutter belonged to the same man who'd rescued her last night. Patrick Garraty.

She didn't know where he'd gone after Ryan had taken her to Burnham's. In fact, she hadn't thought about him since, except in gratefulness that the men of Burnham's Landing had been kind enough to come to their aid.

Now that he was back, Emma couldn't tear her gaze from him. He plunged his oars into the water deeply and steadily. He didn't appear to be straining, as if he were out for a leisure ride to enjoy the new leaves and lush green vegetation of the June morning. Yet the speed with which he approached the village spoke otherwise. Soon his boat pulled alongside one of the docks. He vaulted out and secured the bowline.

Then he lifted out a young boy, who couldn't have been more than two years of age. His face was chubby with the remains of his baby fat, and a mop of reddish-orange hair poked out in all directions, half hanging over his eyes. Where was the boy's cap? Surely on such a sunny day the boy's mother wouldn't have let him out of the house without putting a cap on his wee head.

From where she sat, Emma could hear the tiny boy's steady chatter. His father didn't respond, or if he did, his answers were short. Instead, Patrick heaved at something within the cutter, slowly lifting out a crudely built wooden box. When he finally straightened with the long box braced in his arms, Emma shuddered and flattened herself against the log cabin.

He was carrying a coffin.

From the strain of his arms and the slump of his shoulders, she had no doubt there was a body inside.

Patrick started down the dock with the little boy following behind, none too steady on the wobbly platform. When the toddler reached land, he stumbled up the slope after his father, who was taking long strides in spite of the weight of his burden.

Patrick cast a glance over his shoulder at his son. "Come, Josiah," he admonished gently. "Stay close to me."

The boy's legs pumped faster in an effort to catch up with his father.

It had been too dark earlier that morning to take notice of Patrick's appearance, and she'd been too dazed. But now, in the light of day, she could see that Patrick was a handsome man. Underneath his hat, his dark brown hair was short. His face had several days' worth of whiskers, and his chiseled features were rugged and sun-bronzed.

When Patrick reached a plot dotted with headstones, only then did she notice a fresh pile of dirt with a shovel wedged in it.

Who was in the coffin?

At a rustling behind her, Emma stood.

There in the cabin doorway stood a petite woman. She was hunched over, a gray crocheted shawl draped over a black dress. She wore a tight-fitting bonnet, and her hair fell in two severe braids over her shoulders. Her face was pale and her cheeks drawn.

Emma had glimpsed the sick woman earlier that morning when she was warming herself in front of the stove. Bertha Burnham had been lying in bed under heaps of covers in the cabin's one bedroom when her mother-in-law, the widow Burnham, had delivered an onion poultice and a cup of hot broth to the sickroom.

The widow Burnham hadn't spoken much, but it had been enough for Emma to learn that Bertha wasn't only sick with influenza but was grieving the recent death of her cousin and couldn't be disturbed.

As Bertha emerged into the sunshine, Emma moved into the shadows of the cabin.

The woman barked a command to a boy standing near a wood-pile onshore. "Go tell your father it's time for Delia's funeral."

He called back, "Yes, Mam," then darted off on bare feet, heedless of the rocks and wood chips that littered the ground.

Bertha Burnham's shoulders shook with a deep cough before she lifted her head and gave Patrick a sharp look. "Snake," the woman muttered under her breath. "Too bad you didn't die instead of Delia."

Emma glanced at Patrick's shadowed face, at the sadness creasing his forehead. Had Delia been his wife?

Bertha shuffled toward the grave, as though everything within her resisted the idea of going near the coffin.

A few moments later, a man on horseback arrived. Wearing a black vest, matching overcoat, and dark felt hat, he gave Emma the impression he was a preacher. When the man pulled a Bible out of his saddlebag, her feeling was confirmed.

His long white beard and spindly white hair gave him the look of St. Nicholas, though a much leaner version. He went to the open grave, held out his arms wide, and embraced Patrick. The reverend then turned and greeted Bertha, as well as the other men and boys who'd gathered around the coffin.

"Poor wee one," Emma whispered, watching Josiah as he stood bravely next to his father, peering up at him, as if he didn't know what to make of all that had happened. He was certainly too young to realize the significance of his loss—if the person in the coffin was indeed his mammy.

Emma had been ten when her mam had died, and she'd felt the loss all the way to her soul. Mam had always been the one to keep her and Ryan and their dad from despairing too much, to remind them of God's presence, to point them back to Him whenever life became too hard.

It was almost as if when Mam died, the solid foundation of their family had been ripped away. From then on they'd had nothing but crumbling, shifting sand. Emma couldn't stop staring at Josiah with his unruly red hair. No child deserved to be without a mammy.

The reverend spoke for a short time and then read from his Bible. Emma thought about moving closer so that she could hear what he was saying. If she hadn't prayed in a long while, well, it had been even longer since she'd heard God's Word read aloud.

The funeral was over within minutes, which was a good thing, since Josiah was already fidgeting and eyeing the dirt pile. Several of the men lowered the coffin into the ground and began the task of shoveling soil over it.

Bertha made her way back to the cabin while leaning heavily on the arm of her husband. She was dabbing her eyes with a handkerchief and murmuring, "My dear cousin, my poor dear cousin." The woman disappeared inside the cabin without so much as a look in Emma's direction, which only sent another unwelcome chill over Emma.

Back at the graveyard, the reverend carried on a steady stream of conversation with Patrick. Neither seemed to pay any attention to the little boy, who had played in the dirt with fascination before turning away and following the trail of a flittering butterfly.

As Josiah wandered farther from his father and closer to the Burnham cabin, Emma waited for the boy to notice her. He froze when he was just feet away, his eyes widening at the sight of her.

"Hello, little love," she said with a smile.

Up close, she could see his face was in need of a washing. Dried jam caked the sides of his mouth, and dirt or ash or *something* smudged his cheeks.

His clothes were worse. She could hardly see the jam stains on his shirt through the coating of dirt, and the knees of his trousers had dark splotches from crawling around somewhere muddy.

"And how are you today?" she asked.

"Mommy in box," he said.

A sharp pain pierced Emma's chest. "Oh, sweet baby. I'm so sorry."

But the boy was already pointing one of his chubby fingers in the direction the butterfly had flown, around the cabin to the woodland beyond. "Buf-fly. Gone." His sad greenish-brown eyes regarded her, as if somehow she could make the butterfly appear again.

Sorrow filled her heart, sorrow for herself and sorrow for this sweet motherless boy. She wanted to capture the butterfly for him, to offer him a small measure of comfort. But there was nothing but the pliers, the broom, and the brown paper that had held the fresh broomcorn.

"How about if I make you a butterfly?" she offered, picking up the paper.

He nodded. "Make buf-fly."

She knelt in the grass and tore the brown paper. Once she'd shaped it into a square, she folded the paper in half to form a triangle, and then folded it again into a smaller triangle.

Josiah crouched next to her and bent his head close to examine her folding.

"Here's one wing," she said as she folded up the right corner of the triangle.

"Wing?"

She nodded and creased the opposite corner. "And here's the other." She lifted it, letting the paper fall open to reveal the body of the butterfly in the center. "There. It's all done."

"All done," he echoed.

She pretended to fly it by flapping the wings up and down. "See? The butterfly is ready to fly."

Josiah grinned. "Me fly it?"

"Of course, little love." She held the paper butterfly out to him, and he took it carefully between his grubby fingers.

"Fly, buf-fly," he said. He stood, raised it in the air, and swooped it up and down, watching the wings rise and fall like those of a real butterfly. His grin widened.

"Josiah" came a stern but kind voice. "What do you tell the nice lady?"

Emma startled and found herself looking up the stocky length of Patrick Garraty. He placed one of his big hands on top of Josiah's unruly hair to keep the boy from running off with his new toy.

"Thank you," Josiah said.

"You're welcome," Emma replied. She stood to her feet and brushed at the back of her skirt, which was still damp and had picked up twigs, shavings, and grass. She tucked her bare toes out of sight. Her stockings and shoes were still drying in a nearby patch of grass, along with the rest of the clothes and items from the bag they'd carried off the burning steamer.

Patrick crouched so that he was level with the boy. "No more wandering off, lad."

She noticed again his kind eyes—green and wide and framed by thick lashes.

"You must stay by my side or you'll get hurt," he said to his son.

Josiah nodded somberly, but then turned his attention back to the paper butterfly.

Patrick rose to his full height, towering over her by at least six inches. "Thank you for occupying him while I . . ." He glanced at the graveyard, at the mound of dark soil that now covered the coffin. His face creased with weariness.

"It was my pleasure. I didn't mind at all. He's adorable." She tucked a flyaway strand of hair behind her ear, realizing she hadn't plaited it since it had dried. She ducked her head, self-conscious of how she must appear to this man, her rescuer, with her hair floating about her shoulders and down her back, about as unkempt as Josiah's. "I'm sorry for your loss," she offered.

He nodded and shifted his attention to the lake, but not before she caught a glimpse of pain in the depths of his eyes.

He didn't speak for several awkward moments. She squirmed, wishing she could take back her comment. Josiah's chirping rose between them as he flapped the butterfly up and down.

Finally, Patrick cleared his throat. "It looks like you're faring better."

"Aye," she said too hurriedly, her nerves tying themselves into bundles. "I'm doing much better now that I'm mostly dry and warm."

"Good."

"And Mr. Burnham gave Ryan a job chopping wood and put him to work right away this morning." She was talking too fast, but she couldn't slow herself down. "He said with the steamers coming through and buying fuel, he always has a need for chopped wood."

She'd learned that, among other things, the Burnhams sold wood as fuel to the steamers that docked in the harbor. While some of the boats were moving to coal for fuel, many still burned wood for their steam-powered engines.

That meant steamboats had to make frequent stops—usually every couple of days—to restock on cordwood and keep their engines firing. There were small landings along the lake, like Burnham's, who turned a sizable profit selling wood to passing boats.

Even if the Burnhams paid only pennies for the backbreaking labor, it was a steady job. And they were willing to provide Ryan with a bed in one of the bunkhouse shanties that housed the fishermen.

Josiah started to move away, but Patrick's long fingers spread across the boy's head and pinned him in place. "Will widow Burnham let you stay too?" He'd lowered his voice and looked warily at the widow's half-open door.

Earlier, when Ryan had asked widow Burnham if Emma could stay with them during their time on Presque Isle, the old woman had only complained about the lack of space in their tiny cabin, that it had only one bedroom, already occupied by the sick daughter-in-law, and that she didn't know where Emma would find room to sleep.

The widow hadn't come right out and said no, but Emma could tell she wasn't wanted. Even when she'd tried to make herself useful that morning by helping with the chores, widow Burnham had largely ignored her. Emma had finally taken the broom outside to work on fixing it.

Patrick studied her, as if he'd read her thoughts and could sympathize. "If widow Burnham kicks me out," she said, "then perhaps I'll have Ryan make me a shelter of sticks and pine boughs. It's getting warmer at night now."

She was only half jesting. Maybe her camping on the beach would be the best option. A makeshift lean-to would be better than some of the places she'd had to call home these past years.

Patrick shook his head. "You'll be safer in the cabin."

"That's what Ryan said. Even though half the men here are

twice my age, he said that won't stop them from ogling a woman, since apparently there aren't many in these parts."

Once again an awkward silence descended, making her grateful for Josiah's chattering.

Patrick stepped away and tugged Josiah with him. "Well, I'd best be about my business."

She wanted to reach after the pair and express her sorrow again for their loss, but she held the words back and instead rushed to thank him. "I didn't have the chance to thank you for saving my life."

"You don't have to thank me."

"Aye. I do. I was ready to give up. I don't think I could have hung on another minute."

"You were brave to hang on as long as you did," he said. Then he tipped his hat and strode away.

Josiah stumbled along next to him. When the little boy reached up a hand, Patrick's large work-roughed fingers encompassed the boy's tenderly. This time he matched his pace to that of the boy, their hands swinging together between them.

"Aww," she whispered, her smile growing. She couldn't help feeling sorry for the woman they'd just buried and all she'd had to leave behind.

Chapter 3

"What do we have here?" The reverend smiled as he approached her.

Emma tore her attention from Patrick and his son. She grabbed the broom and inspected the wires, hoping the reverend hadn't caught her staring at the widower.

The reverend paused in the patch of yard before her and mopped his brow. "I hear you had quite the escapade." Beneath bushy white brows his eyes were full of compassion.

She stopped fiddling with the broom. "I've been through many hardships. But none quite like that."

The reverend was small in stature, shorter than her own five-foot-five. He was thin, his bony shoulders poking through the linen of his coat. Yet she could sense a strength about him that belied his size.

"I'm Reverend William Poyseor," he said, his white beard and mustache curving up with a smile. "But people call me Holy Bill."

"I'm Emma Chambers."

He assessed her in one sweeping motion, and then he looked

toward Patrick, who was disappearing inside the low doorway of the fishery with Josiah close behind.

"That, my young lady," said Holy Bill, "is the finest man in all of Michigan."

She had only interacted with Patrick Garraty briefly. After living among the fishing communities of the north these past years and mingling with plenty of men, she'd learned to judge a man's character quickly. It was easy to see that Patrick was a rare breed, similar to Ryan in his kindness and thoughtfulness.

Why then had Bertha Burnham called him a snake? In her brief interactions she hadn't sensed anything remotely snakelike about him. Perhaps the woman merely had a personal grudge.

"I just helped him bury his wife," Holy Bill said.

"I thought as much, but now to hear you say it, I'm truly sorry."

"Not as sorry as I was when I got the news she'd fallen and died."

Emma waited for him to explain more about the woman's death, but instead he turned his attention to the coastline of the harbor. Several kestrels glided above the shore, the sunlight glinting off their blue heads and red backs and tails.

He rubbed at his beard. "Since I received the news, I've been praying for Patrick nonstop that God would bring about a solution to his dilemma." The reverend turned back to her, his brows raised as if somehow she figured into his prayers. "I hear you're in a dilemma too."

"Aye. Thankfully my brother has work and a place to stay until he can earn back what we lost to the pirates." She hoped it wouldn't be too long, but realistically she knew it might take a couple of weeks.

"And what about you?" he asked. "What will you do while

your brother works? There isn't employment for a single young woman here at Burnham's Landing."

"I was hoping I could help with the drying and salting of the fish," she said, trying not to think about the seriousness of her predicament. "But widow Burnham told me the men take care of their own fish and don't need any help."

The shore crew consisted of a few older men, who were walking among the racks of drying fish that lined the beach. They were turning the fish to ensure even drying and also salting them for curing. She'd spent many days from daybreak to dusk among the drying flakes. She'd even learned to do the work of the headers and splitters, growing quite proficient in removing the fish head and guts and cutting out the backbone.

From all appearances this shore crew was keeping up with the daily catch just fine, so she doubted they would hire her for something they could do for themselves.

Holy Bill lowered his voice. "Is widow Burnham agreeable to letting you stay and help her?" His question echoed Patrick's, as if they were well acquainted with the woman's lack of hospitality.

"She's not too happy about my presence," Emma said. "Perhaps you know of someone else in the area who might have room for me."

"I'm afraid to say there isn't anywhere else for you to go, at least not anywhere near."

She swallowed the disappointment. "That's what I figured."

"However . . ." He examined her face again closely, as though trying to see into her soul. "I may have an answer to your problem, a more permanent solution, if you will."

At his statement a glimmer of hope lit inside her.

"Tell me more about yourself." Holy Bill removed his hat, and the breeze rippled the few wisps of hair left on his balding head.

She didn't know exactly where to begin, so she started with Mam's death from starvation. Her dad had never been the same once Mam had died. He'd committed atrocities Emma had tried to forget. He'd done whatever he could, no matter how grisly, to keep her and Ryan from starving to death.

After two years of sleeping on the sides of roads, in abandoned barns, and in workhouses, their dad had found a way for them to emigrate to America. But the guilt of his crimes had taken their toll. He was a broken man and silenced his inner demons the only way he knew how—through drinking. Every night after returning from the day of fishing, he'd drink himself into a stupor, only to wake up and do it all over again.

Until he got himself fired for missing too many days of work, and then they had to move on to another fishing job somewhere else and start over. Finally, after years of suffering, he'd died that winter on Mackinac Island.

Holy Bill's eyes radiated sadness at her tale. "Sounds like it's time for you to settle down and make a real home for yourself."

She nodded, a lump forming in her throat. Holy Bill didn't know just how true his words were. She wanted a home again more than anything.

"I saw how kindly you treated Josiah," he said. "Do you like children?"

"I haven't been around many children. Josiah is adorable, though."

"Appears that you know a fair amount about fishing. What about lighthouses? Know anything about them?"

"Nay," she admitted, "but I'm a quick learner. And I can be handy with tools when I need to be."

Holy Bill paused and stroked his beard. "Patrick Garraty

has a rough past. When I met him, he was a broken man—in more ways than one."

Josiah bounded out of the fishery, his red hair signaling a small beacon of happiness in the somberness of the day. He still flew his origami butterfly, weaving it back and forth more dramatically now. His loud flying noises made Emma smile.

"Let the past stay in the past," the reverend said. "All you need to know is that Patrick Garraty is a good man. You have my word on that."

At the sight of her still in front of the Burnham cabin, Josiah broke into a smile and darted toward her.

"Where are you going, lad?" Patrick strode after his boy while absent-mindedly counting a handful of coins.

"Buf-fly!" Josiah ran closer, holding out his paper creation. After all the bending and flapping, the paper was beginning to droop. Even so, the boy's eyes sparkled with delight.

Who knew such a small token would mean so much to him?

When the boy came near, Emma crouched to meet him. "And how is your butterfly doing, little love?"

"Fly away from spider," he replied.

"Oh, I see. He's trying to escape from the spider that's chasing him?"

Josiah nodded. "Big spider."

"I think I've found a helper for you, Patrick." Holy Bill clapped Patrick on the back.

"Bless you, Holy Bill." The relief in Patrick's voice was tangible. "How'd you manage that so fast?"

The reverend pressed his hat on his balding head and nodded at Emma. "God has provided Miss Chambers."

Patrick's eyebrows arched. And although surprise flitted across his weary features, the kindness didn't waver.

Emma straightened.

"She doesn't have the light-keeping experience like Delia did," the reverend continued, "but I'm sure you can teach her everything she needs to know."

"Then you're a lightkeeper, Mr. Garraty?" she asked.

Patrick nodded toward the distant tip of the harbor opposite from them. "For the Presque Isle Light."

Emma lifted a hand to shade her view. Above a cluster of spruce, she could make out the rising white tower of a lighthouse. A narrow clearing in the trees revealed another building, likely the keeper's cottage.

"He's the best keeper the board could ever ask for," the reverend said. "But it's a tough job to do all alone, especially with a toddler in tow."

She could only imagine. "I'd be more than happy to help." At least it would give her something useful to do until Ryan was ready to move on.

Patrick hesitated with a glance toward the mound of soil that covered his wife. The blackness of the soil attested to the freshness of her death and also his grief.

"I know it's hard," Holy Bill said, "but you said yourself that you can't go on like this. You can't do your job and take care of Josiah at the same time."

The lump in Patrick's throat moved up and down. He managed a nod.

"Miss Chambers is in desperate straits herself," said Holy Bill. "Aren't you, young lady?"

"Aye. Quite desperate. I may not be skilled at many things, but I'll do the best I can to help you through this rough time."

"I know the timing isn't ideal." Holy Bill seemed to be pleading with Patrick. "And it's rather quick after Delia's death. Still, we can't turn down God's answer to our prayers, can we?"

Patrick pocketed his change and then perused her.

Emma wasn't quite so sure she was God's answer to anyone's prayers. She brushed her damp hair off her shoulders and knotted it into a makeshift bun. At her motion, he looked down at his rubber boots, which he twisted into the grass. Her appearance didn't matter, did it? Not for assisting with light-keeping duties.

"I don't want to rush Miss Chambers," Patrick said. "It isn't a decision anyone should make lightly."

"Oh, you're not rushing me," she said. "I've got no other place to go. You'd be helping me as much as I'd be helping you."

"I don't want you to regret it."

"I won't."

He was silent for a long moment. Holy Bill seemed to be holding his breath. Josiah had spread out on the ground on his stomach and was marching his butterfly through the long grass.

A play of emotions flickered across Patrick's rugged face. "I'll only do this if you're comfortable with it."

She smiled and shuffled a tiny step forward. "Lead the way."

"Praise be to God," Holy Bill said, retrieving his Bible from under his arm. "Let's have the wedding so that Patrick can go home and get some much needed sleep."

"Wedding?" Emma rapidly retreated until she bumped into the log wall of Burnham's cabin.

Patrick exchanged a look with Holy Bill.

"Yes, a wedding, to be married to Patrick," Holy Bill said. "What did you think we were talking about?"

Emma struggled to find her voice. "I thought Mr. Garraty needed an assistant."

"He does," Holy Bill said. "But you can't live with Patrick at the lighthouse without being married. It wouldn't be appropriate for either one of you. The board would never approve of it."

"So you want to marry me, Mr. Garraty?" she squeaked.

"Only if you're willing."

Her cheeks flushed, and she shifted her attention to Josiah and pretended that his hopping butterfly was the most important thing in the world.

No wonder Patrick had inspected her. If she was to be his wife, he'd surely want to know what kind of woman he was marrying. Obviously he could see she wasn't anything special. After his perusal, she was surprised he'd still wanted to marry her, not when he could have any other woman.

But that was the problem, wasn't it? There weren't any other women. She was it. His lone prospect.

"As I said, Patrick is a good man." The reverend's eyes beseeched her to give Patrick a chance, to refrain from passing judgment. But judgment about what? "He's given his life to the Lord completely, and during these past few years I've seen him grow into one of the godliest young men I know."

"I've got a long way to go," Patrick said. "I'm no saint."

"You can't go wrong with this man." Holy Bill grabbed Patrick's arm and wrapped him in a half hug. Patrick started to protest when the reverend added, "What do you think? Do you still want to go through with it?"

A crash, followed by a disgruntled shout, came from inside the log cabin behind her.

She certainly didn't want to stay with the Burnhams, not when she wasn't wanted. But was that the right reason to marry a complete stranger? Then again, this could be the opportunity she'd been waiting for.

Shyly she raised her gaze to meet Patrick's. Embarrassment

flitted over his features, and she could sense that he was as uncomfortable with the idea of marriage to a stranger as she was.

"May I speak with Miss Chambers alone for a moment?" he asked Holy Bill.

"Of course." The reverend bent and patted Josiah's head. "Come on, sonny. Let's go down to the beach for a while. I'm sure you'd like to throw some rocks into the water."

At Holy Bill's words, the boy sprang up. "Me throw rocks." He raced for the shore, his little legs stumbling in his eagerness. Emma smiled, and she realized if she married Patrick, she would become Josiah's new mammy.

The thought, while surprising, wasn't unpleasant. The boy needed a woman's care—not that she knew all that much about caring for young ones. She knew, though, how to launder clothes, comb hair, and wash a face—which was apparently something Patrick was at a loss to do, at least with the child.

Patrick cleared his throat and watched Josiah and Holy Bill as they headed toward the beach.

She waited for him to say something, anything to break the silence between them. He obviously didn't know what to say, even though he'd been the one to initiate their private conversation.

"I'm sorry for the confusion," she began.

"It's my fault," he said. "I shouldn't have assumed . . . I should have known it was too good to be true."

Too good to be true? Did he think *she* was too good to be true? She, as in ordinary Emma Chambers? She who'd never had a proposition of marriage before?

Even if the proposal was out of necessity rather than love, at least it was something when she'd never had anyone decent offer her the slightest attention. And now here was this godly handsome man offering to marry her and finally make all her longings come true. How could she refuse him? She had no other prospects except a life of more moving around.

Though Ryan had promised they would settle down in Detroit, he was still too restless. He wouldn't be satisfied working on the docks or in a fishery in Detroit forever.

And where would that leave her? Single, childless, and homeless. Again.

"You just took me by surprise, that's all," she said, her heart suddenly welling with the need to be married. "I'm not against the idea of getting married to you."

"You're not?" His eyes widened.

She shook her head. "I've been wanting to get married for some time now. I guess I just assumed it would be to someone I'd gotten to know and . . ." She wanted to say *love*, but the word stuck in her throat.

Did love really matter at this point? Plenty of couples got married out of need, for reasons similar to Patrick's.

"Then you'll consider my offer?" he asked.

"I'm thinking." She peered into his eyes, the eyes that had been nothing but kind and caring, despite all that had happened to him recently. She had Holy Bill's word that he was a godly man. She'd witnessed the sweet way he treated Josiah.

She'd be a fool not to marry him right here and now. Besides, maybe after they were married a while, love would have a chance to grow between them.

She studied his face, starting with his unshaven cheeks and moving to his eyebrows to the tiny scar above one of them, down his slightly bent nose—likely broken at one time—to his lips that were full and strong.

She'd never kissed a man. If she married him, would he kiss her today? Tonight? The very thought made her insides quiver.

Lest he see the direction of her thoughts, she let her focus drop to his boots.

"You don't have to worry," he rushed to say, his voice tinged with embarrassment, as if guessing the nature of her thoughts. "I wouldn't expect anything. You'd get no pressure from me. . . ."

She had the feeling he was referring to the intimacies of marriage, of which she knew next to nothing. And since he'd been married before, he obviously knew everything. Yet he didn't say anything more, and she knew that was all the conversation they would have about that particular subject, at least for now.

"I'm not a man of many words. So this is hard for me to say." All the pain and heartache was back, making the green of his eyes dark and murky. "I'm not the saint Holy Bill makes me out to be. I've done some things I'm not proud of—"

"It's all right," she cut in. "Holy Bill mentioned it already. He said we should leave the past in the past." She wasn't proud of her past either, that she'd never done anything to stop her father from stealing and killing. She could have been stronger, could have told him that she was willing to die to live rightly. Instead, she'd turned a blind eye.

"I can't have both Josiah and my job," Patrick went on. "I'd have to give one up. Unless you marry me."

The stark truth of his words gave her pause and reminded her that he wasn't all that concerned about physical attraction. He needed her as a mother for Josiah and a helpmate for his job. At least he was being honest about his intentions.

"In return," he said, "I promise I'll take care of you and make sure you have a good home."

Maybe he wasn't making any promises of love or happiness, but he was offering her a home. She smiled. A home was all she needed, all she'd ever wanted. "I accept."

His brow rose. "You do?"

"Aye."

"Then you'll marry me today?"

Part of her conscience cautioned her to wait and talk with Ryan first, that she shouldn't rush into this without her brother's approval. But the other part of her warned her that he wouldn't agree to her marrying a man she'd just met, that he'd demand she wait and learn more about Patrick first. If she didn't want to lose her one and only opportunity for marriage, then she would have to act fast, before Ryan interfered with her plans.

She took a deep breath to silence all the anxious fluttering in her stomach. "Let's get married right now."

Chapter 4

The lake breeze teased Emma's hair so that loose curls tickled her neck. Her bare toes squished against the rocks and sand of the beach, and her damp petticoat stuck to her legs.

She was getting married. The sunshine pouring down upon her bare head was like a blessing from heaven—at least she hoped so. Only hours ago she'd thought she was drowning, that she'd lost all chance of having hope and a future. Now here she was at the edge of Lake Huron, getting ready to take her vows.

She stole a look at the man who was about to become her husband. The brim of his cap cast a shadow over his face, lending him a handsome ruggedness.

He cocked a brow. "Are you sure you're ready?"

Next to him, Josiah had both hands full of rocks of various sizes. Apparently throwing rocks could entertain him as readily as the paper butterfly she'd carefully tucked into her pocket.

"I'm ready." She forced a smile, trying to ignore the quavering in her legs. Was she really doing the right thing?

Holy Bill opened his Bible and flipped through the thin pages.

"Ah, here we are." He stopped, smoothed the book reverently, and cleared his throat. "'Two are better than one, because they have a good reward for their labor,'" he started, reading from the text. "'For if they fall, the one will lift up his fellow: but woe to him that is alone when he falleth, for he hath not another to help him up.'"

Woe to him that is alone. That was certainly true in Patrick's situation. He was doomed without her help. But was that reason enough to bind herself to a man in matrimony? After all, it was a lifetime commitment.

Holy Bill continued to quote from the Bible. "'Again, if two lie together, then they have heat: but how can one be warm alone?'"

If two lie together, then they have heat. She resisted the urge to squirm at the words. She couldn't imagine lying together with Patrick. At least not until she got to know him better.

"'And if one prevails against him, two shall withstand him; and a threefold cord is not quickly broken.'" The reverend looked up and smiled, first at her and then at Patrick. "Marriage was ordained by God in Eden and confirmed by Jesus His Son at the wedding in Cana of Galilee, and is declared by the apostle Paul to be honorable among all men. Let's begin by asking God's blessing on your marriage."

When both Holy Bill and Patrick bowed their heads, Emma lowered hers in imitation. She had the desperate wish that God *would* bless her marriage. But how could she start praying to Him now and asking for blessings when she hadn't talked to Him in years?

At the reverend's amen, Patrick echoed him softly in agreement with Holy Bill's words. Patrick shifted to face the reverend, and Emma did likewise. Near the water's edge, bunches of goldenrod grew in clusters among the sea grass, dotted with purple thistle—flowers for her wedding. And the rhythmic crashing of the waves was the music for the occasion.

Maybe she didn't have a pretty dress or a church, but the shoreline was like an outdoor cathedral. She couldn't ask for anything better, even if the familiar stench of fish wafted over them, and the old men working among the drying racks had stopped their work to stare at the scene.

Holy Bill turned to Patrick. "Patrick, wilt thou have this woman to be thy wedded wife, to live together after God's ordinances in the holy estate of matrimony? Wilt thou love her, comfort her, honor and keep her in sickness and in health? And forsaking all others, keep thee only to her as long as you both shall live?"

"I will." His response was low, but it rumbled deep in Emma's soul nevertheless.

Holy Bill looked at her. "Emma, wilt thou have this man to be thy wedded husband, to live together after God's ordinances in the holy estate of matrimony? Wilt thou obey him and serve him, love, honor and keep him in sickness and in health? And forsaking all others, keep thee only to him as long as you both shall live?"

Keep him as long as they both lived?

The cool wind blowing off the lake lifted the tendrils at the base of her neck and crept down her back. She peered out over the lake that stretched out forever like an ocean. Her thoughts tossed and tumbled with the waves.

"Emma?" Holy Bill said. "You need to say *I will.*"

She nodded and forced the words out before she changed her mind. "I will."

Holy Bill reached for Patrick's right hand and then took hold of hers, placing it on top of her husband-to-be's. The moment her fingers brushed against his roughened skin, she sucked in

51

a breath. The contact was warm and too forward. She could only stare at their touching hands as he repeated the rest of his vows after Holy Bill.

Somehow she managed to repeat her vows as well.

"I pronounce that you are man and wife together." Holy Bill closed his Bible and bestowed a satisfied smile on them, one that lifted his long white beard and mustache. His crinkled eyes sparked with happiness. "And finally, the best part. Patrick, you may kiss your bride."

Emma stiffened in surprise.

Patrick started to shake his head, but Holy Bill cut him off with a laugh. "You may as well start things off right, Patrick, and get used to kissing your pretty new wife."

Pretty? She started to contradict him, but Patrick spoke first.

"I don't want to rush anything—"

"It's too late for that." The reverend slapped Patrick on the back. "Besides, Emma isn't Delia. I'm sure Emma won't object, will you?" Holy Bill's smile encouraged her to agree with him.

The whole exchange left her confused and just a little breathless. And when Patrick peeked from beneath his lashes at her as if to gauge her reaction to Holy Bill's suggestion, she realized she couldn't object. She didn't want to start off their relationship by refusing a kiss at their wedding.

She lifted her face to Patrick. Her stomach did several funny flops at the thought of him pressing his lips against hers. He stared at his boots and dug a hole in the sand with the toe of one.

What if he didn't want to kiss her? Maybe he was still grieving over Delia and couldn't imagine having to kiss anyone else. Or maybe he didn't find her attractive enough to kiss.

Should she turn away and object, saving him the embarrassment of having to reject her?

She started to lower her face, but then he jerked his head up, reached swiftly for her cheeks, and cupped his hands on either side, the tips of his fingers brushing against her hair. Determination mingled with his flushed embarrassment as he stared directly at her mouth.

Her breath caught in her throat.

When he bent his head closer to hers, she couldn't move, couldn't think, couldn't do anything but wait. His breath hovered above her lips for a long moment, and she almost believed he wouldn't do it, that he couldn't.

Then, gingerly, his mouth met hers.

Her eyes closed, and her heart nearly stopped. She savored the gentle intimacy. The sweetness of his touch was like nothing she'd ever known before.

But it was over before it had a chance to begin. Before she could respond, before she could give in to her body's sudden longing to kiss him back, he pulled his face away and stepped back.

She wanted to lift her fingers to her mouth, to trap the warmth and the memory of his lips there, but didn't want to cause any more awkwardness between them.

Holy Bill grinned and slapped Patrick on his back again. Patrick only ducked his head.

"What in the name of all that's holy is going on?" called a voice from farther up the shore.

She swiveled in time to see Ryan charging down the beach toward them like an angry bull.

"Uh-oh," she whispered.

Ryan flew toward Patrick, his fists balled and raised. "Did I just see you kissing my sister?"

Patrick had stiffened at the sight of Ryan's fists, but he didn't move. Unlike Holy Bill, who sprang out of her brother's path.

"I've never let any man take advantage of my sister," Ryan said, almost shouting now. His eyes were wild, his face flushed with anger. "Rescuer or no, I'm not going to stand back and let you get away with this!"

"Ryan, stop!" she said.

But it was too late. Ryan leaped at Patrick. Even though her brother was lankier than the lightkeeper, he was no weakling. His fist connected with Patrick's jaw with a crack that reverberated through Emma, rattling her down to her bones.

"Don't hit him!" she cried.

Ryan then took a swing at Patrick's gut. His fist bounced off the man like a wave hitting a rock. Patrick didn't move, didn't even blink.

Ryan heaved a breath and swiped his sleeve across his forehead. Dust coated his cheeks, and his hair stuck to his head where his hat had been. He'd obviously been working hard, while she'd been sitting in the sun trying to get warm and dry.

Guilt prodded her forward. "Please, Ryan, I can explain."

But he lunged at Patrick again and struck him in the chin. "No one touches my sister, do you hear me?"

Patrick's head swayed at the impact, and he gritted his teeth.

Was the man just going to stand there and let Ryan beat him without defending himself?

Patrick's eyes narrowed, and his nostrils flared. As Ryan pulled back his arm to level another punch, Patrick stiffened but didn't raise a hand to block the blow.

She darted between the men, spread her arms, and glared at Ryan. "Ryan Chambers, you stop hitting my husband this instant!"

Ryan froze, his arm upraised and poised for another punch at Patrick's face. "Your husband?"

It had felt as strange saying the word *husband* as it did hearing it come from Ryan. Behind her, the warmth of Patrick's torso radiated into her, reminding her of how near she stood to him.

"Aye. We were married just now by Holy Bill." If she turned, she'd be standing mere inches away, as close as they'd been only moments ago when he'd kissed her for the first time.

"You went and got yourself married?" Ryan dropped his fist, and his shoulders sagged.

"It seemed like the perfect solution to our troubles," she said.

He jammed his fingers into his sandy hair, making pieces of it stick out like twigs. "I had the situation under control. You didn't need to go and do a thing like this."

"Emma's right," Holy Bill said, cutting in. "It's the perfect solution for these two people."

"It's *not* perfect," Ryan said. "My sister's married to a stranger now. He could be a criminal for all we know."

At Ryan's words, Patrick flinched.

Holy Bill shook his head. "No matter Patrick's past, you have no worries, sonny. I've met a lot of men during my years as a traveling minister, and I have to say there aren't many as fine as Patrick here. Your sister has got herself the best husband any woman could ask for."

"And what makes you the expert?" Ryan asked.

Emma gasped. "Ryan, please—"

"Haven't I always taken good care of you, Em?"

"Aye, that you have. A very good job. But now it's time for you to live your own life without me holding you back."

"You're not holding me back."

"You could do so much more if you didn't have to worry about me."

"I don't mind worrying about you, Em." His features tightened in earnestness. "I'll worry about you even more now that you're married to God-knows-who."

"I promise to take good care of her," Patrick said.

Ryan glared at him. "You'd better. If I find out you're not treating her right, I'll beat you senseless."

Patrick nodded. "If your sister isn't happy at the lighthouse, I won't hold her to our agreement."

Ryan started as if he would spout off more threats, but as Patrick's words sank in, he stopped. "You'll let her leave if she wants to?"

Patrick nodded again.

Emma didn't understand what Patrick was saying. They were married. It was official. They couldn't change that now, except by divorce. And she wasn't planning on that. Happy or not, she was bound to him. They'd just spoken the words *for better or worse*, until death parted them.

A shout resounded across the beach. Near the edge of the clearing, Mr. Burnham was motioning to Ryan.

"I have to go," Ryan said. "I asked Fred for a break to check on you, and he only gave me five minutes."

"That's not long enough," she said, directing a frown at the big man wiping the back of his neck with a red-checkered handkerchief.

"Beggars can't be choosers, Em," Ryan said.

Exactly, she wanted to tell him. She'd felt the same way about her marriage prospects, which was why she'd wedded Patrick. But instead of arguing, she swept her brother into an embrace. "I'm going to the lighthouse now."

His arms tightened around her. "I'll be out to visit you as soon as I get some time off."

"I'll look forward to it." She clung to him. Even with all her brave words, an ache moved into her throat. This was it. She was finally setting her brother free, and deep inside she knew it was past time to do so.

"After my hard work keeping the men away from you these past few years," he said, his voice gruff near her ear. "I can't believe I left you for a few hours and you ended up married."

She pulled back. "You kept the men away?"

"I threatened to beat up anyone who came calling. I didn't want any of them taking advantage of my sister."

Had Ryan's scare tactics been part of the reason she'd had so little attention from suitors? She didn't know what to say, whether to laugh, cry, or scold him. So instead she said nothing and tugged him into another embrace.

"Are you sure you want to go through with this?" he whispered.

She nodded and squeezed her brother tighter. Right or wrong, rash or not, she was married now. She'd just have to make the best of her new situation. And hope that she hadn't made the worst mistake of her life.

Chapter 5

*P*atrick plunged the oars in and then heaved them up, the water rolling off in a peaceful rhythm. Rowing was such a familiar act, something he could do in his sleep. With the sun shining over him and a breeze caressing his body, he'd already slackened to a restfulness he hadn't experienced in over a week.

If he closed his eyes, he'd be asleep within seconds. But he had to stay awake a few more minutes until they reached the lighthouse.

"Fishy?" Josiah's steady stream of questions was the only thing keeping him awake. Except for once, the questions weren't directed at him. Instead, the boy sat next to Emma in the bow and had chattered with her nonstop.

"Oh, I like that one." Emma peered over the edge of the cutter. "It's more colorful than the last one."

"Fishy fast." Josiah waved his hand in imitation of the way the fish swam.

Emma had her arm around the boy in a protective gesture,

drawing him away from the edge whenever he started to hang over too far.

Thank you, Father. Tonight, when he was tending the light, he'd make sure to pour out his gratitude, but for now in his exhaustion the short prayer would have to do. He drew in a deep breath and let the cool air drive away the sleepy fog threatening his eyelids.

"There's another," Emma said, pointing into the water, her voice tinged with delight.

She wasn't pretending to enjoy the fish watching with Josiah. Her face radiated enthusiasm, and Josiah seemed to be glowing under her attention. Already in the short time since they'd left Burnham's Landing, Emma was proving to be a better mom than Delia had ever been.

Of course, he couldn't fault Delia too much. She'd done the best she could under the circumstances and considering the fact that she'd been an only child and had never been around babies. But the truth was, Josiah hadn't shown any signs of missing her in the past twenty-four hours since she'd died. He doubted the boy understood that she was gone, since she'd never really been all that present in his life anyway.

He supposed that was why he'd been able to agree to Holy Bill's suggestion that he marry Emma. He'd watched her brief interactions with Josiah, the kindness she'd shown his boy when she'd folded the paper, the gentle way she talked on his level. She possessed a warmth and tenderness that Delia never had.

Patrick dug the oars deeper and silently berated himself for his negative thoughts. Delia might not have been the best mother, but he couldn't fault her knowledge of the lighthouse. Besides, maybe Emma wouldn't be quite so warm once she got to know him better.

Even though he was trying to keep guilt from slithering up, it was hissing at the back of his mind. At the moment of the wedding, he'd accepted Emma's polite statement about leaving the past behind them. But now he couldn't keep from questioning exactly how much Holy Bill had told Emma about his past crimes. Probably not enough or she wouldn't have been so willing to marry him.

He steered the boat toward the bend of the harbor, to the bottom of the isthmus that the French explorers had named Presque Isle, meaning *almost an island.*

"Oh, look!" Emma stared between the spruce and pine. "The lighthouse."

Rising above the dark spires was the whitewashed stone tower with the lantern room gracing the top like a polished jewel. The entire structure was conical in shape and was almost forty feet high. The size was somewhat short and squat compared to the seventy-five-foot tower Delia's father managed at Fort Gratiot.

Even if Presque Isle Light wasn't as tall as most other lighthouses, it had been built on an elevated area, so that it could illuminate the mouth of the harbor for vessels traveling either from the north or south.

Like the other lighthouses spread out along the Michigan coastline, it had been built to help ships navigate the treacherous inland lake and diminish the all-too frequent accidents.

"It's lovely." Emma tossed him a smile over her shoulder.

He nodded. Yet having been built almost twenty years ago, the structure was in poor condition when he and Delia had arrived last summer. And now after the harsh winter, there was always something that needed fixing.

"The keeper's dwelling is next to the tower," he said, glimpsing the building through the trees. Though it wasn't connected to the tower like many keeper dwellings, he thought the house sufficient enough; it had kept them safe and dry during the past winter.

Emma strained to see the house. He wasn't sure he wanted to witness her reaction. Delia hadn't liked it, had thought it too small. Of course, she hadn't wanted to move to Presque Isle. She wanted him to wait for a better keeper position, something more prestigious like her father's instead of a tiny lighthouse in the remote wilderness. The fact that Delia's cousin, Bertha Burnham, lived nearby had been the only consolation.

He steered his boat toward the dock. The shore here was dotted with boulders, brush, and wildflowers, similar to the rest of the shore that surrounded the harbor.

When the cutter bumped against the planks, Emma grabbed on and maneuvered the boat closer. She didn't wait for him to secure the cutter before climbing out. She lifted Josiah and, instead of putting him down on the dock, hoisted him to one of her hips, all while staring in fascination at the keeper's cottage that sat back away from the water's edge on a grassy patch of land.

Josiah wrapped his arms around Emma's neck and allowed her to carry him down the dock and onto the shore. She started up the path through the brush and rocks, carrying Josiah as if that were the most natural action in the world.

Panic momentarily panged through Patrick's chest. The house was in disorder, the laundry in piles, the dishes unwashed. He'd had no time to tend to ordinary household chores since Delia had fallen down the winding tower stairway and had hovered between life and death for nearly a week. It had been all he could do to take care of Delia, watch Josiah, and keep the light burning at night.

With fumbling fingers he tied up the boat and then sprinted up the path to the keeper's dwelling. "Wait," he called, but Emma had already opened the front door and was stepping inside.

He bounded after her and nearly ran into her as he entered the front hall. She peeked into the sitting room that doubled as his office. The curtains were wide open, and sunshine spilled across his untidy desk, his logbooks, and the many other journals and records the board required him to update on a daily basis about the weather, storms, purchases, and shipwrecks.

He was behind with logging information from the past week and now had even more to add with the steamer going down last night.

Emma examined the room, which contained his desk, positioned under the window for the natural light, a fireplace, and two chairs facing it—a rocker and a stuffed chair that was faded and worn. She glanced at his basket of neglected whittling, the several items he'd been carving, and tools. Other than that, the room was as sparsely furnished as the day he'd moved in. There wasn't a rug on the floor or a picture on the wall.

"Sorry it's so neglected," he said.

She surprised him by smiling. "It's beautiful."

Josiah was chattering again, his little voice echoing off the bare walls.

Emma murmured to him as she crossed the hallway to the open door of the front bedroom. The curtains were closed, but even so, the sunlight streamed through the crack of calico and illuminated the clothes he'd left strewn on the floor and the unmade bed.

He stepped into the room, swiped up several items, and tossed them onto a bigger pile of dirty clothes in the corner. He shoved aside the clutter on the top of the chest of drawers and placed her bag there.

"Feel free to rearrange things to make space for your belongings," he said. She apparently didn't have much. Even so, he wanted her to feel at home now.

She averted her eyes, but not before he caught sight of the embarrassment that flooded them.

He looked at the bed before him, and his entire body leaned toward it, his knees weakening, his eyes faltering. Exhaustion hit him with the force of a November gale.

"Josiah can show you the rest of the house, can't you, lad?"

Josiah nodded and tugged on Emma's hand. "Show my bed."

She seemed almost relieved to move away from the bedroom.

Patrick stumbled toward the bed, not bothering to shed his shoes or coat. He was already half asleep on his feet. Then he remembered to call after her, "Would you wake me by seven o'clock if I'm not already up?"

She stopped and gave him a shy glance over her shoulder. "Of course."

Without another thought, he closed the distance to the bed, fell across the thin mattress, and was asleep before his head could find a pillow.

Emma swept the kitchen floor, wishing for the broom she'd fixed that morning at the Burnham cabin. The spindly broken bristles on the one she held were useless. Still, she'd had no trouble making a mound of dirt.

"Sweep, sweep?" Josiah asked from his high chair at the table, where she'd finally positioned him with a couple of items from the depleted sideboard—a wedge of cheese and dried beef jerky.

She'd also found a tin half full of flour, a small can of baking soda, and a crock of lard. But since she hadn't known what to do with them, she'd resorted to a simple meal. Fortunately, Josiah didn't seem to mind the plain fare.

It was almost time to wake Patrick. She'd peeked in on him on a couple of occasions and he'd been in the same position each time, sprawled across the bed where he'd collapsed, his feet dangling over the edge. Except for the rise and fall of his chest, she would have thought him dead.

Once she'd considered removing his boots and helping him get more comfortable, but when she approached the bed, a shaft of sunlight had fallen across his scruffy face, the strong line of his jaw and his mouth. She hadn't been able to resist thinking about the kiss he'd given her at their wedding, the softness and warmth of his lips against hers.

Her limbs had quivered with nervousness, and she'd stopped. She didn't want him to wake up while she was pulling off his boots and think she was inviting herself into bed. So she backed slowly out of the room and hadn't gone in again.

Thankfully, none of Josiah's noises had awoken Patrick. None of her banging and scraping had bothered him either, as she'd done her best to scour the kitchen from top to bottom.

It had taken her some time and plenty of failed attempts to light a fire in the cast-iron stove, but once she finally had one blazing, she'd heated water, washed the dishes, and scrubbed the table that had been coated with food spills. Then she'd turned her efforts to the walls, cupboards, and finally the floor.

For the most part, Josiah had played in the kitchen while she worked, often attempting to help her, but usually making puddles or soaking himself in the process. She leaned against the broom handle and breathed in a sigh of contentment. Here she was, in a home of her own, with a husband and a child. This was all hers now, everything she'd always wanted.

The kitchen was as plain as the rest of the house, the faded blue curtains on either side of the lone window being the only bit of color in the barren room. Even though the house was undecorated and lacked a homey quality, the idea of bringing it to life excited her. She'd always dreamed about fixing up a home, and she knew she could make this one warm and welcoming—just as her mam had done in their simple cottage in Ireland.

"More?" Josiah asked as he shoved the last square of cheese into his mouth. The table in front of him was empty except for a few crumbs.

"We say *more, please*."

"More?"

"*Please*," she instructed him.

"Please," he mimicked.

He was in obvious need of a woman's training. Perhaps his mother had been ill for some time. That would explain the unkemptness of the home and her child.

Emma sliced two more pieces of cheese and handed them to the boy. He grabbed one, but she stopped him with a touch of her hand.

"You need to say *thank you*, little love."

"Thank you, little love," Josiah said earnestly.

She couldn't contain the small laugh that bubbled up.

And when he gave her a big scrunched-eye smile in reply, more laughter spilled out. His smile widened as if he knew he was the source of her laughter, although he clearly had no idea why.

What would it be like someday to have a whole houseful of

children? She hadn't wanted to let herself dream about having babies before. It had always been too painful to see women younger than her coddling their little ones. But now that she was married . . .

Footsteps plodded in the hallway, and Patrick stumbled into the kitchen, combing his disheveled hair with his fingers.

"Mr. Garraty," she said, flushing and praying he couldn't read her thoughts. "You're awake."

"What time is it?" he asked in a groggy voice tinged with panic. His eyes were glazed, his clothes rumpled. For an instant she pictured him again on the bed, the mattress bending under his weight. She couldn't keep from thinking about how much it would sag under the weight of both of them together later.

Even if he'd assured her that he wouldn't expect anything, she assumed she was to share the bed with him. They were, after all, husband and wife. And wasn't that what husbands and wives did, share a bed?

He'd placed her bag in his bedroom, indicating that she should unpack her belongings there. Besides, the only other bedroom was Josiah's, and that was hardly bigger than a closet off the kitchen.

She turned away from Patrick, busying herself with sweeping her pile of dirt toward the back door. "Last I checked, it was only half past six."

He grabbed onto the back of one of the two kitchen chairs that flanked the table. He swiped his hand across his face and rubbed his eyes in obvious need of several days' worth of sleep, not just several hours.

"Hi, Daddy." Josiah stuffed his last piece of cheese into his mouth.

Patrick sucked in a steadying breath, and then his shoulders relaxed. "There you are, lad." He reached over and smoothed his large hand across the boy's head. "It looks like your new mam is taking good care of you."

"New mam?" Josiah asked.

"He can call me Emma," she offered. "I know it will be hard to adjust—"

"Mamma," Josiah said, blending *mam* and *Emma* into a new word of his own.

Patrick didn't try to correct him. Instead, he glanced around the kitchen, and his eyes settled hungrily on the wedge of cheese and beef jerky that sat on the worktable.

"I couldn't find supplies for making a meal," she said, wondering if he'd expected her to have a big dinner waiting for him when he awoke. But the truth was, even if she'd had the ingredients, she would've had trouble cooking. She'd never learned how, had never needed to learn—not when she'd lived above one tavern or another over the years.

"We're running low," he said. "I'll make a trip to Fremont tomorrow. Put together a list of what you need."

What would she need? Her mind scrambled to remember some of the things her mam cooked before the famine had started. But her memories consisted only of a constantly gnawing stomach, the frantic pangs of hunger, and the willingness to eat anything, no matter what it was.

"I've made coffee." Coffee was one thing she knew how to make, and she'd located coffee beans in abundance. "Would you like some?"

"Lately, coffee is the main part of my meal," he said.

Emma poured the steaming liquid into a freshly washed mug, drawing in a deep breath of the strong brew. She held the mug out to him. "Here you are, Mr. Garraty."

He wrapped his hand around the mug, his fingers brushing

hers. The innocent contact jolted her, and she couldn't keep from staring at his fingers against hers, his tanned, leathery skin contrasting her paleness.

He took a step back, breaking the connection, probably not even noticing. "Emma." He traced the mug's handle with his thumb. "Why don't you call me Patrick? Now that we're married and everything."

"Oh, okay." She hadn't wanted to appear overly familiar with him. But he was right. They were married now, and living together. She'd have to get used to sharing intimacies with him eventually. . . .

A flush crept onto her cheeks.

Josiah crammed a piece of jerky into his mouth, chewing with his mouth open and watching Patrick's exchange with her with wide-eyed interest.

Patrick smiled at the boy, then bent and kissed his head. "Good night, lad. I'll see you in the morning."

"Night, Daddy," Josiah said, reaching out to Patrick with his mushed-cheese fingers. In spite of the mess, Patrick planted a kiss on one of the boy's hands. He retrieved a wedge of cheese and piece of jerky, strode to the back door, and was almost outside before he turned to look back at Emma. "I'll be in the tower or watch room if you need anything."

She nodded and wished she knew what else to say. But every time she was around him, she turned into a shy, bumbling girl.

After her laughable attempt at dinner, she decided to explore the grounds. The evening was still sunny and warm, and Josiah followed her around as she found a plot behind the cottage that looked like it had been a garden at one time, but was now overgrown in a tangle of weeds. She later discovered a well, a dilapidated hen house, and a shed that had an assortment of equipment and tools. There was also a cellar that had a few remnants of overripe apples and molding onions.

By the time the shadows had lengthened and the sun began to dip in the sky, Josiah had started yawning and rubbing his eyes.

When she stripped him of his filthy clothes and lowered him in a tub of warm sudsy water in the center of the kitchen, he gave a shriek that could have rivaled a fog whistle. Thankfully, he splashed and flailed for only a minute before she thought to give him a cup for playing in the bathwater. While he was distracted with his new task of catching bubbles in the cup, she scrubbed his hair and every inch of his little body.

After she dressed him in pajamas, he didn't offer a single complaint when she laid him in his bed.

"Pray, Mamma?" He looked up at her, fighting to keep his eyelids open. He popped his thumb in his mouth and fingered the edge of a frayed blanket that he snuggled under his nose.

The earnestness of his question took her by surprise. She knelt in the narrow space beside his bed. "Okay. We'll pray."

Without a window, the room was dark and cozy. The fading light of the kitchen cast a warm glow over Josiah. His lashes fluttered, and his thumb sucking halted. Damp strands of red hair curled over his forehead. His face was finally clean, revealing a smattering of freckles across his nose and cheeks.

Her chest swelled with tenderness. This was her son now. And even though she knew very little about parenting, she had to admit, she hadn't done a bad job that afternoon and evening with him. Maybe she could utter a prayer of thankfulness, even if she was a bit rusty when it came to talking with God.

"Thank you," she whispered as she closed her eyes and bowed her head. Gratefulness choked off any further words.

Soon Josiah was asleep, and she slipped silently from his room.

For a while she kept herself busy washing his tiny garments in the soapy bathwater, wringing them out, and hanging them to dry around the kitchen. When she'd finally dumped the dirty water out the back door, the light in the tower was on and cut a long beam through the night sky.

It was amazing to think she'd seen the faint ray last night from the burning deck of the steamer, and that tonight she was on the other side seeing the bright source. Last night she'd been single, homeless, and childless. Now, less than twenty-four hours later, she had everything she'd ever wanted.

When she finally worked up enough courage to approach the bedroom, she could feel herself blushing. In the low light of the lantern, the room appeared less cluttered than earlier in the day. But she could hardly look at the unmade bed, at the imprint left from Patrick's body.

She tentatively opened her sack and pulled out one item at a time. She didn't have much: a brush and comb, another skirt and blouse, several undergarments, a couple of nightgowns. They were wrinkled and smelled of the sea from the soaking in the lake and would need laundering. But for now she couldn't resist unpacking them. It was a sign of permanence that sent a thrill through her.

With a glance over her shoulder toward the half-open door, she slid out the top drawer, revealing a jumble of men's clothing. She caught a waft of Patrick, a scent she hadn't realized was his until she opened the drawer. It was a mixture of the lake, wind, and oil. She bent closer and breathed him in. At the flutter of a moth near the lantern, she jumped back and closed the drawer swiftly.

After a quick search through the rest of the drawers, she found an empty spot in one of them where she tucked her few belongings. Then with a racing heart, she changed as fast as she could into her nightgown.

Breathing hard from her nervous exchange of garments, she approached the bed. When she reached the edge, she froze. Could she really lie down with a man? But what other choice did she have? She couldn't very well crawl into bed with Josiah or sleep in the rocker in the sitting room.

This was it. She'd made the decision to marry Patrick, and she'd have to take *all* that came with it.

She extinguished the lantern, scrambled into the bed, and covered herself from head to toe. Within seconds she lay stiffly, staring in the darkness at the ceiling.

Maybe if she didn't move, he'd think she was already asleep. Maybe he'd fall into bed exhausted, as he had earlier.

She clutched the sheet, the coverlet tucked beneath her chin. She tried to still the trembling in her limbs, reminding herself that he was kind. Surely he would treat her in the bedroom with as much consideration as he'd already shown. Surely she had nothing to worry about.

Even so, there was something unnerving about the thought of sharing unknown intimacies with a man who was still a stranger—even if he was the handsomest man she'd ever seen.

Minutes passed, and at each slight sound she stopped breathing to listen more carefully. But as time dragged on and he didn't make his appearance, her grip on the sheets began to loosen, and her body settled into the dip of the mattress.

Maybe he was giving her time to relax before coming to share the bed.

She dragged in a deep breath. Her lashes fell against her

cheeks, fatigue settling over her. She hadn't slept much the previous night before the pirate attack had awoken her. And after the long day, weariness crept into her bones and muscles.

The last thought she had before drifting into oblivion was that maybe he'd kiss her again. If he did, she wouldn't mind in the least.

Chapter 6

*E*mma awoke to the low rumble of a manly voice, along with the scent of fried fish. She bolted upright and raked a mass of tangled hair out of her eyes. The light coming from between the curtains told her it was morning.

The covers on the opposite side of the bed were undisturbed. The door was still open a crack, the way she'd left it. Patrick had obviously not come to bed with her. In fact, from all appearances, he hadn't even stepped into the room.

She jumped out of bed and grabbed her skirt and blouse from the chair where she'd draped them. After shedding her nightgown, she thrust her limbs into the garments, but she didn't have the same urgency she'd had last night.

Maybe the grief over his wife was still too fresh to think about sharing intimacies with another woman. She could only imagine how hard it would be to marry someone so soon after burying a beloved spouse. Or maybe he was following through with his promise that he wouldn't expect anything of her. Whatever the case, she was relieved he hadn't visited the bedroom.

She rushed into the kitchen still braiding her hair. When

she saw him standing in front of the stove, his back to her, she halted abruptly. He'd shed his coat and rolled up his shirtsleeves, revealing his tanned, well-muscled arms.

Two pans sizzled on the griddle before him. In one, he was browning several fillets of fish, and in the other he was flipping griddle cakes. Dismay chilled her, and she crossed her arms over her chest. She should have risen earlier and had breakfast waiting for him. It didn't matter that she didn't have any idea how to make the griddle cakes or where to find the fish. It was her job, and she'd failed to do it.

"Hi, Mamma." Sitting in his high chair, Josiah was fully dressed and in the process of shoveling a whole griddle cake into his mouth.

At Josiah's greeting, Patrick swiveled, a long-handled spatula in one hand and a knife in the other. His eyes looked tired still. But when he saw her, he nodded.

"Good morning," he said. "I hope we didn't wake you. We were trying to be quiet."

"Me quiet," Josiah said through the mass of food in his mouth, his shoulders straight with the pride of his accomplishment.

"I should have been up earlier." She started across the kitchen. "Would you like me to finish so that you can attend to other things?"

"I don't mind." He turned back to the stove. "I've always cooked breakfast."

His words stopped her, and she stared at his rippling muscles as he flipped one of the golden cakes.

He pointed the spatula toward the coffee grinder on the sideboard. "Would you like to make the coffee again?"

She was too surprised by his proficiency at the stove to do anything but nod and do his bidding. By the time the coffee was perking, he had plates loaded with fish and griddle cakes. Her stomach rumbled at the tantalizing fried aroma that filled the small kitchen. She didn't think she could have resisted sitting down in the chair across from him even if she'd wanted to.

She picked up her fork, ready to stab a piece of fish, but stopped when Patrick reached out a hand toward both her and Josiah. The boy laid down his half-eaten griddle cake and placed his hand in Patrick's big one. "Pray, Daddy?"

"Yes, lad."

Josiah reached a hand toward her too, his sticky fingers mingling with hers. Apparently they were in the habit of praying before meals and holding hands while doing so. She glanced at Patrick's outstretched hand waiting for hers.

She edged her hand nearer, letting her fingers slip around his. At the warmth and solidness of his touch, her whole body heated. The green of his eyes was bright, almost curious. She lowered her head, hoping he wouldn't see her reaction.

After a hesitant second, his grasp tightened. Her stomach turned strangely taut.

"Heavenly Father," he said softly. He spoke to God naturally and effortlessly, almost the same way her mam had prayed, like God was really there listening and waiting to answer. "We thank you for providing this meal and for blessing me with a new helpmate and Josiah with a new mamma."

Her heart flooded with warmth. Patrick thought she was a blessing. She didn't hear the rest of his prayer, except for the amen, echoed by Josiah who wiggled his hand from hers, eager to get back to his breakfast. She expected Patrick to pull his fingers away from hers just as rapidly. But even as she started to back away, his fingers lingered, sending another lurch through her stomach.

When she lifted her head, he was staring at her again. Was he sensing her strange reaction to him?

She slid her hand away from his and wrapped it around her coffee mug. She'd already embarrassed herself enough by oversleeping. She didn't need to gawk at him like a silly little girl.

During the simple meal, Patrick ate quietly. Thankfully, Josiah kept them entertained and prevented any awkward silences.

After his plate was clean, Patrick pushed away from the table. "I'll be going to Fremont now and possibly to Thunder Bay Island." He pulled a folded paper from his pocket, along with a pencil. "I've started a list of supplies. Write down anything you need, and I'll see if I can find it there."

She smoothed out the paper to reveal his scrawled handwriting in a short list of things like fishing hooks, nails, wicks, and other items needed for the upkeep of the lighthouse.

Once he'd left the kitchen, she took a deep breath. His presence had been overpowering. She couldn't think with him so close, with his body exuding such strength, with his eyes so intense.

Josiah squirmed in his chair, ready to be set free. Once she'd washed his hands and face and turned him loose, she tried to corral him in the kitchen while she washed the dishes. But he seemed to sense that Patrick was readying to leave, and he followed his daddy around like a shadow.

When Patrick finally headed down the path that led to the cutter, Josiah rushed after him. And as Patrick clambered into the boat and began untying the dock line, Josiah held out his arms. "Me go. Me go."

Patrick shook his head. "Not today, lad. You stay with your mamma."

Emma reached for the boy, but he dodged her and perched on the edge of the dock, dangling his legs into the prow.

"Come with Mamma, little love." But Josiah climbed down in the boat, scrambling toward his daddy, crawling over the thwart and oars.

Patrick had been winding up a rope with his back turned, and when he spun to find Josiah in the boat, instead of getting angry, he surprised Emma by crouching next to the boy and giving him a hug.

"I know you'd like to come today, lad." Patrick laid a kiss against Josiah's red hair. "But on the return trip, the boat will be very full."

Josiah buried his face into Patrick's shirt.

"Besides, I want you to help your new mamma."

Josiah still didn't move.

Patrick locked eyes with her above Josiah's head, cocking one of his brows as if to ask, *Now what?*

Emma glanced around the shore, to the open waters of Lake Huron to the east and Presque Isle Bay to the southwest. Her mind frantically searched for something, anything, to distract Josiah, to make him want to stay home with her, a stranger, rather than traveling to town with the man he most admired and loved in the world.

A sandpiper and its mate scurried through the cattails that bordered the rocky embankment. The morning sunlight glinted off the water, bringing a gentle breeze.

"Would you like to throw rocks, Josiah?" The rock throwing had occupied him yesterday during the wedding. Maybe it would work again.

But Josiah shook his head.

A knot of desperation tied in her stomach. Even though she was inexperienced with raising children, she didn't want Patrick knowing that and regretting his decision to marry her. She wanted him to think she was confident and able to handle a boy a quarter her size, because certainly she could. She'd done well so far.

After all, how difficult could a two-year-old be?

She knelt next to the boat that was swaying in the waves. "I know you'll enjoy helping me dig up the garden to get the dirt ready for planting."

At the mention of dirt, Josiah peeked over his shoulder, interest sparking in his face.

"You're planting a garden?" Patrick asked.

"Aye. If you don't object." She'd added seeds to the list of supplies earlier.

"Not at all," he responded. "It's just that Delia wasn't interested in one . . ." His voice trailed off, and he focused on Josiah's flyaway hair.

"I don't know much about gardens myself," she admitted, "but I thought it might be fun to plant a few things. I can start with beans and cucumbers and carrots and onions and whatever other seeds you can find."

"What do you say, lad? You can help your mamma ready the garden."

Josiah stood silently for a moment, then shook his head. "Me go with Daddy."

Patrick exhaled a sigh and stood. He hefted the boy up. Josiah wrapped his arms around his daddy's neck and rested his head against his shoulder.

Josiah didn't want to be with her. What must Patrick think of her now? She'd been here less than twenty-four hours and his son had decided he didn't want her for a mamma.

She took a step away from the boat. Maybe it would take more time. After all, he'd just lost his mammy. She couldn't wade into his life so soon after the beloved woman's death and take her place in his heart.

Patrick kissed the boy again. "I love you, lad." He whispered in Josiah's ear, though Emma could hear the tender words anyway.

To her surprise, he pried the boy's arms from his neck and held him toward Emma, gazing solemnly into Josiah's face. "You need to obey me now and stay home with your mamma."

Josiah's eyes rounded, yet he didn't say anything. Emma took the boy, settled him on her hip, and was relieved when he didn't protest.

Quickly, Patrick propelled the boat away from the dock. "I'll be back by dinnertime tonight," he called. And with that, he settled himself on his bench, picked up the oars, and began to make rapid strokes away from the shore.

"Daddy . . ." Josiah's bottom lip stuck out and trembled.

"He'll be back soon," she reassured, infusing her voice with cheerfulness. "In the meantime, we're going to have a very fun day together. We can plant the garden, scrub the laundry, clean your bedroom, and maybe even do some more exploring."

She'd started to turn away from the retreating boat when Josiah gave a small cry and extended a hand toward his daddy. She stopped and smoothed his hair from his forehead. She could wait with him if he wanted to watch his daddy leave. Maybe that would console him.

But the farther away the boat got, the louder Josiah's whimpering grew. And when the boat became a speck along the distant shore of the bay, Josiah was crying in loud gulping sobs.

"Now, now, little love." She hugged him closer.

But instead of letting her console him, he arched his body and threw back his head. He struggled against her so fiercely, Emma was afraid she would drop him.

"Oh, little love," she murmured, doing her best to soothe him. But his cries became more insistent and angry. Somehow she managed to carry him off the dock without losing her grip. When she reached the rocky shore and a patch of long sea grass and cattails, she almost collapsed under the weight of his writhing body and was forced to kneel down and let go of him.

Once on the ground, he kicked his legs, flailed his arms, and screeched at the top of his lungs.

"Heaven have mercy." She wiped the perspiration that had formed on her brow.

She'd never known any child to react this way. She would have believed he was in great agony and dying if she hadn't just watched him climb into the cutter without any problem.

She watched him with a growing helplessness. Finally, after several long minutes of listening to his wailing and realizing he didn't seem to be planning to stop anytime soon, she steeled herself, hoisted him up, and hauled him back to the house.

While she cleaned the sitting room, she attempted to distract him with everything she could think of, from playing in a bucket of water to pounding a drum made out of a pan and wooden spoon. He didn't stop crying until she carried him to the garden plot and offered him a small hand shovel, which he stuck in the soil she'd loosened for him. He filled a shovelful of the dirt and dumped it into his lap, his sobs finally quieting.

Emma crouched next to him, her chest tight, her cheeks wet with her own tears.

He dug his shovel into the ground again, hiccupped a half sob, and scooped more dirt into his lap. He patted the dirt with one hand and then went to work more earnestly digging a hole.

She sat back on her heels, relief overwhelming her and making her want to sob. She hardly dared to move for fear of setting him off again. For a long while she just watched him, not even caring that his freshly washed outfit was growing filthier by the minute or that he'd wiped a dirty hand across his runny nose and now had mud streaked across his cheek.

"Hole," he said, glancing up at her, his face beaming with pride at his hard work.

"Aye, that's a fine hole. The finest hole I've ever seen." At that moment, she'd praise anything he did, so long as it kept him from crying.

She picked herself up, brushed the soil from her skirt, and with trembling legs started clearing the weeds from the garden—keeping one eye on Josiah as she worked and hoping he wouldn't start wailing again.

Patrick studied the overcast sky and attempted to gauge the position of the sun. Instinctively he knew he had several hours before he needed to light the lamp. Even so, he plunged his oars deeper, urging the little boat to go faster.

It rode low in the water under the weight of all the supplies he'd purchased. His muscles burned with the effort of rowing it hard, but he was almost home. He could see the copper dome of the tower with its vent ball topped with the lightning rod and weather vane.

Maybe he should have taken Josiah with him. But he wanted Josiah to learn to accept his new mamma and her authority, which wouldn't happen if he coddled the boy.

The cutter drew nearer the dock, and the anxiety that had been nagging him all day swelled like the crest of a wave. If he were honest, he was more worried about Emma's reaction to Josiah than about getting home in time for his nightly duties.

Josiah could be strong-willed at times and had the energy of a whole ship's crew. He certainly didn't want the boy throwing one of his temper tantrums and causing Emma to second-guess what she'd gotten herself into. She'd do plenty of second-guessing in the days to come without Josiah adding to it.

Emma seemed like a sweet girl, and he'd thanked the Lord more than once during his prayer time last night that He'd sent her to his rescue. But as before, he couldn't keep from wondering exactly what Holy Bill had told her. Probably not enough, otherwise she wouldn't have been quite so accepting.

Of course, Patrick had confessed everything to the Lighthouse Board and Delia's father when he'd been hired as an assistant keeper down at Fort Gratiot. He'd been honest with them from the start.

Still they'd all agreed—including Holy Bill—that wiping the slate clean was the best way for him to move forward. They'd cautioned him against sharing too much with anyone for fear of starting rumors and bringing about reprisals.

He'd only told Delia about his crimes and in the most general of terms. She'd eventually consented to marrying him, even though she'd been hesitant. As it turned out, even the little she'd known about him had been too much. Not many weeks after they were married, he stopped visiting her bed because he'd hated the way she stiffened whenever he lay next to her, as if his merest touch repulsed her.

He didn't blame Delia in the least. He hadn't deserved her anyway. And he certainly didn't deserve Emma now.

Guilt prodded him to share more with Emma. At the same time, he didn't want to push her away. He'd already alienated one wife. Did he have to with this one as well? Couldn't they live in accord without him having to open up the stinking refuse of his past?

His thoughts turned to ice at the memory of the worst ghost of all, the pale face of a woman marred with purple bruises, with streaks of dried blood across her lips and cheek.

"Oh, God, please forgive me," he whispered, just as he had a thousand times since the morning he'd awoken to the battered body in his bed.

With a last heave, he guided the boat alongside the dock. He jumped out and did little more than secure the cutter before sprinting down the dock and up the rocky path. He hadn't quite reached the end of the short trail when he heard Josiah's screams. His heart sank into his rubber boots. The screams penetrated the open windows of the house and rang out over the isthmus.

He didn't stop to wipe his feet, but instead bounded through the front door, down the hallway, and into the kitchen. There, kneeling on the floor in a puddle of soapy water, was Emma. In the washtub next to her sat Josiah, crying and writhing and batting at her hands as she attempted to wash his muddy face.

For a moment, neither Emma nor Josiah noticed his presence.

"I'm home," Patrick announced from the doorway.

Josiah's sobbing came to an immediate halt. "Daddy?" He squirmed and craned his neck around Emma. And when his eager eyes met Patrick's, his freckled face broke into a smile that rivaled sunshine. "Daddy!"

Patrick couldn't muster a return smile. Worry cramped his gut.

Slowly, Emma shifted, her eyes filled with mortification. Weariness drew lines across her forehead, and her shoulders sagged.

Patrick crossed the floor with its muddy puddles and Josiah's dirt-covered clothing strewn here and there. He crouched beside the tub until he was level with the boy.

"Hi, Daddy," Josiah said, giving him another toothy smile that melted him.

"Hi, lad." He tousled the boy's wet hair.

Josiah held out his arms to him, clearly expecting to be rescued from Emma.

But Patrick didn't move. "You're giving your mamma a hard time."

"Daddy give bath."

"No, lad. Your mamma will finish. And no more crying." Josiah looked down at the murky bathwater, his lower lip trembling.

"When you're done, if you've been good, you can help me carry supplies."

Josiah's head shot up. "Me be good."

Patrick rose and nodded. "You need to be good for Mamma all the time."

His lower lip trembled again.

Patrick didn't want to make the boy cry, but he hoped to send the message that Josiah needed to treat Emma with respect.

Gratefulness flashed across Emma's features, features that were sweet and youthful and prettier than he remembered from when he'd seen her that morning.

He expected to see frustration in her eyes, perhaps even anger at leaving her alone with Josiah all day. Instead, she merely gave him a faint smile.

When he retreated to the cutter to start unloading, he kept one ear tuned to the open windows. He released a long sigh when the boy didn't fuss any further. Minutes later, Josiah came charging down the path toward the boat at full speed with Emma rushing after him. He was barefoot, but at least he was clothed.

Dangling the boy's shoes from her fingers, she wiped a dripping sleeve across her loose hair and stared helplessly as Josiah hurtled himself into Patrick's arms.

"I'll put his shoes on," Patrick offered. "And I can watch him while I unload."

She hesitated, taking in the way Josiah clung to him, his arms wrapped tightly around his neck. Then she nodded, set the shoes on the shore, and started back up the path, her shoulders slumped and her feet dragging.

Patrick wanted to call after her, to thank her for tending to Josiah all day. But the words stuck in his throat. Weariness had descended upon him like a heavy fog, and he knew he would need to sneak in a couple of hours of sleep before ascending the tower to light the lantern.

He made quick work putting away the supplies, even with Josiah trailing along with him. Afterward he stumbled to the bedroom, fell across the bed, and was asleep the moment he closed his eyes.

Patrick awoke with a start.

"Daddy" came Josiah's whisper next to his ear.

Had he overslept? That was always the first question that hit Patrick every time he woke. It was the question that haunted his sleep too, the fear that eventually he would wear himself out so much that in his exhaustion he would pass out for days. And then he would neglect the lantern and be the cause of a shipwreck.

Fortunately, the fading light of evening indicated he still had time before he needed to turn on the lamp. In spite of the harshness of the long winter, he'd quickly realized that living in northern Michigan had some benefits, including the long-lasting light of the evenings. The closer the days drew to the summer solstice, the longer the days grew, so that he didn't need to light the lantern until after nine o'clock.

"Mamma tell me to wake you," Josiah said.

Patrick pushed himself up and stifled a yawn. "Thank you, lad." His stomach gurgled from hunger. He took a deep breath and caught the acridness of burnt bread, or something like it. "Go tell your mamma I'll be ready for dinner in a few minutes."

Josiah toddled out of the room, obviously proud of his messenger duties.

Patrick smiled as he sorted through the items of clean clothes left in his drawer. He changed clothes, ran a comb through his hair that was in need of a trim, and ignored the scruffiness on his chin.

He could see that Emma had tidied the room, picking up the clothes from the floor and washing them and making the bed. The sight helped to release some of the tension in his shoulders. Maybe he was worrying for nothing. Maybe he didn't need to say anything more to Emma about his past. Maybe if he kept silent, things would be different from what they were with Delia.

He started down the hallway. Taking a deep breath, he found himself choking on smoky air. As he stepped into the kitchen, he blinked hard through the haze that filled the room.

Josiah was seated in his high chair, oblivious to the fact that the kitchen was burning down before their eyes. "Hi, Daddy." The boy smiled with a mouthful of food, something black.

A quick perusal of the kitchen told Patrick the smoke was coming from the two pans on the stove in front of Emma. As far as he could tell, there wasn't a fire but just smoke rising from whatever she was attempting to cook.

"Eat, Daddy," Josiah said, biting the edge of a charred circle of what might have been a biscuit or griddle cake if it hadn't been completely burnt and unrecognizable. Josiah chomped away and smiled with no signs that he'd spent the day throwing one temper tantrum after another.

Emma's back was stiff, and she was attempting to flip something in one of the griddles but only managed to keep half of it in the pan. The other half slid onto the stove and sent another billow of smoke into the air.

Above the sizzling, she gave a soft cry.

Had she burned herself? He went to her in two long strides and took her hand. "Are you hurt?"

She shook her head with a cough, and other than sticky flour coating her skin, he couldn't see any sign of injury.

He stepped around her and closed the vents on the firebox, then grabbed a rag to hold the hot griddle handle and shoved the pans away from the burning heat. He hurried to the window, pushed it up all the way, and then threw open the back door.

"I'm so . . . sorry," she said while coughing. Soot covered her cheeks, making the whites of her eyes stand out. "I didn't mean to burn everything."

He fanned the smoke out the door with the rag.

"You have every right to be angry with me," she said, her shoulders sagging.

"What?" He closed the distance between them.

She pressed against the cupboard and cringed.

Was she afraid of him? Did she think he was heartless enough to get upset over a burnt meal?

"Ah, lass." He lifted his thumb and wiped away a smudge of soot on her nose. "I'm not angry with you."

Her eyes widened. "You're not?"

"Not in the least." He knew he should move away from her, but he wanted her to know he wasn't an angry man—not anymore.

He lifted his other hand. A loose strand of her hair floated over her face, beckoning him to tuck it behind her ear. He started to reach for it, but then merely rested his palm against the cupboard door next to her head.

"Josiah doesn't like me."

"Give him time."

"And I don't know how to cook." Her voice turned to liquid at her admission.

"Well, Josiah doesn't seem to mind." He glanced over his shoulder to the little boy.

Josiah flashed a smile, showing them both a mouthful of blackened griddle cake.

Emma gave a soft laugh.

A grin tugged at Patrick's lips.

As if realizing he was the source of their amusement, Josiah scrunched his eyes and gave them an enormous grin, the specks of black making him look as though he were missing several teeth.

Emma laughed again, this time louder.

Patrick's grin broke free. He wasn't sure what he liked more, the sound of Emma's delighted laughter or Josiah's silly antics. Instead of watching Josiah, he let himself study Emma's face—the gentle curve of her chin, the pertness of her nose and mouth, the delicate lashes that framed her eyes.

What was she really like? What were her interests? Her past?

There was so much he didn't know about her. But now all he could think about was getting to know this woman who had come into his life. He realized that even though she hadn't been a part of his and Josiah's lives very long, he didn't want her to go.

"You were a saint to put up with Josiah's crying all day," he told her.

At his words, her body melted, and her eyes warmed to rich coffee. She brushed at the loose wisp of her hair and averted her eyes shyly, as if she'd been thinking about him and remembering that they were married, that he was a man and she a woman.

She'd let him kiss her yesterday at their wedding. In fact, she hadn't seemed to mind. And heaven help him, he'd found pleasure in it. Much more than he'd wanted to admit. The contact had been brief, but it had stirred manly longings deep inside him, longings he'd tried to bury three feet deep with Delia.

He didn't realize that he'd leaned closer until Emma pressed her head back against the cupboard. Her smile faded, and she glanced nervously around his face.

He removed his hand from next to her head and took a step back. He forced himself to turn to the stove before she could see the effect she had upon him.

He'd told her he wouldn't expect anything of her, and he needed to stay true to his word. Besides, he wasn't worthy of her. It would save them both heartache if he didn't pretend otherwise.

Chapter 7

*J*ust one seed at a time," Emma said again to Josiah.

But the little boy spilled several into the hole, heedless of her instructions.

She sat back on her heels in the garden plot she'd finally cleared as an all-too-familiar helplessness swept over her. Josiah was an angel whenever Patrick was home, but any time Patrick left, the boy became nearly impossible to handle.

She peered beyond the tower to the rocky beach that formed the bend of the isthmus. In the clear blue of the day, the lake went on forever without a boat in sight—not even Patrick's. It was almost time for him to return from fishing, and she wasn't sure who was waiting more anxiously for him, her or Josiah.

After almost a week, it hadn't taken her long to recognize a pattern to Patrick's schedule. He came down from the lighthouse at sunrise after turning off the light. He fixed breakfast, then headed out in his cutter to fish until the early afternoon. After he arrived home and ate the leftovers from breakfast, he'd fall into bed and sleep for five or six hours until the evening when he'd spend time with Josiah before he had to head back to the tower.

She wanted to ask him why he hadn't taken the time yet to show her the workings of the lighthouse, but she dreaded hearing him say that he thought she was overwhelmed enough just taking care of Josiah and the house, and that she wasn't capable of learning about the light too.

It was almost as if he was going out of his way to avoid interacting with her. She wanted to believe it was because he was busy, or that he simply didn't have time for her, or was still grieving the wife he'd lost. But she wasn't so sure.

"Daddy home?" Josiah stood and stared at the lake.

"Not yet, little love."

His lip slid out and wobbled. She'd quickly learned that was the sign he was about to cry.

"How about if you help me cover the seeds?" She inwardly chided herself for looking at the lake and reminding the boy about Patrick's absence. "Let's get your shovel, so you can scoop the dirt."

Josiah shook his head. "Me throw rocks. See Daddy." He moved away from the garden.

She sighed. She didn't mind standing at the lake's edge and watching for Patrick if that was what it took to calm Josiah and keep him from crying. The trouble was, she needed to finish planting the beans and then try to salvage the mess Josiah had made in the mounds of cucumbers she'd planted yesterday.

"Wait, Josiah," she called after the boy.

But he was already skipping away as fast as his little legs would carry him.

She stood, grabbed his cap—which was a battle to keep on his head—and raced after him. If only she could finish one thing before Josiah moved on to some other interest or task.

The clopping of hooves and the crunching of wagon wheels

stopped the boy. He spun so fast that he fell on his bottom in the long grass.

She was surprised too at the sight of a wagon coming down the barely visible path that wound through the woods stretching to the west of the lighthouse. She shielded her eyes and caught sight of the thin frame of a woman driving the team of horses.

Emma waited with growing anticipation as the wagon pulled into the yard. She smoothed her skirt, brushed away the soil that clung to it, and straightened her straw hat, hoping she didn't have any dirt on her face.

This was her first visitor to her new home. She'd always dreamed about a moment like this, welcoming company into *her* home, and now here it was.

"Good afternoon," she called with a wave and a smile.

The petite woman nodded curtly and brought the team to a halt, her bony arms straining against the reins. The woman's face looked familiar. Was this the sick Bertha Burnham she'd seen before the funeral?

"You the new Mrs. Garraty?"

Mrs. Garraty? Hearing her name on the woman's lips sent a warm sensation through Emma. Even if she wasn't Mrs. Garraty in the truest sense, the sound of the name coming from someone else was still pleasant. "Aye. I'm she."

The woman stared down at her from beneath the brim of a bonnet. Her face was narrow, her eyes sharp. "I'm Mrs. Burnham. Mrs. Bertha Burnham. Folks call me Bertie."

"I'm delighted to meet you, Bertie. I hope you've recovered from your illness."

"My head hurts, my bones ache, and I still have a cough. But the work doesn't wait, does it?" Bertie frowned at the half-planted garden, the tools scattered in all directions, and then beyond to the basket of wet laundry that Emma had yet to hang on the line.

"The work doesn't wait," Emma agreed, wishing she'd stowed the damp clothes out of sight. "But I can't seem to get much done with Josiah needing my attention." If she could hardly manage with Josiah and all his energy, how did mothers with a whole houseful of children ever get anything done?

Bertie leveled a stern look at the boy.

He sidled against Emma and wrapped one arm around her leg, twisting her skirt and smearing dirt from his muddy hands. He popped his thumb into his mouth and peered up at Bertie.

For a reason Emma couldn't explain, his simple act of drawing comfort from her somehow reassured her, and she rested her hand lightly on his head. Maybe she was making more progress in gaining his affection than she realized.

"I have four boys." Bertie started to climb down from the bench. "And I never had any trouble getting my work done."

"Four?" Emma searched the woman's tiny frame, noting the two thin brown braids that hung down her back and reached to the waist of her black dress. Bertie didn't look matronly enough to have had four children. The woman was as flat as a washboard, not at all the rounded body of a woman who'd born children.

"The oldest is fifteen and youngest ten," Bertie said, pressing her hands to her shapeless hips. "I always said that the best thing for them, besides the switch, was hard work. They've been fishing and chopping wood since they were knee-high."

Josiah's hold tightened, and he sucked his thumb noisily.

"Josiah is certainly a hard worker, aren't you, little love?" Emma squeezed him with a half hug.

The boy was too busy sucking his thumb to speak.

"First thing you need to do," Bertie said, "is make the boy stop sucking his thumb. He's not a baby anymore, so you don't treat him like one."

Emma gave a start and glanced at Josiah's lips puckered around his thumb. "I had no idea he was too old for that."

"If you want him to grow up, then you can't baby him."

"Oh . . ." Emma didn't quite know how to respond. Her inadequacies about parenting rose up to taunt her once again. Perhaps she could learn a great deal from this mother of four, who obviously had much more experience.

"I told that to Delia too, but no matter how much she tried, Patrick had a mind to spoil the child."

Emma thought back to Bertie's harsh words at the funeral when she'd called Patrick a snake. She'd also indicated that Delia was her cousin. It seemed something had happened to cause hard feelings between Bertie and Patrick.

"I'm sorry for your loss," Emma said. "It's never easy to lose a loved one."

Bertie's face hardened. "It's very difficult. Delia was much too young to die." Bertie again looked around the yard and then up at the tower, pursing her lips tightly.

Even though Emma was curious to know more about Patrick's first wife and the circumstances that had led to her death, she held back her questions. Asking Bertie anything more would be prying, and Emma didn't want to start off a new friendship on the wrong foot.

"How's Ryan?" Emma asked, the familiar ache for her brother pressing in her chest. She'd been busy that week and hadn't had the time to think about him too much. But every time she did, she missed him and wondered how he was faring at his temporary job.

"Ryan's doing fine. Good thing he's a hard worker. Can't say as much for the other survivors who have been hanging around this week. Mighty glad that the passel of them has sailed out."

Emma hoped she would at least have the chance to say good-bye to Ryan before he moved on.

"Now, let's get these chickens unloaded." Bertie turned back to the wagon.

"Chickens?"

"Patrick said you wanted chickens." Bertie lifted a crate, and there was a sudden flurry of flapping wings and squawking.

Emma hadn't mentioned anything to Patrick about chickens. Yes, she'd started making repairs to the hen house a day or two ago, though she hadn't realized he'd noticed.

"When he delivered his catch to the fishery yesterday, he stopped by and bought you five of my new hens and a rooster." Bertie placed a crate on the ground, then turned to reach for another. "I told him I'd deliver them because I've been waiting to meet you ever since I heard you up and married him. I only wish I'd been well enough to talk to you and warn you not to make such a foolish mistake."

Foolish mistake? Emma stared at Bertie.

"Unfortunately," Bertie continued, setting the other crate on the grass, "what's done is done. And now we'll have to try to make the best of it and do what we can to keep you safe."

A curved beak poked from between the slats in the crate.

Josiah pulled his thumb out of his mouth and pointed. "Chicken?"

"Aye," Emma responded absently.

Foolish mistake? Keep her safe? What could Bertie possibly mean? After a week of living at the lighthouse, she couldn't speak of any regrets about her rash decision to marry Patrick. Everything was going as well as could be expected.

She'd even lost her nervousness at night, finally understanding that Patrick wouldn't show up at dark, not when he was tending the light.

Josiah circled the crates, hopping with uncontainable excitement.

Patrick had even purchased chickens for her without her having to ask. He was as considerate as he was kind. Surely Bertie was completely wrong in her assessment of Patrick.

"You carry one crate." Bertie nodded to the boxes. "I'll carry the other."

Emma approached tentatively. She'd never tended chickens before. She and Ryan and her dad had never lived anywhere long enough to consider it.

She gingerly lifted the crate, hoping the fowl wouldn't peck her fingers through the slats. "What would you like to name the chickens?" she asked Josiah, holding the crate well away from her body as she followed Bertie toward the hen house.

"No naming the chickens," Bertie called over her shoulder. "They're not pets."

At the flapping and squawking, Emma stretched farther from the crate and careened after Bertie.

When they reached the wire-fenced area, Bertie opened the top of her crate, revealing a medium-sized rooster and two smaller, speckled black-and-white hens. They squabbled as if scolding her for cooping them up. In seconds they were out in the grass and strutting around.

Josiah clapped his hands and squealed. "Chicken!"

Emma followed Bertie's example and opened her crate, allowing three more hens into the grassy area.

Josiah shrieked again, his eyes wide, the sunshine highlighting his freckles. Emma couldn't keep from smiling at the boy's delight. She pushed down all the qualms Bertie's remarks about Patrick had elicited and simply tried to enjoy the moment of watching Josiah and the chickens.

"Patrick purchased a bag of feed too." Bertie reached for the crates and started back toward the wagon.

"Wait," Emma called as she raced after Bertie. She pushed down the anxiety she felt over being left alone with six chickens. "Can you tell me what I need to do? I don't know anything about chickens."

As Bertie replaced the crates and tended her horses, she rattled off a long list of dos and don'ts, including how much to feed them, when to check for eggs, and how to make sure the nesting boxes were dark. Emma nodded, hoping she'd be able to remember everything.

"I can't stay long," Bertie said, heading toward the house with a spring in her step, her braids bouncing against her back. "I've got too much work waiting for me back home. But I suppose I can sit a short spell with you and have a cup of coffee."

"Aye, come in, won't you?" Emma turned first toward the house and then back to the chicken coop, completely flustered. How could she have been so stupid not to invite her guest inside? Even if this was her first home and visitor, she should have known better.

"Come with Mamma, Josiah." She reached for Josiah.

"No!" He pointed at the hen house, resisting her with the force of a full-grown ox. "Chickens. Me see chickens."

Emma tugged him toward the house. "Come, little love. We need to go inside now and serve our guest. Maybe you can have something to eat."

Josiah wiggled to free himself from her grasp. "No! Me see chickens!" His pitch rose a notch.

"I'll make you a smiley-faced griddle cake." She'd used maple syrup to draw faces on the round cakes once before to get him to stop crying.

Out of the corner of her eye she could see that Bertie had stopped and was watching her interaction with Josiah with narrowed eyes.

"Or how about if I make you another creature out of paper?" The butterfly she'd folded for him had become nothing more than a torn, dirty mass of paper. "I'll fold you a kitty this time."

A sob slipped from his lips. In only seconds he'd be on the ground, flailing his legs and screaming.

She had to do something to stop him. She'd only just met Bertie. She couldn't let Josiah scream now, for once he got started it was difficult to console him. She didn't want Bertie to think she was completely inept at everything, even though that was close to the truth.

He jerked against her hold and let loose a scream that was as loud as a ship's whistle. Just as he'd done previously, he threw himself to the ground. But he'd hardly had time to kick his legs and pound his fists when Bertie was at his side.

"Young man," the woman said, grasping his arm and yanking him back to his feet. "You get in the house right now." Her thin face was a mask of calm fury, her eyes fierce.

Josiah was so startled that he gulped down his sobs and turned immediately silent and ashen-faced.

"I won't put up with any of your nonsense," Bertie said, louder this time. "And your mother shouldn't put up with it either. If I were her, I'd have taken a switch to your backside by now."

Bertie half dragged, half hauled the boy into the house, her steps firm and quick, her lips pinched together. Emma followed after them, her face burning. What must Bertie think of her?

The woman plopped Josiah into his seat and then situated herself in the chair next to him, glowering as if daring him to make a sound.

Josiah looked at Bertie, his lashes glistening with the wetness of unshed tears. Emma had the urge to stare at Bertie too. She'd never met a woman quite like her, and she wasn't sure whether to be frightened alongside Josiah or laugh at the absurdity of the situation.

Instead, she rushed to the stove, to the coffee she'd left warming on the burner from earlier. She poured two mugs and searched for anything she could serve Bertie, anything at all. Other than the fish and griddle cakes that sat in the greasy pan from breakfast, she had nothing. She swallowed the dismay that kept surfacing and forced a smile as she turned.

"I wish I had something to serve you besides coffee," she said, setting the mug before Bertie. "But your visit caught me by surprise."

Bertie examined every inch of the kitchen before settling back in her chair and reaching for her mug. Emma was glad she'd made an effort to dress up the kitchen a little with a canning jar of cattails and wildflowers and a few colorful and uniquely shaped rocks she'd found along the shore.

"To be honest, I'm not much of a cook." Emma sat down across from the woman. What she wouldn't give to learn how to make a meal or two for her new family, instead of having to resort to leftovers of the meals Patrick prepared.

"Not to boast," Bertie said while taking a sip of coffee, "but I've gained quite the reputation for my baking abilities. If you need any tips or receipts, I've got plenty."

"Oh, I could use all the tips you could give me." Emma slid to the edge of her chair in her eagerness. "I'd be forever grateful if you could show me how to make biscuits or bread or anything really."

Bertie peered over the rim of her mug. Her eyes lacked warmth, and her cheeks pinched as though she had swallowed vinegar instead of coffee. "Young lady, it looks to me like you took on a job here that you can't handle."

Emma traced a dark coffee stain on the table. She couldn't deny Bertie's assessment. She dreaded that eventually Patrick would realize just how inept she was and regret he married her. "I'd be much obliged if you could teach me everything you know."

Josiah was taking tiny bites out of a cold griddle cake. He continued to stare at Bertie as though she might reach out and bite him if he moved.

"Would you have time to give me a receipt or two today?" Emma asked.

"'Course I can," Bertie said, her voice echoing in her mug as she took a gulp. "That's what friends are for."

Emma was writing the last of the ingredients for biscuits and fish chowder when the front door opened.

"Daddy?" Josiah called, squirming in an effort to get out of his chair.

"Sit, young man!" Bertie ordered. "You wait for your mother to lift you down."

Patrick's squeaky boots sounded in the hallway with his approach. Emma removed Josiah from his chair, knowing how important it was for him to see his daddy upon his return home. Once his feet touched the floor, he charged forward, arms outstretched as Patrick entered the kitchen.

Patrick's face lit up with a grin. He swept the boy up and lifted him above his head. "There you are, lad."

Josiah giggled.

Patrick lowered him into a big hug and brushed a kiss on top of the boy's head.

Bertie had risen from her chair and was watching the display, her expression stormy.

Emma never tired of witnessing Patrick's gentleness with the child. Truth be told, she couldn't imagine anything more beautiful than a father showering love on his son.

Patrick's eyes met hers above Josiah's neatly combed red head. He seemed to be checking on her, making sure she was still there. And at the sight of her, he released a slight breath.

"Thank you for the chickens," she said.

"I hoped you wouldn't mind," he said, focusing on Josiah.

"You were very kind to think of it." She wanted to tell him that no man had ever given her anything before. Even if the chickens were for all of them and not just her, it still felt like she'd been given a precious gift.

She had the urge to run over to Patrick like Josiah had and throw her arms around him in a grateful hug. But Bertie cleared her throat loudly, drawing their attention and reminding Emma that she still had company.

At the sight of their visitor, Patrick took a step back, his face hardening. He exchanged a few terse words of greeting with Bertie before excusing himself. "I'll take Josiah along with me," he offered, as he usually did when he returned from fishing.

Bertie watched him go, her lips growing thinner until Patrick and Josiah disappeared.

"Delia told me the board doesn't pay Patrick enough for his

light keeping," Bertie said in a hushed voice. "That's why he has to get the extra income from fishing."

Emma nodded and tried to pretend that the news didn't surprise her. Patrick hadn't shared much about himself or his personal life with her yet, and she didn't suppose a wife ought to concern herself with her husband's financial situation the first week of marriage.

Bertie leaned forward, peeked down the hallway, and then bent closer to Emma. "Delia also suspected that Patrick needs the extra money because he's secretly giving it to someone. A woman."

Emma recoiled at the words. "Who? And why would he?"

Bertie held up her hand as if to stop Emma's questions. "I don't like to gossip, so I won't say any more except that I've never liked Patrick."

"I don't understand." Although she wanted to shut the door on Bertie's words, to block out everything negative the woman said, so that she could continue to live in blissful oblivion, something inside her demanded to know the truth.

"My dear cousin wasn't one to speak much. She was quiet. And it's no wonder she was melancholy having to live with Patrick," Bertie said, brushing at invisible crumbs on the table. "But she did say to me on several occasions, 'Things aren't what they seem, Bertie. Things aren't what they seem.'"

Emma's stomach flipped. "What did she mean by that?"

"Like I said, I don't want to gossip." Bertie started for the back door. "But I will say, you best watch your back. And if I were you, I'd go through his things and see what I could find."

"I don't know what I'd be looking for. I feel completely safe here."

Bertie halted abruptly and spun so that her thin face was only inches from Emma's. "I personally don't believe Delia's fall was the accident Patrick claims it was."

A stunned quiet fell over Emma.

Bertie's eyes gleamed with anger again. "Maybe she was pushed . . . or maybe she got in the middle of a lovers' quarrel."

Emma shook her head, unwilling, unable to listen to another word. "Please, Bertie. I don't think we should say any more—"

"My thoughts exactly." Bertie opened the door. "I did want to warn you, though. You should know exactly what you've gotten yourself into by marrying Patrick Garraty."

Emma followed Bertie outside to her wagon. Josiah was chattering and following Patrick around as he stowed his fishing supplies in the shed. She didn't dare look Patrick's way lest he read the confusion battling inside her.

She stood by the side of the wagon as Bertie climbed aboard and situated herself on the bench. "Watch for those pirates," she called to Patrick.

Half in the shed, his back stiffened.

"Heard just this morning that one pirate boat in particular is harassing steamers passing through the area. Captained by a man named Mitch Schwartz. Quite dangerous from what people are saying."

Patrick turned slowly. His face was shadowed by the brim of his flat cap. "Thank you, Bertie. I'll be on the watch for any problems."

Emma's mind flashed with the vision of flames that had engulfed the steamer and nearly killed her and Ryan. "Do you think they're the same pirates that set fire to the steamer Ryan and I were on?"

Bertie held up a hand again and cut off Emma's inquiry. "Don't want to speculate. Just wanted you all to be aware that there could be more attacks headed our way."

The woman flicked a sharp riding whip across the team of horses. The wheels rolled forward in the tall grass as she veered the wagon toward the woodland path. She called to Emma over her shoulder, "Pepper. Put pepper on that boy's thumb. That'll make him stop sucking it in no time."

Emma nodded and gave a last wave to her new friend. A part of her wondered if she should chase after Bertie and demand that she take her with her back to Presque Isle Harbor, back to Ryan. Maybe she wasn't safe at the lighthouse with Patrick after all.

But she could only watch Bertie's wagon lumber away and pray that none of the woman's words of caution were true.

Chapter 8

*P*atrick ran a jack plane over the crumbling caulking above the windowpane. The crack was in need of sealing to prevent a leak during the next storm. After the long winter, the whole tower was in sorry shape, with stones loose in the lower two-thirds and the bricks wasting away in the upper part. The structure was bordering on unsafe, and he didn't know how it would survive another Michigan winter without collapsing completely.

Of course, the board hadn't sent out the Lighthouse Service tender crew yet, even though he'd mailed his request to Mr. Yates, the district superintendent, when the lake had thawed, once again allowing communication with the outside world. Since Patrick hadn't heard anything back, he'd been forced to attempt his own repairs.

From his spot in the gallery, he could hear the steady tap of a hammer. He glanced down into the backyard to where Emma knelt next to the hen house. She held several nails between her lips and hammered at the holes in the roof with a precision that had him looking in her direction more than he should.

She'd come outside to work after putting Josiah to bed. In fact, he'd noticed that she worked most evenings scrubbing clothes, cleaning, or tending the garden until darkness forced her to stop. A niggling of guilt told him she had no choice. During the day, Josiah was still giving her a hard time and preventing her from getting much done.

Patrick looked to the west, over the towering white pines, spruce, tamarack, and hardwoods that spread over the Presque Isle isthmus. The sun was sinking, the sky streaked with an array of oranges and pinks. A warm breeze stroked his cheeks, signaling the coming of summer.

For all the hardships that came with his being a lightkeeper, the beauty of evenings like this made everything worthwhile. He took a deep breath, and his soul offered a prayer of gratitude. God had been good to him, had blessed him much more than he deserved. And he couldn't forget it.

He forced his attention back to the repairs he'd been neglecting. He dug through the toolbox issued by the Lighthouse Service and found a caulking iron. He stared at the crack. How could he fill the enormous gap?

With a sigh, he dropped the caulking iron and picked up a hammer and a piece of crumbled caulk from the gallery. He pushed the jagged part back into the hole it had vacated at some point that spring and then swung the hammer against it. But instead of hitting the narrow strip, the hammer slammed against his thumb.

A mutter escaped his lips before he could prevent it. He let the hammer fall with a clatter to the catwalk that surrounded the tower windows. He stuck his thumb in his mouth and at the same time glanced at Emma, hoping she hadn't seen his stupidity.

But of course she'd paused in her own hammering to peer up

at him. She spit the remainder of nails into her palm. "Looks like you could use a hand," she said, rising to her feet and sending a smile his way.

He knew he should protest, but she'd already started across the yard toward the door in the base of the tower. Maybe he should let her come up, for then he could use the opportunity to apologize for anything Bertie had told her about him.

Ever since the Burnham woman had driven away in her wagon earlier that day, Emma had regarded him with a hesitancy that hadn't been there before. And he couldn't help but wonder what Bertie had shared with her.

He knew Delia had never revealed much to her cousin. Delia had been embarrassed about his past and his family and wanted to keep matters private. In fact, Delia had been the one to warn him not to say anything to Bertie about his history. He'd been all too happy to comply.

Even so, he wasn't sure what information Bertie had weaseled out of Delia during the past year. Most likely the busybody had come to her own conclusions. Even if she didn't know anything, Bertha Burnham made a full-time job out of gossiping, and most of it was just plain hogwash. Most of it . . .

His muscles stiffened again, as they had every time the name Mitch Schwartz replayed in his mind. His blood had turned cold and he'd been paralyzed the moment Bertie had spoken the name. He prayed this was another of those times when the woman was simply spouting nonsense. He hated to think what could happen if Schwartz really was in the area, if he discovered that Patrick was keeper of the Presque Isle Light.

"Please no, God," he whispered.

At a movement inside the lantern room, he squeezed through the narrow door that led back inside. Emma was already poking her head through the hatch in the floor and scrambling through. She focused on the Fresnel lens that took up the major part of the small lantern room.

Patrick let his eyes linger on the dozens of heavy glass prisms mounted in bronze that made up the lens, which stood two and a half feet high on a cast-iron pedestal. The platform made the lens level with the large panes of glass that formed the lantern room. "She's a beauty, isn't she?"

Emma walked slowly around the impressive object. "It's larger than I imagined."

"It's only a fourth-order lens, not as big as some. But for a small tower like this, it's a decent size."

She studied it with the same awe he remembered feeling when he'd first set foot in the lighthouse at Fort Gratiot, where he'd been the assistant keeper under Delia's father. The tower there had a smaller fifth-order lens, a fact Delia often forgot when she'd complained about the inferiority of the Presque Isle lens compared to the one where she'd grown up.

"The prisms are shaped to concentrate the light from the lantern. The bigger bull's-eye lens in the middle helps focus the light into a solid beam that can be seen more than ten miles away."

"I saw it from the steamer before Ryan and I jumped," she said. "We were following it while trying to swim toward shore."

He nodded, wishing he were a smoother talker and that he didn't get so tongue-tied around her, a very pretty woman.

She circled the lantern again. He stood back, giving her room and noticing that her hair had come loose as it usually did from the knot she wore at the back of her neck. The blond wisps floated around her neck and gave her a wind-tossed, carefree appeal.

When she completed a half circle, she turned her attention to the windows that surrounded the room. She gazed out at the lake. "What a magnificent view."

He leaned back against the door and smiled, content to watch her dart from window to window, taking in the spectacular sight with the excitement of a child on Christmas morning.

"No wonder you're up here so much," she said, lingering on the west side and looking at the fingers of color streaking the sky. "It's like having a bit of heaven on earth, isn't it?"

She finally looked at him, and seeing that he was staring at her, she quickly turned toward the lake again, to the ebb and flow of never-ending waves.

He did the same. "On nights like this, it's heaven. But it's not quite as nice during a storm."

The first time he'd gazed upon one of the Great Lakes, he thought somehow he'd gotten mixed up and was back at the ocean he'd crossed from Ireland. The lake seemed to go on forever with no end in sight, and it had waves just as high as the ocean.

Even though the waves looked the same, he'd learned over the years since first sailing the lakes that freshwater waves have a different motion to them. They're sharper; they jump and tumble rather than roll smoothly like the denser saltwater waves of an ocean.

She nodded toward the lantern. "Have you ever missed lighting it?"

"Not yet." His body had ached to skip a night during those long days and nights after Delia's fall, but he'd forced himself up the tower steps every night regardless of how exhausted he felt.

"Maybe sometime you can show me how to light it," she

offered. "Just in case . . . you know, you're not here, or you're sick or something."

"I've been meaning to, but I didn't want to make too many demands of you right away."

She smiled and nodded, and he was relieved that the hesitancy of before seemed to have faded.

"It's not hard to learn," he added. "You have to make sure it has enough fuel, unlock the weights that drive the gears, and then use the hand crank to start a new descent."

"Sounds complicated."

"It's not." Even though it wasn't quite time to light the lantern, he could get it going a little early. "Would you like me to show you now? Tonight?"

She started to nod eagerly, but then stopped and glanced down at the house. "What about Josiah?"

"He'll be fine. He's a sound sleeper."

For all the boy's antics, at least Patrick rarely had any trouble with the boy waking up at night. As he went through the process of lighting the lantern, Emma studied his every move and listened intently. He explained the steps for setting the gears that would rotate the lens into motion. Then he showed her how to trim the wick and where to pour in the oil.

When the beam was finally revolving out over the lake, he stood back. "There you are."

She watched the light reflected through the prisms with a look of wonder. It filled the lantern room with a brilliance that was almost blinding. "Thank you for showing me. I hope I can get it started if I ever need to."

"Maybe you can come up again sometime," he said hesitantly. "To practice." He didn't want to force her, but it would put his mind at ease to know she could handle the light if anything should happen to him. He'd never had to worry about that with Delia. She'd known more than him and would have been a fine keeper were she a man.

He was relieved to see Emma smile. "Of course. I can come up again to help you with the repairs too."

"I admit I'm lousy with a hammer."

"Aye." Her smile broadened. "I was worried you'd take off your thumb."

Dusk had begun to settle outside, and he knew it was too late for her to return to her own repairs. "I'm sorry you couldn't finish your work today."

She shrugged. "It'll wait."

He liked the way her cheeks flushed and her eyes sparkled.

"How old are you, lass?" The question came out before he could stop it.

She shifted and looked down at the floor that he kept immaculately swept and scrubbed.

"I'm sorry," he rushed to say. "I shouldn't have asked. It's just that you seem so young—"

"I'm twenty-two. Practically an old woman."

"Old woman?" He gave a soft laugh. "I would have guessed eighteen and not a day older."

"That's probably because I don't know how to do anything."

He couldn't keep from laughing again, appreciating the way the light from the lantern highlighted the reddish tint to her hair. And he liked her smile, the gentleness of it.

For a long moment she didn't say anything. He wanted to find the words to express his appreciation for all she'd done over the past week, yet he felt as if he'd swallowed a bucket of sand.

Though he knew he should stop staring at her, he couldn't

make himself look away. In the cramped quarters of the room, her smile turned shy. She lowered her head and took a half step toward the hatch and the ladder that led down to the landing of the stone stairway. "I guess I should get going."

"I suppose Bertie had some things to say about me," he blurted.

She stopped, her expression turning serious. "Aye. She doesn't seem to like you much."

"And do you feel the same?" He knew it shouldn't matter; he knew Emma would be better off guarding her heart from a man like him.

Emma studied his face and then offered him a little smile. "I'm not one to form my opinions based on what others say. I like to make my decisions based on what I see for myself."

The muscles in his back relaxed.

She nodded, looked as if she wanted to say more, but instead she descended the first rung of the ladder. "Good night, Patrick."

"Good night, lass." He knew he should say more too, and yet something held him back.

As she disappeared down the ladder, he resisted the urge to follow her, an urge he'd never had with Delia. He hated to admit that he'd always been relieved when Delia would leave him to himself. It wasn't that she was always arguing with him. But she'd had a silent way about her, one that left him feeling inadequate, as if he could never please her. He didn't think any man could please her, except perhaps her father.

In hindsight, he realized he probably shouldn't have moved away from Fort Gratiot, that he shouldn't have forced her to leave the one person in the world she loved—her father. She hadn't wanted to go when Mr. Yates had offered him the position at Presque Isle, even knowing she'd have her cousin nearby. But he'd been excited about the prospect of advancing from assistant to a full-fledged keeper.

And more than that, he'd been anxious to put more distance between himself and his past. He was willing to face many things, including any number of hardships, but his past was something he never wanted to meet up with again.

Chapter 9

*P*retty rock, Mamma?" Josiah held up a gray plain-shaped rock like all the others he'd found.

"Aye." She gave him a nod before digging through the assortment of more colorful rocks at her feet.

The waves crashed nearby, constantly weathering the smooth stones that lined the shore. She picked up a rock that was oblong and a shade of pink. She turned it over, brushing off the sand before dropping it into her pail with the others.

"Here, Mamma." Josiah dumped several of his rocks into the bucket. Next to the vibrant and unique ones she'd collected, his looked like lumps of dirt.

She couldn't hold back a smile of amusement at his definition of pretty. "Thank you, little love. You're a big helper to Mamma."

He smiled and stuck his thumb in his mouth, even though his hands were coated in sand. She waited for him to spit it out and make a fuss about the sand, but his mouth worked furiously around the thumb while he stared off into the distance, in the direction Patrick had gone when he'd left to go fishing a little while ago.

Josiah had wanted to linger like usual on the beach after watching his daddy row away. Emma didn't mind. She enjoyed the cooler morning air before the heat of the day set in. And she never turned down the chance to explore, to hike farther up the isthmus. She always seemed to find something she could use to decorate the house.

She settled Josiah's hat on his head more squarely, noting his tired eyes. He'd woken up crying during an early morning thunderstorm and hadn't gone back to sleep. She could only hope his tiredness wouldn't make him too difficult that day, because Patrick would be gone longer than usual.

After cooking breakfast for them all, he'd left for his fishing as he usually did, but he'd told her not to expect him back until later in the day, that he had some business he needed to tend to. He hadn't told her where he was going or what he was doing.

As he prepared to leave, he appeared distracted and even nervous. She couldn't stop thinking about Bertie's insinuation the previous afternoon that Patrick was involved with another woman. Then she quickly swept the thought from her mind. The Patrick Bertie had described didn't match with the man she was beginning to admire.

What about Bertie's advice to wean Josiah of his thumb-sucking? Should she try it? She imagined Bertie would expect her to have accomplished something by the time they met again.

Gently she tugged the boy's thumb out of his mouth. "You're getting to be a big boy now, Josiah. Maybe it's time you stopped sucking your thumb."

He stared at his thumb and then up at her. "Me not a big boy."

"Aye. Even your britches are getting too small." She'd noticed they were above his ankles and had thought about asking Patrick to buy her material to sew him a new pair.

Josiah stared down at his trousers and shook his head. "Me suck thumb."

She started to correct him, but when he stuffed his thumb back in his mouth, she stopped. Standing before her on the wide open beach with the lake spreading out to the horizon, he appeared so small and forlorn in his tiny cap and freshly laundered shirt and pants that she couldn't muster the wherewithal to argue with him or force him to give up his thumb-sucking.

If it brought him comfort, who was she to challenge that? Not when he must still need it, and not when she'd only been his mamma for such a short time.

"Daddy?" Josiah's face lit up, and his thumb fell out of his mouth. He stared up the shore and pointed to a boat that had moored to the north of them.

Emma frowned. It was much too early for Patrick to return. And besides, there were several men milling about the rocky area, hauling something ashore and poking about the brush.

They didn't appear to be fishermen. They didn't have rods or nets or crates or anything else remotely related to fishing. They weren't wearing the usual gear. If they weren't fishermen, then who were they and what were they doing?

She glanced back over her shoulder in the direction she'd hiked. She'd wandered far enough north that the tower and keeper's house were out of sight. A rustling of wind in a patch of sea grass nearby made her jump.

Josiah raised a hand. "Daddy!" he called, waving. "Daddy, Daddy!"

"Nay, Josiah," she said. "That's not your daddy."

But he bolted forward. At his calls, the men swiveled to stare at her and Josiah.

Emma couldn't make out their faces, but there was something

about them that tightened her muscles and sent her racing after Josiah. She easily caught up with him and swooped him into her arms.

He protested with a cry and attempted to wriggle out of her grasp. She locked her arms around him and cupped a hand over his mouth. "That's not your daddy!" She spun and stalked away as quickly as she could, which was no easy feat on the rocky shore while holding a boy who was squirming like a slippery fish.

"Stop!" someone shouted.

She looked over her shoulder. One of the men had broken away from the group and was running toward her.

Emma picked up her pace. By the time she reached the keeper's house, her legs and arms burned and her breath came in heaving gasps. She stumbled inside, slammed the door closed, and collapsed to her knees.

Thankfully, Josiah had ceased struggling and was sucking his thumb and staring at her with large frightened eyes.

"Mean guys?" He spoke with his thumb in his mouth.

"I don't know, little love. But we're safer here. Until your daddy gets home."

Josiah didn't answer except to suck his thumb again.

She smoothed a hand against his freckled cheek. She knew then she wouldn't—couldn't—make him stop sucking his thumb. The poor wee one had experienced too much loss lately. And he didn't need any more.

Emma dropped the last biscuit onto the baking pan. Her fingers stuck together with the mixture, flour dusted every inch of her apron, and she couldn't see the table through the smears of dough that remained where she'd attempted to roll it out and cut the biscuits evenly.

Josiah was covered from head to toe in flour and sticky dough too. When she started her new baking adventure, she thought she'd keep him occupied if she let him help. But he was only interested in helping for a few minutes, and after making a disaster of the kitchen and himself, he decided to make handprints on the wall. Then he'd thrown flour into the air to pretend it was snowing. And when she'd promptly put an end to his wasting food, he'd started to cry.

She attempted to occupy him by filling a pail with water and showing him how to wash the walls, hoping he'd have just as much fun removing his handprints as he had putting them there.

"All done," he said through a big yawn. He stood by the pail, his shirt and sleeves dripping wet.

"Now you can wash the table for Mamma." She stepped over a puddle and carried her pan to the oven.

"No." His voice was sulky. The day had been more difficult than she'd anticipated. She'd stayed inside, wanting to avoid a confrontation with the men who'd landed down the beach. But Josiah had too much energy to be inside for any length of time.

She blew out a weary sigh and focused on the cast-iron stove. She still didn't know much about using it, but slowly she was figuring out how to heat the stove so it wasn't too hot to burn everything or too cold to do much good.

"Me wash floor."

"Not now, little love." She opened the oven door and slid in the pan of biscuits.

She'd done it. She'd created her first pan of biscuits. A sweet sense of accomplishment engulfed her. Lifting the lid of the fish chowder she'd made earlier, she breathed in the steaming aroma of the fresh trout, sage, and potatoes. She'd made her first real meal all by herself. Wouldn't Patrick be surprised when he walked in and found biscuits and soup? She hoped he'd be pleased.

Warmth spilled through her stomach at the thought of earning another of his smiles, the same kind of smile he'd given her last night when they were in the tower together. The weathered skin at the corners of his eyes had crinkled, his lips had turned up with an adorable quirk, and he'd seemed genuinely happy to be with her. She craved another smile just like it.

"Wash floor," Josiah said again.

She replaced the kettle lid in time to see Josiah tipping the bucket. "Josiah, Mamma said *no*. We're not washing the floor right now."

He looked at her with his mouth set while continuing to tilt the bucket so that some of the water dribbled onto the floor.

"Please obey Mamma, little love."

More water spilled out, and his eyes flashed with defiance. Dark circles under his eyes testified to how tired he was. Even so, she couldn't let his tiredness be an excuse for outright disobedience, could she?

She hesitated. How would an experienced mother like Bertie handle the situation? Emma forced her mouth into what she hoped was a stern frown and then she made her voice sharp. "No more, young man. I want you to put the bucket down this instant."

Josiah's chin lifted higher, and in one swift motion he dumped the bucket the rest of the way, sending water in a web across the floor.

Apparently she hadn't imitated Bertie well enough.

She had no idea what she should do next. Clean up the spill? Make Josiah clean it? Discipline him? Ignore his misbehavior?

She felt positive Bertie would have disciplined Josiah, perhaps punishing him with the switch. But she couldn't make herself do that.

"Oh, Josiah." She breathed out all the anticipation she'd felt only moments ago. Her shoulders sagged with the discouragement that had been building over the past week of trying to be a good parent to him but never quite knowing how. "I wish you would have obeyed Mamma."

He ignored her, squatted and slapped his hand in the water, which sprayed up into his face. He gasped and jerked his head back. It would have been almost funny had the situation not been so serious. For a moment, he didn't say anything, and she was afraid he'd burst into sobs.

But he surprised her by slapping the water again and sending another spray into his face. He sucked in a breath as he did before, but this time it was quickly followed by a giggle.

Emma was tempted to laugh too, and she smothered her smile behind her hand. Everything inside her told her she had to do something to chastise him for dumping out the water. If she didn't, he would think he could always disobey her.

"Josiah . . ." She went to him, her mind scrambling to find the appropriate discipline.

"Me 'plash water." He looked up at her with a delighted smile.

She crouched next to him. "Josiah," she said, in a stern but kind voice she'd heard Patrick use, "Mamma told you not to dump out the water, and you disobeyed."

"Me 'plash!" He hit the water with both hands this time. "'Plash, 'plash, 'plash!"

"And now because you disobeyed, you'll need to . . . you'll need to . . ." She paused and glanced around the kitchen for any solution to her problem. She saw the open door of Josiah's closet bedroom and his tiny bed. "You'll need to sit on your bed for a little bit and repent for not doing as Mamma said."

He kept his head down and waved his hands sideways in the water, causing the puddle to spread out across the floor.

This was going to be hard.

She took a deep breath and reached for his hands. "Come with Mamma to your room."

He shook his head and tried to pull away from her. "Me play in water."

"Nay, little love. You must sit on your bed now."

The moment she steered him away from the water, he started crying. He fought her every step of the way into his room, his cries growing louder until he was screaming. When she tried to lift him to his bed, he arched his back. And when she finally plopped him amidst the feathery mattress, he climbed off.

She hefted him back on, only to have to repeat the process several times, until finally she sat down on the edge of the bed, wrapped her arms around him and held him on her lap, even though he struggled against her and sobbed hoarsely.

A bead of sweat trickled down her forehead, and she was breathing as heavily as if she'd been climbing up and down the tower stairway. "Oh, Lord," she whispered, her heart aching more than her body, "why is this so hard?"

Now that she'd started the battle with Josiah, she had the feeling she needed to finish it. She couldn't give in and let him have his way, or things would only get worse with his disobedience.

He wrenched against her, but she didn't budge her hold. He gave a deep, angry growl.

"Lord," she cried, this time louder. She'd never felt more alone or inadequate in her life. "What am I doing wrong?"

For several long moments, he strained and thrashed. Then

slowly, as if someone had pricked a hole in his anger, it began to leak out, his body was less rigid, and his crying grew softer. Finally he stopped fighting her altogether and just lay in her arms, resting his head against her shoulder, sobbing.

Tears slipped down her cheeks, falling upon his red hair.

She sat up and sniffed the air, catching the bitterness of something burning. "Oh no!" she cried, setting Josiah aside on the bed. "My biscuits!"

With a frantic burst, she dashed out of Josiah's room into the kitchen to the oven. "Please, please, please don't be burned," she said. But when she opened the oven door and looked inside, she let out a wail. "They're burned. Every single one of them!"

Using a rag, she yanked out the pan and flung it on top of the sideboard with a clatter. A dozen smoking black lumps leered at her. Her beautiful biscuits. Ruined.

The ache in her chest expanded into her lungs. A sob burst out, but she caught it in her palm. Bertie had been right when she'd said Emma had taken on a job as wife and mother that she couldn't handle. Another sob tried to escape, but she forced it back.

At the sound of Josiah's broken cries, Emma's shoulders slumped, and she retreated to the bedroom where she'd left him. She couldn't bear to look at the charred biscuits. All she wanted to do was gather the boy into her arms again and cry with him.

She lay down next to him on the bed, cuddled him and stroked his hair and cheeks, letting her tears mingle with his. He nuzzled closer, and his cries gradually tapered. His eyelids grew heavy until they fell. His breathing turned steady with the rhythm of slumber, and his sucking became jerky around his thumb.

She leaned in and pressed a kiss against the softness of his hair. She started to pull away from him when he grasped her hand and snuggled his fingers against hers, as if he didn't want her to leave him.

She closed her eyes and let her body sag into the mattress. A tiny breath of peace settled over her.

Josiah didn't hate her for disciplining him. He hadn't pushed her away. In fact, just the opposite had happened. He wanted her there with him. No matter how hard it was being a parent and a wife, maybe there was still hope.

Chapter 10

Hoping to get a few hours' sleep, Patrick opened the door wearily. A smoky haze and the odor of burnt food greeted him. That wasn't anything new. Emma had a knack for burning just about everything she cooked.

A grin tugged his lips at the remembrance of the first time she'd attempted to fry griddle cakes. Even something as simple as that had ended up charred and inedible.

What had she tried to cook today?

A strange silence hovered in the house. His grin faded, and the hairs on the back of his neck rose. It was too quiet.

What if she'd left? What if she'd somehow figured out the truth about him and run away?

He headed straight for the kitchen and stopped abruptly at the disaster that greeted him. Water on the floor, flour on the table, and the source of the haze—burned biscuits on the sideboard.

The mess didn't concern him. He was immaculate with the tower and the light, because the *Instructions for Light-Keepers* manual spelled out strict regulations for its daily upkeep. But when it came to the house, he was much less organized. He just didn't have the energy to worry about it.

He'd tried to sweep and wash and maintain some order, but it had always been low on his list of priorities. And housekeeping had been the last thing Delia had wanted to do.

Emma, on the other hand, had worked hard to clean up the place. Every time he came in, he could see new evidence of her womanly touch: a new bunch of flowers on the table, colorful rocks on the windowsill, a wreath on the sitting room wall she'd woven from sea grass, cattails, and Queen Anne's lace.

She'd decorated the house more in one week than Delia had done in a year.

No, he couldn't condemn Emma for a messy kitchen. But after such a short time living with her, he realized the mess was uncharacteristic of her. Combined with the silence, it left him even more unsettled.

He made his way around the spilled water to the back door and peered outside. The clothes she'd washed yesterday hung on the line and flapped gently in the breeze. The newly turned soil of the garden was dark and well tended. The chickens strutted about their fenced-in area, pecking at the grass. But there were no signs of Emma and Josiah.

His pulse raced faster, and he spun away from the back door. Through the doorway of Josiah's room he caught sight of the familiar floral print of Emma's skirt, and relief washed over him. He went to the bedroom and halted at the door.

The two of them were asleep on the bed. Josiah had curled into a ball against Emma's body. Her arms surrounded him like a blanket, and her chin rested against his head.

For an eternal moment he couldn't tear his attention from

them. The sight was so precious it caused his breath to hitch in his chest and tears to sting at the back of his eyes.

If only Josiah's real mother had been as loving and sweet . . .

The splotchy red spots on Josiah's face were the telltale signs that he'd thrown another crying fit and given Emma a hard time—which would explain why she'd had to leave the kitchen in such disarray.

Emma's delicate lashes fanned out against her pale skin. Her lips were parted slightly with the soft breathing of slumber. And the long curve of her neck was exposed, an expanse of fair, beautiful skin. He had the sudden desire to graze his fingers along its curve, to test for himself how soft it was.

But he held back and instead allowed himself to look upon her—her face and her very womanly form. She was lovely, and she was his wife. Longing stirred in him.

She must have sensed his presence because her eyes flickered open and connected with his, and he found himself sinking into their warm brown depths.

He didn't say anything but took a small step back, chastising himself for being too bold. "How are you?" he whispered.

She lifted a finger to her lips and glanced sideways at Josiah. The slight protective action on her part reminded him of the good mother she already was, even though the lad had been making life difficult for her.

Patrick nodded and waited silently as she attempted to extricate herself without waking the boy. But at the movement of her arm, Josiah yawned and his body stiffened into a long stretch.

It took only a moment longer for him to open his eyes and see Patrick in the doorway. "Daddy home?" he asked in a sleepy voice.

Patrick smiled at the innocence of the boy's expression. Looking at his angelic face, it was hard to believe he was the cause of all the trouble in the kitchen. But he had no doubt that Josiah had misbehaved for Emma again.

"I'm home, lad."

Josiah pushed himself up and away from Emma, crawled over the edge of the bed, and flung himself at Patrick. He caught the boy and drew him to his chest.

Emma stood and looked past them into the kitchen. She gave a barely audible sigh as she brushed a lock of hair behind her ear.

"I'll take Josiah with me for a little while," he offered. "It looks like you could use a break."

She nodded, but before she could speak, Josiah pulled back and said, "Me naughty."

"I can see that," Patrick replied, "and that makes your daddy sad."

"Me 'pent on bed."

"Pent?" Patrick glanced at Emma.

"Repent," she said. "I had him sit on his bed to repent."

He nodded his understanding and then held Josiah by his shoulders so he could look him in the eyes. "I'm glad you repented. That's what God wants."

Josiah stared up at him. Patrick wasn't sure how much the boy grasped, but he'd decided it wouldn't hurt to start teaching the boy while he was young to walk in the ways of the Lord. That way the boy would have fewer regrets when he grew up.

"Repentance is important, lad. But you need to listen to your mamma the first time."

Josiah's shoulders sank, and his face fell. Then he did something that surprised Patrick. He turned to Emma and said quietly, "Me be good boy, Mamma."

She smiled at him. "Aye, you will."

Patrick was tempted to ask her if she wanted help cleaning the kitchen, but he sensed he'd help her more if he took Josiah outside for a while and gave her a rest from his boundless energy.

For at least an hour, he kept Josiah occupied with chores. Finally, Patrick's stomach couldn't resist the gurgling and rumbling for food. He hadn't eaten anything since breakfast.

He cracked open the back door and peeked inside. The kitchen was spotless now, as Emma had made quick work of bringing the house back to order. The table was set for supper, and she was busy at the stove, stirring something in a kettle.

When she saw him, she swiped at her cheeks. Was she crying?

He didn't know what to say or whether he should back away and return later.

Then Josiah squeezed past him and dashed to the table. "Hungry!"

"Good," she said too cheerfully, "because dinner is ready."

The two of them sat at the table as she placed what appeared to be a bowl of soup before Patrick, though he wasn't sure since it was covered with a film of black flecks as if it had burned to the bottom of the kettle. She then brought a plate of tiny brownish lumps and set it on the center of the table. He suspected the lumps were the burned biscuits, and that she'd cut away all the blackened parts, leaving only the middle.

After they prayed, Josiah eagerly took one of the lumps and ate it in one bite. "More?" he asked Emma through a mouthful.

"More, *please*," she instructed him.

"More please," he repeated.

She gave him several more, since they were hardly big enough to feed a mouse.

Patrick stirred his soup and found that it contained more

black than any other color. But he was too hungry to care. He sensed her attention upon him, and he didn't want to take his first bite while she was inspecting him, just in case he grimaced.

Instead, he reached for his steaming mug of coffee and took a sip. He savored the strong flavor, just the way he liked it. "That's good coffee."

At his words, a sob slipped from her lips. She pushed away from the table, her chair scraping and falling backward in her haste to get away. She covered her face with her hands and rushed out the door, letting it slam behind her.

Patrick stood. All he'd said was that the coffee was good. Wasn't that a compliment? He stared at the door, not sure if he should go after her or give her time to calm down first.

"Mamma sad?" Josiah paused in devouring another biscuit and strained to see out the kitchen window that overlooked the backyard.

"Yes, lad." Patrick watched Emma cross the grassy lawn to the clothesline, where she began to take down and fold the items with jerking motions. Her back faced him, but he could tell she was still crying by the way she brushed at her cheeks.

Every time she swiped, his heart squeezed. He had an overwhelming urge to run outside and pull her into his arms.

"Mamma?" Josiah called to her through the window, his brow wrinkled in worry.

"She'll be all right," Patrick said, praying that was the truth but knowing somehow he'd hurt her. "Let's eat, and we'll give Mamma some time to herself."

They ate their meal in silence, and even though the soup was speckled with burned fish, he had to admit it was tasty. He tried one of the miniature biscuit centers and realized it was moist and delicious too.

She'd obviously tried hard to make a nice meal, her first attempt at something besides leftovers. Even if it hadn't turned out perfectly, he could have made an effort to praise her for the effort.

That was why she was upset. He was sure of it. And now he wanted to hit himself across the head for being such an idiot.

He just hoped it wasn't too late to apologize and make it up to her.

Emma kneeled in the garden and pulled the weeds that had sprung seemingly overnight. She'd cried herself out and was now feeling drained. She knew she should go back inside and clean up dinner, but she couldn't muster the strength to do it.

She was embarrassed by her outburst. What must Patrick think of her? She'd not only proved her inadequacy in the kitchen, but she had served him a nearly inedible meal. To top it off, he'd seen the messy kitchen and her inability to control Josiah. If he hadn't regretted marrying her yet, he surely would after today.

She paused in her weeding and brushed her sleeve across her forehead. A sudden swell of longing rose for her brother. It was so sharp she nearly lost her breath. She hadn't seen him in a week, which was the longest she'd ever been apart from him.

"Oh, Ryan," she whispered through trembling lips, "I miss you."

Maybe she should ask to stay with the Burnhams. Then she could return to the previous plan of moving to Detroit with Ryan. If she left voluntarily, she would save Patrick the unpleasant chore of having to broach the awkward subject. After all, he was probably too polite to say anything about her inadequacies. The kind thing—the right thing—was to give him a way out of their marriage now that he knew exactly what he'd gotten in the bargain.

With a sigh, she dug her fingers into the soil, letting the cold damp earth crumble against her touch.

"Emma . . ." His voice came from behind her and startled her. She hadn't heard the back door open or his footsteps. She glanced over her shoulder and found him standing at the edge of the garden, his hands in his pockets.

"How's Josiah?" she asked, keeping her face turned away from him, so he couldn't see her puffy eyes or splotchy cheeks.

"He's asleep now."

"Oh. Thank you for laying him down." She should have gone in to kiss Josiah good-night. But then why make things harder if she was leaving? Because if she were honest with herself, it would be hard to say good-bye to the little boy. As difficult as he could be at times, he was still adorable and she'd already grown attached to him.

Patrick was silent, but out of the corner of her eye, she could see him wade through the rows until he stood in front of her and blocked her path forward. She didn't dare look up at him. She was too afraid of what she'd see in his eyes.

"Emma," he said again softly.

She sat back on her heels and let the dirt sift through her fingers.

He lowered himself until he was kneeling in front of her.

She bit her lip.

He lifted his hand to her chin and tipped up her head, so that she had no choice but to look at him.

One glance into the beautiful green depths was enough to remind her of what she would lose, and she couldn't prevent her lip from trembling.

He brought his hand to her cheek. His eyes wouldn't let go

of hers, and she wished desperately she hadn't disappointed him, that she'd been able to please him.

"Come here," he said. And without waiting for her permission, he tugged her near and slid his arms around her. He'd long past shed his coat and wore only his light cotton shirt. It was cool against her cheeks, and his chest beneath was solid.

She thought she'd cried all the tears she could, but at his gentleness the tears pooled again.

"There, there, lass." His voice was as tender as a caress.

She blinked back the tears, not wanting to dampen his shirt. But he held her close, enveloping her and beckoning her to lose herself within his hold. After only a few seconds of trying not to cry, she let her body sag into him and let her tears find release.

He didn't say anything. He just held her.

"I'm sorry, Patrick," she finally said through a snuffle. "I know I'm not what you were expecting in a wife and mother. And you can row me back tomorrow to Burnham's Landing so that you can start looking for someone more capable—"

"You made a good soup, Emma." He pulled back and locked eyes with her. "I'm sorry I didn't tell you that sooner."

His words gave her pause, and she examined his face, the sincerity creasing his brows and the apology radiating from his expression. "I never had a mam to teach me how to cook or how to take care of a wee one. It was just me and Ryan and my dad for many years—"

"You'll learn," he said.

"But what if I don't? What if I can't?"

"You're a kind woman, and you're good to Josiah. That's what matters most."

"Now that you know what an inept wife you got, I won't hold it against you if you want to find a different woman."

She was surprised when he lifted a hand and brushed at one of her stray strands of hair. He let his fingers linger against it before tucking it behind her ear. "I don't want anyone else," he said quietly. "Neither of us is perfect." A shadow flitted across his face. "Me least of all." He paused and cleared his throat. "I told you, though, that you could leave if you weren't happy here. And I'm a man of my word. I'll let you go if that's really what you want."

She wanted to shout that what she really wanted was to stay with him. Yes, it had been a hard first week, but she'd also been at peace. When she'd cleaned the house, she was delighted to know it was her home too. When she'd readied the garden, she was relieved that she wouldn't have to move before she saw the fruits of her labor. And when she'd fixed the chicken coop, she was excited to think about next spring and the possibility of seeing the new chicks hatched.

She'd thought about Patrick showing her more about the light and how it worked and how rewarding it would be to spend her life helping him save lives. And sometimes when Josiah was especially cute or good, she even pictured the day in the not-so-distant future when she'd have a baby of her own. Maybe several children.

Aye, this place, this lighthouse, it was the home she'd always dreamed about. And Patrick was better than any husband she'd ever attract on her own.

He waited for her answer, his brow furrowed, his eyes sad.

She wished she was bold enough to stroke his cheek and reassure him. Instead, she offered him a small smile. "If you're sure you don't mind all my faults . . ."

"As long as you're willing to put up with mine," he said.

"Aye, since you're terribly hard to put up with." Her smile grew.

Seeing her smile, he gave a half grin. "I'm more terrible than you realize."

"But at least you can cook."

"And you make wonderful coffee."

She laughed softly. "At least I do one thing well."

His expression turned serious. "You do many things well, Emma." He lifted his fingers but hesitated before gently brushing another loose piece of hair off her face.

Only then did she consider the fact that they were kneeling just inches apart, that his face was a hand's span away from hers.

Maybe he would kiss her again.

As embarrassing as the idea was, and as tempted as she was to duck her head, she forced herself not to move. How else would he know that she wouldn't mind his attention if she always turned into a shy butterfly around him?

As if he'd heard her thoughts, his gaze dropped to her lips and he stared for a long moment. His breathing turned ragged, and his chest rose and fell more rapidly.

She was sure he would lean in closer. She wasn't the expert at reading desire upon a man's face, but surely that was what was written in his features.

She held her breath and waited.

And when he finally wrenched away from her and stood stiffly, she released a whoosh of air but found that she was strangely disappointed.

"I need to head up to the light," he said in a strained voice.

She nodded and stared at his boots.

He didn't move. "There's something you should know about me. About my past . . ."

"It's okay, Patrick," she assured. "We agreed to let the past stay in the past—"

"I have a criminal record."

His words slammed into her and took her breath away. She waited for him to go into more detail, to tell her what he'd done. But he stood silently as if his pronouncement were a death sentence in and of itself.

Apparently he hadn't been joking when he'd said he was more terrible than she realized.

She dragged in a breath and tried not to let him see her trembling hands. She couldn't look him in the eyes, yet she knew she had to say something.

"I stand by what I said before—let's keep the past in the past."

For a long moment he said nothing. Then he sighed. "Good night, lass."

"Good night, Patrick."

As he walked away, her mind raced. Exactly what kind of man had she married?

Chapter 11

mma picked up Patrick's coat from the end of the bed where he'd shed it after changing out of his work clothes into his Sunday best. He'd said that even though they didn't have a church building in the area, he held his own worship service every Sunday morning.

Occasionally, when Holy Bill was in the area, the reverend would lead a service. Yet that was only once a month or so, as he had to split his time between the various communities along the lakeshore.

She could hear Josiah chattering to Patrick in the sitting room as they waited for her to join them. She'd asked them to spare a moment while she changed into her Sunday best too—not that she had anything fancy. Nevertheless, she'd donned her cleanest shirt and newest skirt, and she'd twisted her hair into a knot, trying to capture the runaway wisps with pins.

She hadn't been able to stop thinking about Patrick's confession from the night before. She'd lain in bed trying to decide what crimes a man like Patrick had committed. After ruling out almost everything from murder to thievery, she'd finally decided he probably hadn't done anything too terrible. If he had, he'd be in prison. Surely whatever he'd done had been only minimal, some petty crime.

Even so, Bertie's warning echoed through her head. *"Things aren't what they seem."* What if Patrick had a side to him that she hadn't yet seen? A more volatile side . . .

Emma rubbed her hands over his coat. Did she dare search his pockets? Hadn't she promised him she wouldn't bother with his past? Besides, she only had to think of how he'd come to her in the garden last night, of his tenderness when she'd been upset, the way he'd held her and comforted her and reassured her that he wanted her to stay. She couldn't imagine how Patrick could be capable of anything other than the utmost kindness.

No matter his past, she liked the man he was now. Perhaps she was going against her better judgment, but she wanted to give him a chance.

Aye. She wanted to pretend he'd never said anything about being a criminal. Why couldn't she? Holy Bill had given his word that Patrick was a changed man. And from what she could tell, the reverend was right.

She couldn't find any faults with Patrick, not yet anyway.

She clutched his coat. Then, with a glance toward the door, she brought the garment to her face in what she could only describe as an immature and girlish need to have more of him.

In spite of the new revelation, her mind brimmed with the memory of being in his arms, the hardness of his chest, the steadiness of his heartbeat against her cheek. She had a keen need to be in his arms again.

"What am I to do?" she whispered into the quietness of the bedroom as that strange physical longing returned to her.

At their wedding he'd told her he wouldn't expect anything

of her, and she'd understood that to mean in the physical sense. But now that she had a real home, she wanted a real marriage too. She'd never had a relationship of any kind with a man other than with Ryan and her dad.

How was she supposed to act? What kinds of things was she supposed to do in order to let Patrick know of her interest in him? After all, they were husband and wife. Why couldn't they be together as such eventually, especially if she ever hoped to have more children?

She pressed her face into his coat. It was all him. It had his shape, his touch, his warmth. She sucked in a deep breath and caught his unique aroma of wind and sea. A faint wisp of something else lingered. She lifted the coat higher, following the scent to the collar where it grew stronger.

It was an exotic scent of jasmine or some other woman's perfume.

Emma flung the coat back on the bed and took a quick step back. She stared at the dark linen, and another of Bertie's warnings clanged in her head. *"He needs the extra money because he's secretly giving it to someone. A woman."*

It couldn't be true that Patrick was involved with another woman. Aye, he'd been gone all of yesterday and he hadn't told her where. But he didn't seem to be the kind of man who would spend his free time and hard-earned money visiting loose women.

Then again, he'd confessed to being a criminal. What if his cavorting with women had been part of his crimes?

She turned away from the coat, refusing to look at it again. She had to stop imagining the worst about him. As she left the room and tried to forget about the womanly scent on the coat, she struggled to put aside the panic that had come over her.

When she stepped into the sitting room and Patrick glanced up at her warily from his chair near the unlit hearth, her heart pinched with the realization of how little they knew about each other.

His dark brown hair was combed neatly. The crisp whiteness of his shirt brought out the tan of his skin and the green of his eyes. He exuded strength in every limb. He was an attractive man, as sweet and sensitive as he was handsome. How could she compete for his affection with another woman?

Not that there was another woman, she reminded herself.

As she listened to him read Scripture, lead them in prayer, and then close with a hymn, she resolved to do a better job not being so shy. Maybe she could find ways to gain his attention, to make herself more appealing to him. And maybe if they got to know each other better, she could put to rest Bertie's warnings.

Patrick closed his well-worn Bible and fingered the lettering on the front reverently. Emma sat in the rocking chair opposite him and held Josiah. She'd been surprised when the boy had climbed on her lap and was even more astonished when he'd snuggled against her and listened attentively to Patrick. Of course, he'd sucked his thumb the entire time. But he'd seemed content to be in her arms instead of having to sit with Patrick as he usually demanded.

Perhaps her attempt at disciplining him yesterday hadn't been a failure after all.

"What we do now, Daddy?" he asked, sliding forward on her lap.

The June sunshine coming in the sitting room's open window had warmed the room, and yet Emma relished the coziness together. This was her home now. She'd swept and washed the floor until it shone. She'd dusted away the cobwebs. She'd even added a few decorations, like the tall crock she'd found in the shed that she filled with a bouquet of cattails, and the pair of tin candle holders she'd polished and placed on the mantel.

Patrick took a sip of his coffee left over from breakfast. "I think we should let your new mamma decide what to do today, don't you?"

Josiah nodded, then cupped her cheek with his tiny hand. "What do, Mamma?"

She looked at Patrick for his interpretation this time.

"We take turns picking an activity to do together on Sunday," he explained, setting his Bible on the desk, which was still in disarray. "Sometimes we go hiking or take a boat ride or visit with neighbors down at Burnham's Landing."

She nodded and sifted through the possibilities the day held.

"Maybe you'd like to visit your brother?" Patrick offered, rising from his wing chair.

A lump formed in her throat. "I'd be grateful for the chance to see him, but I don't want to trouble you."

"It wouldn't trouble me, Emma."

"If you're sure . . ."

"Last I saw Ryan, he was asking about you."

"He was?" She smiled at the thought that Ryan missed her too. "I hope he wasn't *asking* you with his fists."

"Close."

"Then for your safety I'd better go visit him and reassure him I'm doing well."

"That would be mighty nice of you." Patrick grinned. The relief in his expression told her he was glad they were bantering again, that he'd been worried about her reaction to his confession.

She felt it would be unfair to shun him now that he'd told

her more. The truth was he'd tried to warn her before they got married. For her part, she'd been too excited, too desperate to pay much attention.

And now that they were married, she would have to take the good with the bad. After all, he was accepting her despite her faults. Shouldn't she do the same for him?

When they arrived at Burnham's Landing, she was disappointed to discover Ryan had gone hunting with the Burnham men farther inland. But Bertie Burnham invited her into the cabin for coffee and biscuits.

Sunshine poured through the doorway, lighting the hovel and revealing the unswept floor, the faded curtains that were in need of a good wash, the heap of cold ashes on the hearth, and an unwashed kettle on the table. They apparently hadn't used the broom she'd fixed.

After they were seated, Bertie perched on the edge of one of the kitchen chairs like a barn owl. Her sharp eyes seemed to take in every detail of Emma's appearance, from her wind-tossed hair to the damp hem of her skirt.

"Nope." Bertie's bonnet covered most of her head, except for her long narrow braids. "Don't expect them back until nightfall. I told Fred I wanted victuals besides fish to fill my belly and that he shouldn't come home until he had something."

"Has Ryan said anything about when he's planning to leave?" Emma asked, breaking off a bite of the perfectly flaky biscuit and trying not to think of her own burnt biscuits.

"He doesn't seem to be in a big hurry," Bertie said. "What do you think, Mother?"

The widow Burnham sat in a rocker positioned near the window, her knitting needles clicking at top speed. Her lips were pursed tightly. She didn't seemed any more pleased to see Emma now than she had when Emma stood wet and shivering in her doorway the first time they'd met.

"Besides," Bertie said, not waiting for her mother-in-law's response, "I keep telling Ryan to stay off the steamers right now. It's too dangerous with that pirate boat lurking in the area."

Emma nodded, letting hope inflate her heart. Maybe Ryan would stay longer until the threat from pirates had subsided, at least until she had the chance to see him again and give him one last hug good-bye.

Bertie glanced to the open door of the log cabin, as if to be sure they were alone, and then sat forward. "Maybe you're having second thoughts about staying out there with Patrick?"

"Of course not." She hoped her words didn't come out too fast.

"I don't suppose you've noticed anything suspicious?" Bertie asked, probing further.

"Nay," Emma said. Did she dare say anything about Patrick's criminal past? She had the feeling Bertie didn't know about it, otherwise she would have already told Emma. Perhaps Patrick's first wife, Delia, hadn't revealed anything to her cousin.

Whatever the case, Emma decided she needed to hold Patrick's confession in confidence as well.

But would it hurt to mention Patrick's trip yesterday and the perfume on his coat? She hesitated and then decided that for now she'd keep those details to herself too.

"Patrick has been very good to me. I can't complain about anything. Except . . ."

Bertie's bony shoulders stiffened. "Except what?"

Heat flamed Emma's cheeks. There would be nothing wrong with asking Bertie for advice on how to make herself more attractive to her husband, would there? The woman had conceived four sons. She obviously knew something about capturing the attention of a man. She could surely give her some ideas for how to win Patrick's favor.

Emma picked at the thin golden crust on the top of the biscuit. She had to ask now before she lost her courage. "I know Patrick's busy and he works at night." Her voice dropped to a mere whisper. "But most of the time he's aloof and he hasn't shared the bed with me . . . yet." Emma didn't dare look up. She couldn't bear to see what Bertie thought of her now that she knew the truth.

Bertie harrumphed. "I'm not surprised."

"I'm sure he misses Delia." Emma rushed to speak, hoping to cover her embarrassment. "I guess I shouldn't expect him to be interested in me yet, not when he's still in love with the wife he just lost."

"He didn't love Delia." Bertie spat the words. "And he certainly doesn't miss her."

Emma glanced up at the woman in time to see anger flash in her eyes.

"I bet it has to do with that other woman I told you about," Bertie said. "He's probably getting his needs met in some other woman's bed and has no desire for yours."

Emma wanted to protest, but how could she? Not after his disappearance all of yesterday and the scent of perfume on his clothes this morning. Still, there was something overly cynical in Bertie's assumption, and it stirred her need to defend Patrick. "I don't think he's unfaithful. He's much too kind—"

"Anyone can put on an act. The fact is, he needs a mother for Josiah. And he needs an assistant to help with the light. That's it. He doesn't need you for a wife. He didn't need Delia for a wife either."

Emma took a sip of her coffee to hide her confusion. She knew

Patrick had married her for practical reasons, but what if those were his *only* reasons? What if he'd never had any intention of having a real marriage? Maybe that had been his arrangement with Delia too.

It would certainly account for the fact that he didn't seem all that sad about her passing. For that matter, neither did Josiah.

"As I told you before, I'm not one for gossiping." Bertie spoke through a bite of biscuit. "But I don't want to see a young lady like you suffer unnecessarily."

Emma hadn't suffered yet, not in the least. "Maybe I can try to make him want me for a wife. Maybe you can give me a few tips . . . tips for attracting a man . . . ?"

Bertie chortled. The older widow Burnham stopped her knitting to glare at Emma. It was the kind of look that said she thought Emma was nothing but a hussy.

The room became stifling, the scent of fried fish almost too much to bear. Emma started to rise. "I'm sorry. I'll just go. I knew I shouldn't have asked."

"Sit down, young lady," Bertie snapped.

Emma plunked back into her chair and folded her hands on her lap.

Bertie stared at Emma until she squirmed. "You're right," she finally said. "You might as well test him. Maybe you'll gain his confidence enough to find out what's going on."

"That wasn't what I meant—"

"Yes, that's a good plan," Bertie continued. "You can turn on the charm, and if he falls for it, then I'm sure you'll be able to ask him all kinds of questions about everything that happened. And if he doesn't fall for you, we'll know why."

"Why exactly?"

"Why? Because he's in love with another woman, that's why.

Most likely an unsavory woman who he doesn't want any of us God-fearing people to know about."

Emma shook her head. "Maybe there's another explanation."

"Have you searched through the house, through his belongings for evidence like I told you to?"

Emma didn't respond, deciding against telling Bertie she'd almost checked his pockets.

"So, what should Emma do to attract him, Mother?" Bertie asked.

Widow Burnham laughed. "You're speaking nonsense, the both of you. Leave me out of it."

Emma took another bite of biscuit, but it stuck to the roof of her mouth.

"It's been quite a few years since I've had to attract a man," Bertie said, flinging first one braid and then the other over her shoulders. "But I was quite good at it in my day."

"What did you do?"

"Not to boast, but mostly all I had to do was look real purty."

Emma tried hard to picture the thin woman with her dour face as pretty. It was hard to imagine. But then again it had been long ago, and time and hard work had a way of changing people's appearance.

If Bertie had once been able to make herself look pretty, maybe there was hope for Emma. Maybe she could try to fix her hair nicer or keep her fingernails cleaner.

"And when you get him alone," Bertie said, "don't be shy about giving him a kiss."

"Me? Kiss him?" Emma's voice squeaked, and her stomach quivered at the scandalous nature of their conversation. She hoped Patrick and Josiah wouldn't decide to show up at that moment.

Bertie nodded. "You just go on and give him a kiss, and that'll be all the invitation he'll need to sweep you up in his arms and carry you to the bedroom."

"Oh my." Emma fanned her overheated face with her hand. "I just can't imagine myself doing such a thing."

"If he hesitates, then you'll know he's got himself another woman. Ain't no man who can resist a young woman like you throwing herself at him unless he's blind or has himself a lover already."

"Thank you, Bertie. You certainly are wise in these matters." Emma's body sizzled with embarrassment, and she was desperate to change the subject. "Now perhaps you'd be kind enough to give me more of your cooking wisdom too."

Later, when Patrick and Josiah came for her and they started back to the lighthouse, she couldn't look at Patrick for fear he'd see the bold thoughts running through her mind. All she knew was that there was no way she could throw herself at Patrick and initiate a kiss with him. Never.

When they reached the dock in front of the light, Patrick secured the cutter while Emma hoisted Josiah onto her hip.

"What do now, Mamma?" He squinted at her through the sunlight gleaming off the silver waves. Already in the short time she'd known the boy, his freckles had multiplied from his exposure to the sun.

She used her fingers to comb back his hair and then pressed his cap back onto his head. All that day he'd worn his cap. He hadn't resisted like he usually did. It was almost as if the battle from yesterday had brought them to a new place in their relationship.

Perhaps she'd gained some ground in him seeing her as his mamma, as a real mamma. And maybe by sticking to her word and not giving in to him, she'd earned some authority.

"What do, Mamma?" Josiah asked again.

She looked to Patrick, still in the boat, and raised her brow. The gurgling in her stomach and the position of the sun told her it was past noon. Patrick would probably want to sleep at some point, since he hadn't had the chance yesterday.

He was winding extra rope around his arm. Even with the waves lapping and the breeze blowing against him, he stood as nimbly as if he'd been born in a boat. "We have time to do something else together. If you'd like, that is."

Aye. She'd like spending more time together. There was nothing she'd like better. But what could they do? What would be something Patrick and Josiah would enjoy?

She looked around at the open beach that rounded the bend of the isthmus. Sea gulls perched on several of the boulders that rose out of the lake near the shore. She pictured her mam resting on a blanket on the beach not far from their home in Ireland, Dad's head on her lap, and the two of them smiling as she and Ryan waded and splashed in the sea.

Emma couldn't remember how old she'd been or what else they'd done. All she remembered was the happiness in her parents' eyes.

"How about a picnic on the beach?" Emma said. During one of her hikes with Josiah farther up the beach, she'd found a spot that was sandy.

Once she explained what a picnic was, Josiah became enthusiastic about the idea. She wasn't sure what Patrick thought, but since he didn't protest, she made quick work of packing the few biscuits Bertie had sent home with them, along with the leftover fish from breakfast.

After they'd walked a little ways, Patrick helped her spread out a spare blanket. Though the June sun had disappeared behind a covering of clouds, it was still warm.

They ate their picnic meal, and when they'd devoured every last bite, they built a tower out of rocks and sand. Then she waded in the water with Josiah, hoisting her skirt but still unable to keep the hem from getting wet. Patrick rested on the blanket, reclining on one elbow and watching them. When his eyes wandered to her exposed ankles, she dipped her chin and pretended not to notice. But somehow she had the feeling she needed to take advantage of his interest, so she settled Josiah back at the stone tower to play and dig some more and then lowered herself onto the blanket next to Patrick. She situated herself so that she could keep an eye on Josiah.

Maybe she wouldn't be able to throw herself at Patrick and kiss him the way Bertie had suggested, but at least she could sit near him.

A few moments passed and she found herself telling him about Ireland and the picnics she'd taken as a child, trying to cover her nervousness with chatter. Finally she fell silent and couldn't think of anything else to say.

Patrick watched Josiah too, as if he didn't quite know what to say either. At last he said, "I have to admit, I've never been on a picnic before."

"Not even as a child?"

"No." There was a bitter note to his voice that she'd not heard before. With his soft brogue and Irish name, she guessed that he'd immigrated to America just as she had.

"Did your family suffer a great deal during the famine?"

His face hardened, and then he looked away.

"I'm sorry, Patrick. I shouldn't have asked—"

"My family was already a disaster before the famine." He closed his eyes as if to block out the painful memory.

"You don't have to talk about it." She watched the way the breeze teased his hair.

"When we moved to America, the sins moved with us." For once the lines in his face made him look older, as though he'd lived through more in his days than most saw in a lifetime.

She didn't say anything, but instead touched his arm. It was only a brief contact, the merest of grazes. And she wasn't sure why she did it, except that she sensed the turmoil raging through him and wanted to offer him a measure of comfort.

At her touch, his eyes opened and met hers. He seemed to be trying to read her expression and see into her heart. Even though she was tempted to glance away, she forced herself to stay steady, to look him in the eye. She wanted to be bolder, to let him know that despite his confession of the night before, she wouldn't refuse his attentions.

But her stomach quivered, and a flush stole up her cheeks. After only a few seconds she shifted her attention to her hands, twisting in her skirt.

He released a soft breath, then flipped over on his back and rested his head against the blanket.

Inwardly she chided herself. She had to stop being so shy around him. "During our picnics back in Ireland, my dad would use my mam's leg as a pillow. If you like, you could . . ." But she couldn't finish. She focused again on Josiah piling rocks.

Instead of speaking, Patrick scooted closer and lifted his head onto her lap. As he situated himself, she held her breath and didn't move.

He closed his eyes and sighed.

After several seconds, she allowed herself to breathe again. And before long she could feel his shoulders relax against her thigh.

"You make a comfortable pillow," he said, folding his arms across his chest. "I might fall asleep here."

"I won't mind." She was glad he couldn't see the embarrassment that was sure to be brightening her face.

Soon he was asleep, his expression peaceful.

When Patrick's chest began to rise and fall with the rhythm of deep sleep, she knew he wouldn't waken easily. She lifted her fingers to his hair and grazed the brown strands that lay against her skirt. It was softer than she expected. She pulled her hand away and watched his face to gauge whether he'd noticed. His eyes remained closed and his breathing steady.

She skimmed his hair again. Still gaining no reaction from him, she let her hand linger. Gradually her touch turned bolder and moved deeper, until she combed through his hair much the same way she did Josiah's.

When Josiah grew tired of building castles and throwing rocks, she interested him in a caterpillar crawling near their blanket. While the sky had grown more overcast and the air damper with the sign that rain would soon be upon them, she didn't want this moment with Patrick to come to an end.

She bent over his face and wished she were brave enough to trace the scar on his forehead or run a finger down his slightly bent nose. Her pulse raced faster at the thought of stroking his full lips. She knew she'd never be brave enough to take such liberties were he awake.

But since he was asleep, he wouldn't have to know she'd touched him. Josiah was bent over and talking to the caterpillar. The boy wouldn't have to know either.

With a surge of daring, she brushed her fingers against Patrick's forehead. She traced first one brow and then the other.

She stopped, hovering above him, waiting for him to awaken and catch her touching him so intimately.

Yet he didn't budge, not even to move an eyelash.

She released a pent-up breath and ignored a raindrop that fell on the back of her neck. She allowed herself a small but shaky smile. She was overcome with wonder that this handsome man lying in her lap was her husband, and that only a short distance away was their home.

Her life was full. What more could she ask for?

Patrick tried not to move, but with each passing moment it was growing more difficult to pretend he was asleep. He'd awoken to find Emma's fingers in his hair. Her gentle touch had stirred his blood, but he'd sensed that if he opened his eyes, she'd pull away from him faster than he could blink.

And so he'd kept himself motionless. Then when she stroked his forehead and his eyebrows, desire had surged through him, causing his breath to hitch, even more with the knowledge she hadn't pushed him away in spite of what she'd learned about him.

He knew telling Emma about his once being a criminal had been the right thing to do, no matter how much it might have cost him. And while she'd been clearly shocked, she hadn't seemed repulsed. In fact, here she was even now, touching him. His relief was beyond measure, and her gentle caresses were filling him with longing.

He couldn't keep up the pretense much longer before he did something reckless like pull her down on top of him and kiss her. And then he'd definitely scare her away.

Yet as her hand moved to his cheek and lightly brushed the

whiskers along his jaw, he leaned closer for more of her. He couldn't hold himself back any longer. He reached for her hand, captured it, and brought her fingers against his lips.

She gasped and started to pull away from him.

His eyes flew open to the mortification spilling across her face.

"I'm sorry," she whispered, leaning back, her cheeks flushed.

He didn't let go, but instead brought his lips to her fingertips again, hoping she'd read the message written on his face that she needn't be sorry for anything.

At the kiss, she stopped struggling. She held herself stiffly, but at least she wasn't attempting to escape him.

Fat raindrops began to plop against his face. Although he knew they should pack up and return home before they all got soaked, he wasn't ready to break this connection with her. He wasn't satisfied with a few kisses against her fingertips; he wanted so much more.

He swallowed the rising desire and pressed her hand back against his cheek. He held it there, wanting her to know how much he'd welcomed her caresses.

Her eyes grew rounder.

"Rain, Mamma," Josiah said. "Me wet."

At Josiah's simple statement, she broke away and scrambled backward, so that Patrick had no choice but to sit up. He rubbed a hand across his face, trying to wipe away the stark desire that radiated there just as surely as the Presque Isle Light beamed in the darkness.

Thankfully she turned her back to him and busied herself with Josiah. As the rain began to fall in earnest, they gathered everything and ran back to the house. Stumbling into the kitchen, panting and laughing, rain dripped from their garments and formed puddles on the floor.

"Me wet," Josiah said again. "Change clothes." He dropped the half-squished caterpillar onto the table and toddled toward his room.

Emma started after the boy at the same time Patrick did, and they almost collided. "I was going to help him," Emma said.

"I was too," he said softly.

She was only inches from him.

The rain pattered hard on the roof. It was a soothing sound, not at all like the thrashing of some of the storms that buffeted the lighthouse. In the cloudiness of the late afternoon, the kitchen was dark, shadowing them both, giving the room a cozy air.

Even in the dimness, he couldn't help but notice that her wet clothes clung to her. Her shirt plastered her rounded curves, and the rapid rise and fall of her chest only served to draw his attention to the outline of her body.

She followed his gaze downward, gave a soft gasp, and took a quick step back while crossing her arms over herself. "Maybe I should get changed too," she whispered.

He gave himself a mental shake and forced himself to focus on her pretty face. She started to move past him. He knew he should let her go, but when her shoulder grazed him in passing, he took her by the arm and stopped her.

She sucked in a breath. In the stillness of the room, with only the tapping of rain above them, her soft gasp did something strange to his stomach. He moved sideways until his face brushed against her wet hair. His mouth hovered near her ear. For the longest moment he couldn't move. She didn't move either, except that her breathing turned more rapid. The sound of her quick intakes only stirred him until his heart raced with a frenzy he'd never felt before.

"Emma," he whispered against her hair.

She didn't say anything in reply. Then slowly she turned her head so that her lips were near his. Her warm breath came in bursts that mingled with his.

He was going to kiss her. He couldn't help it. His lips grazed hers, as light as a sprinkle of rain.

When she didn't move away, he gently brushed against her again. He knew he shouldn't rush things, though he wasn't sure how much longer he could go without taking her fully and crushing her under the weight of a real kiss.

He pulled back slightly and touched his nose to hers. Again she didn't turn away.

He leaned in for more of her . . .

"Mamma, help!" came Josiah's muffled voice, breaking through the charged air that surrounded them.

Emma jumped back.

They both swiveled toward Josiah's bedroom. He stood in the doorway, naked except for his shirt, which he'd pulled up over his head where it had become wedged at his chin.

"Stuck," the little boy said through the wet linen.

Emma's mouth dropped open.

For a moment, Patrick was as speechless as Emma, still struggling to return to reality. She gave a stifled laugh, pressing her hand over her mouth.

The lad made quite an amusing sight with his chubby white body capped by his shirt sticking straight up over his head.

Emma laughed again, unable to contain her mirth.

Patrick grinned, and then before he knew it, he was laughing with her. Sensing that he was the source of their laughter, Josiah started prancing around and giggling.

Finally, Emma crossed to the boy and freed his head from the shirt, and afterward Patrick scooped him up in a hug.

"Go ahead and get changed first," he said, tossing Emma a smile, "while I take care of this little clown of ours."

He knew he shouldn't stare at her, but as she crossed the kitchen, his eyes trailed after her. And when she peeked at him over her shoulder, her smile of pleasure sent a burst of hope through him.

Maybe things would turn out differently from the way they had with Delia. Maybe he'd been worried for nothing. He might not be worthy of Emma, but he could only pray he'd do his best to make her happy.

Chapter 12

The little house shook from a deafening clap of thunder. Emma bolted upright in bed and rubbed the sleep from her eyes.

"Mamma!" Josiah's terrified cry echoed through the house.

She swung her feet over the edge of the bed to the cold wood floor as a streak of lightning lit up the night sky and was again followed by a bang of thunder that seemed intent on beating down the walls of their home.

Josiah screamed.

Without taking the time to wrap a robe around her thin nightgown, she rushed out of her bedroom, feeling her way through the dark hall and kitchen until she was in Josiah's room. She gathered his shaking body into her arms and carried him back to her bed.

It took some time for him to stop crying. When he was finally quiet, he lay next to her, sucking his thumb. She'd wrapped her arms around him to comfort him, but as the storm continued to rage, her own fear mounted.

She'd heard sailors talk about the storms on Lake Huron,

how they were the most violent of all the Great Lakes. And even though she'd experienced a few squalls during her time on Mackinac Island, none could compare with the one raging outside.

The wind rattled the entire house as if to blow it right out into the lake. It whistled under the door, down the chimney, and through every crack in the windowpanes. At a ripping noise overhead, she drew Josiah closer. The roof was breaking apart.

If the storm was tearing at the house, she didn't want to think about what it was doing to the tower in its dilapidated condition. Her insides trembled at the thought that Patrick might be in danger.

She wanted to pray for him, that God would keep him safe, that the tower wouldn't blow away into the sea with Patrick inside. But she wasn't sure that she could.

She only had to think of Patrick's bowed head at breakfast every morning, of the sincerity and humility with which he offered his petitions, and she knew she had to try to pray again sometime. Her voice and throat, though, were still rusty, long neglected when it came to prayer.

At dawn, the storm finally blew itself out over the lake, leaving a steady patter of rain against the windows. She waited for the squeak of the back door, signaling that Patrick was done with his keeper duties for the night. But as the minutes passed and the house grew lighter, he still didn't come.

With Josiah asleep again, she dressed silently and tiptoed outside. She told herself she was only assessing the damage to the house, but the first place she looked was up at the tower.

Through the pelting rain and overcast sky, the beam was still rotating. She searched for the outline of Patrick's form through the tower's windows, but couldn't spot him.

As the rain spattered her face, she tried to quiet the rapid thud of her heart, hoping he'd left the light burning longer because the morning was unusually gray. He would be turning it off soon.

After waiting and watching a few moments longer, she decided she needed to know that he was all right. She dashed to the tower and raced up the winding stairway until she reached the ladder that led to the lantern room.

"Patrick," she called through gasping breath. She pushed open the hatch and popped her head into the room.

The howling of the wind was the only reply she received.

She scrambled to her feet, taking in the deserted room. She stopped short at the sight of a trail of water and shattered glass spread across the floor. One glance at the window told her the wind had blown in a pane, allowing the rain to pour into the tower. It had come precariously close to the lantern.

With growing dread, she crossed to the narrow door that led to the catwalk. She shoved it open against the pressure of the wind. "Patrick!" she shouted, grabbing the rail and fighting the gusts to stay on her feet.

In the distance, huge waves hurled themselves against the shore. She shuddered at the sight. What if Patrick had gone out to save someone and hadn't returned?

"Please, God, no," she whispered as she shuffled forward for a better view.

She didn't want to lose him. She'd only just realized her dream of having a place she could call home, and had only just started to connect with her new husband.

She was still mortified that he'd awoken yesterday on the beach to find her stroking his face. Why had she done it? Even though she kept chiding herself, part of her was glad he caught her. He didn't seem to mind. In fact, he'd kissed her fingertips in response.

And later he'd shown his affection in the kitchen.

Her insides warmed again at the thought of how close they'd stood together, of his hot breath on her lips. Just the thought of that soft kiss made her stomach do a little flip.

She rounded the catwalk, making her way toward the broken window. At the sight of him lying on the gallery, facedown and unmoving, she gave a cry and rushed forward.

"Patrick!" She fell to her knees beside him.

A puddle of blood pooled next to his head, blood mixed with rain.

Shaking, she carefully turned him over. His normally tan face was ashen and smeared with streaks of blood. She pressed her ear against his chest and listened for a heartbeat. After hearing a faint *thump-thump*, she released a pent-up breath.

The broken window and the hammer and canvas wedged against the tower told her he'd likely come out to repair the window or at least nail up the canvas to keep the rain from blowing into the lantern, and somehow he'd taken a tumble.

She examined his head, slicking back his hair until she found a deep gash. Spinning around, she saw a piece of heavy iron lying near the edge of the gallery, a piece that had broken loose from the damaged window. Maybe he'd been struck by the metal, or maybe he'd slipped and fallen against the rail. Whatever the case, she needed to get him down from the tower and into bed.

He moaned and stirred. When finally he opened his eyes, they were glazed.

"We need to get you home," she said. "Can you stand?"

He nodded slowly, allowing her to wrap her arms around his waist and raise him to his feet. She half carried, half dragged him into the lantern room, out of the rain and the wind, and then inch by inch she helped him down the ladder and stairway. Together they staggered across the small yard, making their way back to the house.

With Patrick leaning heavily on her, Emma stepped through the back door and headed toward the bedroom. Just as they reached the bed, he slumped and became unconscious again. She removed his wet coat and boots and managed to get him out of his damp shirt. But she hesitated at the clasp of his trousers. She couldn't bear to think what Patrick might think of her if he awoke to find himself completely unclad.

Instead, she washed his head wound, bound it with clean strips of linen, and made him as comfortable as possible. By then, Josiah had awoken, so she dressed and fed him, tended to the most basic household chores, and resumed her care of Patrick while trying to keep Josiah busy.

All through the rainy morning she felt as though she were being pulled in a dozen different directions at once. She gained a new appreciation for what Patrick had gone through after his wife had died and why he'd been so desperate to have help.

She couldn't keep from thinking about what she would do if Patrick didn't recover. Sitting in the chair she'd pulled up next to the bed, she sighed and checked Patrick's bandage again. At least the wound had stopped bleeding. His breathing was shallow, and he was still very pale. He'd obviously lost a great deal of blood before she'd found him. There was no telling how long he'd lain there on the gallery unconscious.

At a rap on the front door, she started, jumping up from the chair. Josiah jumped up too from his spot on the floor, where he was playing with the newest origami creature she'd folded, a swan.

She didn't know who would be out visiting on a rainy day like this, but she would be glad to see anyone. Maybe they would know how to help her with Patrick. At the very least they could send for a doctor.

She hurried to the door and swung it open, bringing in the cool damp scent of the lake. Two burly-looking men stood side by side, wearing knee-length leather boots and oilskin coats.

"Well, hello there," said one of the two, a man with curly black hair and a scraggly beard. Rain dripped from his cap in a steady stream. He raked her over from top to bottom, and his lips curved into a smile. "Aren't you a pretty one."

Pretty? She almost glanced over her shoulder to see who he was talking to. The second man stared at her too, and there was something in his face that was hard, that set her on edge.

"Good day to you," she said with a smile. "What brings you out on a day like today?"

The curly-haired man shared a look with his companion and then nodded toward the tower. "We saw that the light there is still on and figured something must be wrong here."

Josiah sidled against her and wrapped his arm around her leg, twisting her skirt. He stuck his thumb in his mouth and peered up at the men with curious eyes.

She placed a hand on his head to reassure him as much as herself that everything would be all right. "Aye. My husband was hurt last night during the storm. I was so busy tending to him, I forgot all about the light."

How would she turn off the light? Patrick had showed her how to turn it on, but she had no idea how to shut it down. Regardless, she had to give it a try. Patrick would want her to help as much as she could.

"Is he hurt bad?" the stranger asked.

"He lost a lot of blood and is unconscious. I'd be obliged if you'd fetch the doctor for me when you head back to the harbor."

"Sure," said the one with the curly black hair. "'Course we can let the doctor know he's needed."

"Oh, thank you." Relief sifted through her. "My husband needs my help and I don't want to leave him."

"Then he won't be able to tend the lantern tonight?"

"Even if he regains consciousness, he'd be too weak to climb the tower stairs and spend the night on watch."

"Are you able to light-keep yerself?" The rain continued to trickle off the brim of his hat. The bulging outline of a gun showed beneath his coat.

She started to shake her head and then hesitated. They were sure asking a lot of questions. "I can give it a try. To be honest, I don't know much about the light."

"We know enough that at least we can shut it off for you."

She nodded. "I'd appreciate it." It would be one less thing for her to worry about.

"Not to worry, ma'am. And when we fetch the doctor, we can also spread word that you need help with the light. I'm sure someone can come out and give you a hand until your husband recovers."

"Would you? That would be perfect." Perhaps one of the fishermen at Burnham's Landing would know enough about the lantern to help her get it going again in the evening.

Emma couldn't say why she was relieved that the men didn't ask to come in and dry off and warm up for a spell, but when they left after only a few moments, she let out a long breath and watched as they headed to the tower.

After some time, the beam stopped rotating, and a couple of minutes after that she saw the two men amble down the rocky path to the dock. The one who'd done all the talking limped just slightly. The other turned to stare at the tower one last time before they disappeared through the trees.

She waited expectantly all day for help to arrive. When evening came and the sky began to grow dark, she finally stopped watching out the window for the arrival of the doctor and any other fishermen from Burnham's Landing. No one would venture out after nightfall, especially not on a rainy, windy night.

Once Josiah was tucked into bed and asleep, she ascended the tower steps, carrying a small lantern. Even though she tried to imitate everything Patrick had done the night he'd shown her how to light the lantern, she couldn't get it going.

After crying out in frustration during what felt like her hundredth failed attempt, she returned to the house to check on Patrick and Josiah. She climbed the tower stairway two more times to try again during the long night. On the last attempt, she stared dismally out the window into the darkness and hoped there weren't any ships out on the lake in need of the light.

She caught a glimpse of a beam to the north. She paused and stared. The shaft of light swung out over the lake similar to a beam coming from a lighthouse, only thinner and not as intense. Had someone else noticed the Presque Isle Lighthouse was dark? Maybe they'd lit something for safety's sake.

Emma returned to the house and collapsed exhausted in the chair next to Patrick's bed. She buried her hands in her face. What would he think of her when he woke and found she'd failed to light the lantern?

In all his time working at the lighthouse, he'd said that he never once missed lighting it. And now tonight, for the first time, the ships in the area would be at risk, all because of her.

If she'd begun to win his affection, she'd surely lose it now, now that she'd failed him.

"Oh, Patrick, I'm sorry." She reached for his hand. It was cold and limp in hers, but she grasped it anyway. She could only hope that the light she'd seen to the north would suffice.

She rested her cheek against Patrick's hand. She was too weary to do anything more tonight but close her eyes and sleep.

Chapter 13

*P*atrick's head pounded with a ferocity that nearly blinded him. His tongue stuck to the roof of his mouth, and his body sagged with weakness. He felt as though he'd been banged around, punched in the face, and finally knocked down in the last round.

His breath was shallow, just like it had been after his last fight, the night he'd thought he was a goner, the night he'd been rabbit-punched in the back of the head, supposedly by accident.

He tried to take a deep breath, but his chest was caved in, almost as if his opponent had launched several hooks into his gut. He'd sworn he would never fight again, not for any reason, and certainly not for any amount of money.

So what had happened to him?

He started to raise a hand to his head when he realized someone was holding it.

His eyes flew open to the sight of someone slumped half on the bed and half on a chair. The glow of the lantern on the bedside table revealed it was a woman. Blond hair spilled around her face, but through the tangled tresses he glimpsed a pert nose and mouth, such sweet features.

Emma.

She was asleep with her cheek resting against his hand, which was intertwined with hers. He didn't move but was content to watch her, to bask in the revelation that she was by his side. No one except Holy Bill had ever stayed by his side, not even his mother.

She'd always been overworked and harried. And he'd just been another mouth to feed and body to clothe among his ten brothers and sisters. In fact, he'd been the one to raise his younger sister, the baby of the family, because his mom and older sisters were working twelve-hour days in the coat factory, and his dad and brothers were busy working in the sawmills that lined the Saginaw River Valley.

From his earliest recollections, even before they'd moved to Michigan, he'd been left home to watch the baby. At the time, he was only a young boy himself and had done what he could to keep his sister content. But now that he was full grown, he cringed when he thought of all their escapades. He wished he'd been a more responsible big brother. Thankfully, God had since gotten ahold of him, and he could make up for some of his mistakes by being the kind of father Josiah needed.

Emma sighed, and the warmth of her breath sent a tremor up his arm. He had the urge to brush the hair away from her face so he could get a better view and watch her sleep.

Sleep? He pushed himself up and glanced toward the window. What time was it?

At the slight movement, pain ripped through his head and forced him to fall back against the pillow with a moan.

Emma sat up with a start. She released his hand and flipped

the tangled mass of long hair out of her face. She was on her feet in an instant and hovering above him. "You're awake," she said, relief in her voice.

"What happened?" he croaked, trying to make sense of why he was lying in bed and feeling as if he'd just been soundly beaten in a boxing match.

"There was a storm." Gently, Emma touched his forehead, and he could feel the tight roll of a bandage. "I think you were knocked in the head with a piece of metal from one of the tower windows."

His mind spun back to the last moments he remembered, when the rain had been spraying into the lantern room too near the light. He'd gone out to cover the broken window and was trying to nail one of the corners of canvas.

He lifted his hand to his head, to the aching spot on his scalp where he'd taken the hit. He'd slipped, fallen backward, and hit his head against the rail. That was the last thing he remembered.

Once again he looked to the bedroom window and saw the faint light that peeked through a slit between the curtains. From what he could tell, it was now dawn. An urgency compelled him to sit up in spite of the pain. He struggled to move his legs to the edge of the bed.

"You should lie still," Emma quietly admonished.

"I'll need to turn off the light soon."

"It's already off."

"It is? But how . . . ?" His hands turned clammy. "How long have I been out?"

"More than twenty-four hours."

His chest tightened. He didn't want to ask, but he had to know. "And the light?"

Only then did she look him in the eye. Her expression radiated distress. "Some men stopped by yesterday and helped turn the light off. But when I tried to get it started again last night, I couldn't."

Fighting dizziness, he fell back against the pillow and squeezed his eyes shut against the throbbing in his head. He'd failed in his sacred duty as keeper of the light. And the pain of that overwhelmed him more than the pain of his wound.

"I'm so sorry, Patrick," she whispered. "I tried several times to get the light going, but I couldn't manage to make it work."

"It's not your fault," he said.

Her shoulders slumped. "But I should have been able to do more—"

"No." He reached for her hand and tugged her closer to the bed. Even in the dimness of the room, he could tell she had dark circles under her eyes. "You did all you could. I should have prepared you better." He squeezed her hand.

"I kept waiting for help."

"Help?"

She nodded. "The fishermen said they'd fetch the doctor and also find someone who could come out and give me a hand with the lantern. But no one came."

"I'm not surprised."

"Maybe the doctor will come today."

"There's no doctor in these parts." Dread settled deep in his aching bones. "When someone's injured, it's the widow Burnham who is called."

Who had Emma talked to? If the fishermen were from the area, they wouldn't have given her false hope about a doctor and help with the light, would they?

"Maybe the visitors were the ones who set up a light north of here," she said.

He jolted up, and his head rebelled against the quick motion. "What? There was another light?"

"Aye. I saw one beaming over the lake just to the north."

"Near the shoals?"

"I don't know."

Ignoring the hammering in his head, he swung his legs over the side of the bed. "Did these men give you their names?"

"Nay. They said they came because they saw the lantern was still on and wondered if there might be trouble."

"What did they look like?"

"One had curly black hair and walked with a limp."

No . . . His breath snagged in his chest. The description could only apply to one man, Mitch Schwartz—a man he'd hoped never to see again.

"The other had a hard face," she said. "He wasn't as friendly."

Patrick wiped a hand across his eyes, praying she wouldn't see just how shaken he was. "I'm afraid the men didn't come to help." He needed to take a hike up to the shoals, yet he was afraid of what he might find.

"Why did they come, then?"

"They're pirates." He swallowed the bitter taste of bile that rose to the back of his throat. "They wanted my light to stay dark so they could set up a decoy."

Her brow creased.

"It's called moon cussing," he explained, hoping she wouldn't ask him how he knew. "The pirates make sure the lighthouse is out of commission, and then they place a false light in a danger-ous area. The beam fools the ships' captains and causes them to sail into rocks—making it easier for the pirates to rob them."

Her eyes grew wide. "That's awful. Maybe they were the same men I saw on the beach north of here a few days ago when I was hiking with Josiah."

His head pounded harder. "Why didn't you tell me you saw men on the beach?"

She shrank back at the anger in his voice.

"Never mind," he said, swallowing his frustration. He wasn't angry at her. He was angry at Mitch. He had no doubt that she'd caught Mitch hauling a makeshift lantern ashore in preparation for setting up a decoy light. It was a common tactic for pirates, one he knew all too well. "Don't go hiking too far from the house again."

She nodded.

"I'm just relieved they didn't hurt you or Josiah."

She glanced in the direction of Josiah's room, as if more concerned about the boy's safety than about herself. Except for the patter of more rain against the roof, the house was silent. She visibly trembled and lowered herself to the chair again.

"So the men went into the lighthouse?" he asked.

She nodded.

Mitch had probably tampered with the light so that Emma wouldn't be able to turn it on. But did Mitch know that Patrick was here? That was the most important of his unanswered questions. Mitch had left him for dead after the knockout in his last boxing match.

His old friend had no reason to believe he was still alive. And if Mitch knew he'd survived, he wouldn't believe Patrick had given up his wicked ways and turned into a God-fearing man. In fact, he'd laugh in his face if Patrick ever mentioned the fact that he was clean.

Patrick wouldn't blame him. Anyone who'd known the man

he'd once been would find it difficult to believe he'd changed. There were still times he found it hard to believe that God had given him a second chance at life.

He had a new wife, a healthy son, and a steady job he liked. He didn't deserve any of it. Yet he aimed to live the rest of his life doing the best he could with all that God had given him.

He'd just have to pray that Mitch would sail away before the pirate stirred up more trouble. Or before Emma learned the whole truth about the man Patrick had once been and the awful things he'd done.

Chapter 14

"Me bunny," Josiah said as he hopped in the grass near the garden. "Watch, Mamma."

Emma straightened and gave the boy her attention. He grinned and hopped some more. "You're a very sweet bunny," she said while biting back her complaints about the real rabbits that were destroying her new bean shoots.

She'd been so excited to see them poking through the soil a couple of days ago, their tiny leaves unfurling. And now most of the plants were leafless, sticking up like thick blades of grass, completely useless. She needed a fence around the garden plot before she could replant—if Patrick would spare her the cost of the fencing.

Her eyes moved to the top of the tower, where Patrick was perched precariously on the roof, cleaning the wind vent. After almost a week since his injury, he'd taken off the bandage and his gash was healing. Of course, he hadn't stayed in bed beyond a few hours.

After hiking up the shore, he'd discovered a shipwreck as a result of the pirates' moon cussing. The steamer had been robbed, but besides springing a leak in the hull, none of her crew had come to harm.

Patrick found that the pirates had indeed disabled the light. She felt slightly better knowing she wouldn't have been able to get it going no matter how hard she'd tried. He'd easily fixed the misplaced gear. The very next night he showed her again how to turn the lantern on and also off.

She helped him with repairs to the window, as well as fixing some of the crumbling caulking. But through all of their time together over the past week, he'd never once made another move to initiate any intimacy between them. He'd become distant again.

Emma turned back to the garden. She tipped her hat against the afternoon sunshine, reached down and tugged on a weed. Maybe she ought to try Bertie's advice about making herself look pretty. Or maybe Bertie had been right about his reason for marrying her. What if he'd only been interested in her because he needed an assistant and a mother to Josiah?

She swallowed the disappointment that surfaced every time the thought crossed her mind. She couldn't let herself dwell on the possibility. For now, she had to hold out hope that in his own time, he'd be ready to embrace her as his wife.

Josiah hopped through the dirt toward her. "Bunny eat beans, Mamma?"

"Aye, little love. They've been eating all my beans."

He bent his head and pretended to nibble at the bean shoots. "Me eat."

She laughed, and he flashed her one of his impish grins and then took a bite out of the remains of a bean plant.

"Oh, wee one, don't really eat it. Just pretend."

He chomped on the piece of green for a moment. Then he frowned and began spitting it out as fast as he could. "Yucky!"

Shaking her head, Emma laughed again.

"Hey, Em!" came a call from across the yard.

Emma's heart leaped at the familiar voice. At the sight of Ryan striding around the house, she squealed with joy. Tossing aside her hat, she raced across the yard and threw herself at her brother.

He dropped what he'd been carrying and embraced her. "It's good to see you too." He planted a kiss on her cheek.

She pulled back but didn't completely let go of him. "How are you?"

"Fine," he said with a grin. "Working hard, building up my muscles. I know it hasn't been that long since we've seen each other, but I miss you."

"I've missed you too." She hugged him again.

"I'm glad Patrick convinced Fred Burnham to give me the afternoon off," he added after he'd extricated himself from her hug. His smile faded, and he glanced up at the tower.

Patrick had paused in his work and was looking down at them. Ryan waved at him in greeting.

Her husband tipped his hat before turning back to his work.

Ryan studied Patrick for a moment and then stooped down to retrieve the roll of wire he'd brought with him. "He said he needed supplies delivered for a fence, and a man to help build it."

Emma grew silent. Patrick had noticed her rabbit-eaten garden. And he'd given her the help she needed in the form of the one person she most wanted to see—her brother. A lump swelled in her throat.

No matter his past, Patrick Garraty was a good man. A very good man.

She wanted nothing more at that moment than to throw herself into his arms and hug him and tell him thank you. She couldn't keep from looking at him again, taking in the solidness of his arms and back, the strength in every movement. She wished he'd turn around again and see her gratefulness.

"I wasn't so sure about this quick marriage of yours," Ryan said. "But now that I've had the chance to talk with Patrick a few times, I have to admit I like him."

She nodded, unable to speak past the tightness in her throat. She had to agree with Ryan. She liked Patrick too. In fact, she liked him a lot.

The afternoon passed all too quickly. With Ryan's help, the fence went up much faster than if she'd had to attempt it by herself while caring for Josiah.

When they finished, Ryan tousled Josiah's hair. "You're a good helper, little man."

Josiah held up the small hammer Emma had found for him at the bottom of the lighthouse toolbox. He went to the nearest stake and with a serious expression began pounding on it, just as he'd watched Ryan do moments earlier.

Emma shared a smile with Ryan.

"He's cute," Ryan said. "He doesn't look a thing like Patrick, but still he's cute."

Josiah's face was the color of beets from the hot afternoon, and his red hair stuck to his forehead from underneath his cap. She studied the boy's features, trying to see Patrick there. Ryan was right. Except for his eyes, Josiah didn't resemble his father. Yet even the eyes were a different shade from Patrick's. It made her wish she'd known Delia, that she could have met her at least once.

Ryan began to pick up the leftover wire.

"You're staying for supper, aren't you?" she asked, not ready for her time with her brother to come to an end yet.

"Who's cooking?" Ryan asked.

"I am."

"I don't think I'll be able to stay."

She gave him a playful shove. "I'll have you know I haven't burned anything the past two days."

He cocked one of his brows.

"Ryan Chambers, I dare you to try my cooking. It's much improved, believe me."

"I'm a daring man most of the time. But with your cooking?" His tone was skeptical, though his eyes twinkled.

"You'll be amazed," she assured, tugging him inside.

She'd already made Bertie's johnnycake that morning when Patrick had been out fishing. Thankfully she hadn't burned it this time. She also had a pot of rabbit stew simmering from another of Bertie's receipts, a rabbit Patrick had trapped and dressed for her yesterday.

When the coffee was done perking, Patrick stumbled into the kitchen wiping the sleep out of his eyes. She guessed the aroma of the fresh brew was his evening alarm clock. He stopped short at the sight of Ryan at the table in the extra chair she'd dragged in from the sitting room.

"I invited Ryan to join us for supper," she said, pouring him a mug of coffee.

"Good," Patrick replied. He took a seat in the chair next to Josiah. His hair was scraggly from sleep, his eyelids still drooping.

She didn't know how he did it night after night, working so hard and getting so little sleep. She wished there was more she could do to ease his burden.

"She twisted my arm into staying," Ryan said with a wink.

"I wasn't so sure I should eat anything Em cooks, but then I figured you're still alive, so I've probably got a good chance of surviving too."

Patrick's lips quirked into a half smile at Ryan's jest.

She handed Patrick his mug. He gave her a grateful nod, took a sip, and sat back in his chair. "Ahhh . . . that's good coffee."

Her heart warmed at the words he spoke every evening when he took his first sip. Only then did she turn back to the stove and begin to ladle the stew. As she served the men and listened to their conversation, her heart swelled even more.

Seating herself between the two men, she held both of their hands while Patrick prayed. Contentment seeped through her. Who would have guessed a month ago that she'd have her own home and be serving her brother and husband a meal she'd made herself? It was a dream come true.

As they ate, she listened to the men talk about fishing and other matters. Ryan was as talkative as ever and shared about the last hard winter they'd spent on Mackinac after their dad had died.

"Now that I've told you a bit about our family," Ryan said, scraping the last spoonful of stew from his bowl, "please, tell us about yours."

Patrick's spoon halted halfway to his mouth. A shadow fell across his face, and he lowered the spoonful back to his bowl uneaten.

Emma stiffened. Part of her wanted to tap Ryan's arm in warning. But the another part wanted to learn more about this man to whom she'd pledged her life. He'd shared so little about himself, and she longed to know more.

Oblivious of the storm brewing within Patrick, Ryan sat back in his chair and reached for his coffee. "Well?"

"What do you want to know?" Patrick said in a low voice.

"Everything. What part of Ireland is home? When did you leave? Where is your family now?" Ryan took a sip and fastened his attention on Patrick expectantly.

Patrick stared into his nearly empty bowl and twisted the spoon, letting it clank against the side. "Most of my family lives down in Saginaw, working in the sawmills."

Ryan nodded. "What got you interested in light keeping?"

Patrick didn't say anything for a long moment. At last he set down his spoon and locked eyes with Ryan. "Holy Bill saved my life. Once I was recovered, he helped me get the assistant keeper position down at Fort Gratiot."

Emma could sense that each word he spoke was forced.

"What happened?" Ryan continued, apparently not noticing how difficult his questions were for Patrick to answer. "Did you get hurt in one of the mills?"

Patrick shook his head, then looked down at his thick knuckles. For the first time, Emma noticed the scars there.

"I was in a boxing fight," Patrick finally said.

At Patrick's confession, Ryan's brow rose.

But before Ryan could ask any more questions, Patrick pushed away from the table. "I best be heading up to the light. I've a few more repairs to make."

Emma jumped up and darted for the coffeepot. "Would you like to take a cup of coffee with you?" she asked as she'd gotten into the habit of doing after the evening meal. Her coffee was the one thing she'd been able to make consistently without ruining.

He nodded and held out his cup.

She sensed his inner turmoil. After she poured the coffee, she wanted to reassure him that she cared. So he'd been in a fight.

Maybe the fight had even gotten him into trouble. But what did it matter anymore?

He'd shown her such kindness, with the chickens, and now today by providing the fence for her garden and inviting Ryan out to help her build it. The least she could do was to offer him some encouragement.

Before he could move away, and before she let her bashfulness stop her, she reached over and touched his arm.

He looked up.

She smiled, hoping he could read her gratefulness.

He gave her a tired smile in return and then crossed the room and disappeared outside into the evening.

"Not much of a talker, is he?" Ryan said once Patrick was gone.

Emma sighed. "Nay. But I couldn't ask for a better husband."

"Then you're happy here, Em?" Ryan stood and put his hat back on. "You're really happy?"

She knew she couldn't tell Ryan that Patrick had a criminal past. It would ruin all the positive feelings Ryan had developed for her husband. But should she tell Ryan that Patrick hadn't consummated their marriage? Should she tell him she was worried that perhaps Patrick didn't want her as a wife? Maybe he'd be able to give her some advice.

Ryan looked at her intently. "What is it?"

Her cheeks burned, and she couldn't make herself ask.

"I don't want to leave until I know for sure you're happy here."

"I'm happy, Ryan."

He didn't look convinced. "But—"

"Mamma, me all done," Josiah said from the table.

She bustled to the boy, wiped his faced and hands, and lifted him onto her hip, all the while sensing Ryan's eyes on her.

When she turned again to face her brother, she buried her face in Josiah's hair. She didn't want Ryan to see her hesitation. If he did, she knew he'd stay. One of the reasons she'd gotten married was so that she could give her brother his freedom. She wanted him to pursue his dreams and make a new life for himself in America now that they didn't have Dad to worry about.

"I'll be fine, Ryan," she said, hating to admit there was still part of her that wasn't ready to let go of him yet.

"I'm in no hurry to leave," Ryan said. "Chopping cordwood has been a nice change from fishing, and the Burnhams haven't kicked me out yet." He gave her a good-bye hug and kiss. "Don't worry. I'll be here for you if you need me."

After he left, she sighed in frustration. If only she'd answered him more cheerfully when he questioned her. As she cleaned up after supper and prepared Josiah for bed, a sense of relief settled over her nonetheless. She'd get to see Ryan again. Maybe by then she wouldn't hesitate when he asked if she was happy.

After she tucked Josiah into bed and kissed him good-night, she was surprised when Patrick stepped quietly back into the kitchen. The sky was still bright, and it would be another hour before sunset when he needed to turn on the light. Even so, she hadn't expected his return.

He went into Josiah's room. While she swept the floor, she could hear his deep voice mingling with Josiah's as they talked and prayed together. She loved the way Patrick interacted with the boy. He was always loving and yet stern when he needed to be.

When Patrick returned to the kitchen, Emma kept herself busy sweeping. She expected him to simply walk past her and return to the lighthouse.

Instead, once he closed Josiah's door, he turned and leaned against the frame. Her insides squirmed. She propped the broom into the corner and fingered one of the smooth rocks in the windowsill, one she'd collected during her hike on the beach with Josiah. She peeked at him over her shoulder.

"I forgot to tell you that supper was good," he said softly.

She smiled. "Nothing burned this time."

He smiled back. "It was real good."

The words warmed her. "And I forgot to tell you how much I appreciated you inviting Ryan to help me with the garden fence."

"It was selfish on my part. I don't want the rabbits eating what belongs in my belly."

She doubted he could be selfish even if he tried. "It was wonderful to spend the afternoon with him. I can't thank you enough for that."

He glanced down at his boots. "Your brother's a decent man."

"Sorry he was pestering you so much after dinner."

Patrick lifted his eyes, letting her glimpse his shame. "I'm not proud of some of the things I've done."

She longed to go to him and wrap her arms around him and reassure him. But touching his arm earlier was about as brave as she could get. "Your past doesn't matter. It's who you are now that counts."

He held her gaze as if testing her words. Finally he nodded. "Thank you, lass."

She nodded back, her body aching with the need to hold him.

For a second, something flickered in his eyes, and she almost believed he'd cross the room and gather her in his arms.

She held her breath.

When he started toward the door, she released her disappointment slowly.

He paused halfway out and looked at her again. "Will you come up to the tower tonight?"

There was a shyness behind his question, and she wasn't sure why he was asking. Maybe he only wanted to test her knowledge of the lantern or teach her more about his keeping duties. Whatever the case, he'd invited her, and she didn't want to say no.

"Aye. I'll come."

"Good." He closed the door behind him and was gone.

Chapter 15

$\mathcal{P}$atrick jotted another number into the logbook, tallying the amount of oil he'd used in the past week. Then he glanced toward the open hatch and the top rung of the ladder for the hundredth time since night had fallen.

Where was Emma? She said she'd come.

He scratched another number down into the next column on the half-filled page.

What had gotten into him anyway to invite her? Of course, he'd had her come up after his accident to make sure she was comfortable with lighting the lantern in case something should happen to him again. But now that she knew how to operate the light, what need did she have to come to the tower with him? Why would she want to spend time with a man like him?

With a sigh, he jabbed the pen back into the bottle of ink. He should have left things alone. They were doing fine.

It's just that she hadn't been disgusted by his admission about his boxing. She'd even touched his arm. She'd initiated the contact, just like she had that day on the beach. And then again when he'd been injured in bed and she'd held his hand.

She wasn't repulsed by him the way Delia had been.

His chest pinched at the thought of how Delia had cringed whenever he made the briefest of contact with her, even by accident. And she hadn't known the worst about him—about the other woman, about what he'd done. Delia would have abhorred him if she'd ever found out. And Emma would too.

Even if Holy Bill had told him some things about his past weren't worth dragging into the future, he couldn't help but wonder if Emma deserved to know everything. Then while Ryan was still in the area, she could leave with him if she wanted to.

"Patrick?" her soft voice sounded behind him.

He spun around. At the sight of her climbing through the hatch—her cheeks flushed, her eyes warm and curious, and her hair flowing down to her waist—he almost forgot his promise to her that he wouldn't pressure her. He was tempted to heft her up and crush her in his arms.

She hesitated halfway up.

He held himself back and smiled. "You came."

"I didn't know," she said. "I mean, I wasn't sure if you'd be busy."

"I have all night to get my work done." He couldn't tear his eyes from the waves of her hair that fell down her shoulders. It gleamed as if she'd recently brushed it. He'd seen her with her hair loose before, but only when it had been tangled and wet, nothing like this in all its glorious beauty.

"I'd like the company," he said, meaning it. He didn't mind the solitude of the keeper's life. After years of living in a big, noisy family and then on crowded ships, he relished having the space to himself.

He loved the quiet hours before dawn when he could talk to

God out loud without the worry of anyone else hearing him. He could pour out his worries and fears and know that God was there, listening.

But tonight, with her standing there glowing like an angel by the light of the lantern, he realized he wanted to be with her, that he craved the companionship.

"If you're sure I won't be a bother," she said as she climbed up the rest of the way.

"You'd never bother me, lass."

"You're kind to say so, but I've been known to annoy Ryan quite often with my talking."

"Ryan's a good man."

"Aye. I'll be sad to see him go."

After spending time with Ryan today, was she having second thoughts about staying at Presque Isle? Did she want to leave?

She looked past him to the open door. "It's peaceful up here tonight."

"The stars are all out. It's a sight to behold."

She followed him out onto the gallery to the west, opposite the beam of light. The air was warm and humid, while the cool breeze blowing off the lake was soothing, one of the pleasures of being up on the balcony at night.

He'd learned a great deal about the night sky during his years navigating the Great Lakes. For a while she asked him about the stars, and he pointed out the different constellations to her, enjoying her nearness and the way strands of her hair would blow into him.

"So is this what you do at night?" she asked. "Stargazing?"

"Sometimes. Mostly I pray." He didn't look at her for fear of seeing humor on her face. He wasn't used to talking about his new faith, except with Josiah.

She was silent for several long seconds. "I think I stopped believing in the power of prayer after my mam died."

"She died from starvation?" he asked hesitantly.

Emma nodded. "I prayed and prayed and prayed for her. But in those days, people everywhere were praying to stay alive. They were praying just as hard as me. And God couldn't save everyone, could He?"

Patrick stared at the black sky, alight with countless stars. It always amazed him to think that the God who created the universe cared about a sinful mortal like him, that He chose to save him when he didn't deserve anything but condemnation. "I find it incredible that God saves any of us. He doesn't have to, but sometimes He chooses to."

He could feel her full attention on him, and he uttered a silent prayer that God would give him the right words to say. He wasn't wise like Holy Bill, and he wasn't eloquent either.

He forced himself to continue. "Maybe we should stop looking at why God doesn't answer every prayer the way we think He should. But instead we should count it a blessing that He hears our prayers at all."

"I hadn't thought of it that way," she said.

He shifted, and her shoulder brushed against his arm. "Holy Bill told me that God sometimes answers *yes* to our prayers, but sometimes in His wisdom He answers *no* or *wait*."

Whatever the case, Patrick always prayed. Through praying he found peace for his anguished soul, and this alone was enough for him no matter how God answered the prayer.

"You're a wise man, Patrick."

He turned to look at her upturned face. She was smiling. Her hair swirled, the light from the lantern reflecting hints of red amidst the gold. She was beautiful.

Don't look down at her mouth, he admonished himself. If he let himself glimpse her lips, he'd only want to kiss her. It was too tempting not to kiss her now that they were alone, in the dark, on the gallery.

With self-control he didn't know he had, he reached for her hand, and slipped his fingers cautiously around hers.

She didn't pull away but wrapped her fingers around his and clasped his hand. For a long while they stood there quietly holding hands, gazing out at the starry night.

When she shuddered from the cold, he led her back inside and didn't have the nerve to reach for her hand again, though he wanted to keep holding it. She was easy to talk to, full of eager questions. He found he enjoyed her company much more than he should.

"I'll let you get back to work," she finally said, heading back toward the hatch.

He thought about asking her to stay longer, but he knew she needed a good night's sleep. As she started down the ladder, he watched her leaving with a momentary swell of panic. "Will you come tomorrow night?"

"Aye," she said softly. "If you want me to."

"I do." He ached to bend down and pull her back.

But he held himself rigid until she disappeared. Only then did he release a pent-up breath. "I do want you to," he whispered into the empty room. "Very much."

The next day was Sunday, and since Holy Bill had ridden into town, everyone for miles around gathered for a church service at Burnham's Landing. Afterward, Patrick invited Holy Bill to come out to the lighthouse and join them for Sunday dinner.

He didn't know what Emma had planned, but she was agreeable to his suggestion. Before leaving Burnham's Landing, she'd stopped to get instructions from Bertie Burnham for what he guessed was another meal.

"Emma's a nice young lady," Holy Bill said as they walked along the shore a short distance from the keeper's cottage.

"That she is," Patrick said, watching Josiah run along ahead of them, at home among the rocks and tall weeds. He paused to poke at a decaying fish head.

"Praise God for His answer to prayer." Holy Bill had taken off his hat, and a sticky breeze teased the thin white hair left on his balding head.

Patrick agreed. Maybe God's way of answering prayer would always be a mystery. All he knew was that prayer was his lifeline. He needed it more than the air he breathed.

Holy Bill rubbed at his bushy white beard. "Emma seems a bit more agreeable than Delia."

Patrick stopped behind Josiah. He didn't want to speak ill of Delia, but the truth was that living with Emma was like a breath of spring warmth and sunshine after a long, hard winter. "Emma's a sweet lass," he admitted.

"And she's obviously sweet on you," Holy Bill said with a smile curving his bristly mustache.

"You think so?"

"I can tell by the way she looks at you that she admires you."

Patrick's heartbeat picked up a pace. "How?"

One of Holy Bill's bushy eyebrows shot up.

Patrick reached for a rock and tossed it into the water. He could kick himself for sounding as eager as a young lad with his first love and sweetheart.

"What's going on between you and Emma?" Holy Bill asked.

Patrick toed a big rock stuck deep in the sand. He could always count on Holy Bill getting right to the point. And he knew it wouldn't do any good to try to change the topic. Holy Bill would only come back to it.

"After my troubles with Delia," Patrick said, nudging at the unmovable rock, "I'm trying not to pressure Emma."

"I see."

Patrick could tell Holy Bill knew exactly what he was talking about, that he hadn't consummated the marriage yet.

Holy Bill was quiet for a moment before giving Patrick a pat on the back. "So, since you had one wife reject you already, you're afraid of that happening again?"

Was he afraid of rejection? Afraid that Emma would decide she didn't like being married to a convicted criminal? Would his past eventually embarrass and shame her too?

Holy Bill knew how difficult his marriage with Delia had been. The reverend had seen the problems firsthand every time he'd visited. Delia had never cared for him, had married him mostly because that was what her father had suggested. Then after the baby and the move, her apathy had turned to resentment.

"As I said, I think Emma's different from Delia," the reverend said. "Perhaps your fears are unfounded."

"I told her I was a criminal."

Holy Bill grew motionless. "How much did you tell her?"

"Nothing more or less than I told Delia."

"Well, then apparently your past isn't too off-putting. She still seems to really like you."

He hoped so. "But should I tell her everything?"

Holy Bill stared out over the waves toward the few puffy clouds that dotted the horizon. "Maybe you should tell her more. Eventually."

Patrick sighed. He'd hoped the reverend would tell him to stay silent.

"I've always thought that once you're set free from the past," Holy Bill continued, "there's really no reason to keep bringing it up. But pray about it. See what God wants you to do. Maybe He'll give you opportunities to share in bite sizes so that Emma can digest it a little at a time."

The sun beat down on Patrick's navy cap, heating his scalp. He swiped off the hat, dipped his hand into a cold wave, and rubbed the water into his hair to cool himself.

Josiah scooped a handful of water and did the same, giggling as the water coursed down his face.

"Besides, there's no rush," the reverend said. "Maybe you should court Emma first, win her love proper-like, and then you can tell her more."

Court her? Patrick placed his hat back on his head. He'd never considered courting her. In fact, he'd never courted any girl before, not even Delia.

"How do I court?" he asked.

Holy Bill chuckled. "You're asking the wrong person on that one, sonny, considering I'm sixty years old and never been married."

Patrick glanced back at the house, barely visible beyond the tower. A strange yearning squeezed him. He liked Emma more than he'd expected he would, beginning with when he stood beside her on the harbor beach and took his vows.

And now he wanted to see if maybe he could have a normal family, a normal life. Maybe he could be the kind of husband and father God wanted him to be. Maybe he could give Emma and Josiah everything he'd never had when he was growing up—stability, love, and godliness.

Holy Bill slapped him on the back again. "I'm sure you'll find ways to woo her. Give her things, compliment her and treat her real sweet. And maybe someday you'll be able to tell her the truth about Josiah too."

Patrick turned his attention to the boy. He was in the process of dumping another handful of water over his head, heedless of the fact he was soaking the front of his shirt.

Patrick nodded. The reverend's counsel seemed sound. Maybe once he'd courted Emma and won her affection, he'd tell her more. He didn't want to chance her rejecting him now, though, not when things were so new between them.

For the time being he'd have to figure out how to woo his wife. As embarrassing as it had been to discuss the matter with Holy Bill, the prospect of courting Emma was more than a little appealing.

Chapter 16

Patrick kneeled in front of his desk and slid the bottom drawer open. He reached into the deep recess, and his fingers grazed grainy wood and a folded sheet of paper underneath. He pulled both out and sat back on his heels, examining the wood—two pieces of ship wreckage that had been nailed together in the shape of a cross. The longer piece was only about a foot long, and both were dark and roughhewn around the edges.

There wasn't anything extraordinary about the cross itself. It was simple, made by someone who didn't have much skill in woodworking. Rather, it was the sheet of paper that came with the wooden cross that transformed it into something beautiful and hopefully something worthy of giving to Emma.

The late evening sunshine slanted through the window above the desk and illuminated the yellowing paper in his hand. Even now, just looking at it filled him with hope.

He'd discovered the cross during the long days of winter when the blowing snow had buffeted the house and a howling blizzard kept them inside. He'd been rummaging through the desk, sorting through the assortment of items left in it from previous keepers.

That was when he'd read the story for the first time. The story seemed too personal, even though there was a note at the end from the writer encouraging the reader to pass the cross along to someone who needed it. Patrick had carefully tucked the cross and letter back in the drawer where he found it.

Over the remainder of the winter he'd returned to the desk on several occasions with the intention of rereading it and sharing it with Delia. But every time he reread it, he was only able to kneel in front of the desk and that was all.

Now Patrick was glad he hadn't shared it with Delia, because somehow he knew the cross belonged to Emma. With the cross and letter in hand, he stood and moved to the door and then stopped. The house was silent. He'd already tucked Josiah into bed. Only the melody of the crashing waves could be heard in the distance.

Holy Bill's words of the previous day had rolled over and over in his mind that he should court Emma and win her love proper-like. The problem was he didn't know how to start courting her. But he decided he couldn't put it off any longer; he had to set aside his reservations. He needed to show her he liked her and thought she was special.

He hid the cross behind his back and forced himself to make his way out of the house and around the corner, where Emma sat in the grass next to the open cellar door, counting empty canning jars. They were coated in dust and cobwebs. Delia had certainly never used them.

At the sight of him, Emma looked up and smiled. "Is he already asleep?"

"The moment his head hit the pillow."

"I guess all the sunshine and fresh air wore him out."

"And he has a good mamma who keeps him busy."

She shifted her focus back to the jars, but not before he caught sight of the creeping flush on her cheeks.

He leaned his shoulder against the house, did a quick calculation of the number of jars. If her garden did well, she wouldn't have nearly enough for preserving the vegetables. Next time he went to Fremont, he'd see if he could purchase some more.

She traced a finger around the mouth of one of the jars as if waiting for him to speak. Loose hair stuck to her neck, damp with the humidity that wouldn't give them relief even in the evening.

He longed to bend down, push her hair back, and let his fingers feel the skin of her neck. Instead, he held out the wooden cross. "I want you to have this."

Her eyes widened at his offering. Immediately he wanted to kick himself for not thinking of something more romantic to say with the gift. How would she know he was attempting to court her if he acted like a bumbling idiot all the time?

"The cross comes with this." He held out the folded paper.

Her brows rose as she took the sheet.

"I thought it might give you hope," he added.

She twisted the cross in her hands and then studied the paper. "Should I read it now?"

"If you want."

She made quick work of wiping her hands on her apron before carefully unfolding the sheet of paper. She began reading it silently. The slanted strokes of ink were meticulous. A few moments later, she lowered the paper. "What a beautiful story." Her voice wobbled, and her eyes glistened. "Is it true?"

"Stephen Thornton was the Presque Isle lightkeeper about five years ago. I believe Isabelle was his daughter."

She scanned the paper again.

Having read it many times over, Patrick could see the words in his mind, telling the story of Isabelle Thornton, the lightkeeper's daughter. She and her father had rescued a young man from a shipwreck. He was the only survivor and the wealthy heir of Cole Enterprises, a copper mining and lumber magnate in Michigan.

Due to the nature of his injuries, Henry Cole had been stranded at the remote lighthouse, in the days before Burnham's Landing had come into existence. Henry had been rich, spoiled, and carefree. And he'd been anxious to return to his home in New York after spending months away.

He'd made the cross to serve as a reminder to pray for his family to rescue him. But the longer he stayed, the less he wanted to leave. He'd fallen in love with Isabelle, who was unable to resist Henry's charm. She'd fallen in love with him too.

But Isabelle's secrets, as well as Henry's enemies, had forced the couple apart. Through it all, Isabelle had learned not to give up hope.

"It's amazing to think that such a love story happened right here at this lighthouse," Emma said.

Patrick felt himself blush. Would Emma think him too bold for sharing something so intimate with her?

She carefully folded the letter and then held up the cross as if admiring it. "This is too special a gift. I couldn't possibly accept—"

"Please. I want you to have it."

"But it's yours."

"You read the ending. It's not meant to keep; it's meant to pass on to someone who's in need of hope."

"You mean me?"

He pushed away from the house and stuffed his hands into

his pockets. "When you told me about your mam, it sounded like you'd given up the hope of God hearing your prayers."

"Aye," she said. "I suppose I have."

"Maybe this cross and story can remind you to hope again, to know that God is listening to you."

She caressed the cross.

He hoped he hadn't overstepped his bounds. Perhaps he ought to tell her that the other reason for this gift was because he wanted to have a relationship with her similar to what Henry had with Isabelle. But again the words stuck in his throat.

"Thank you, Patrick," she whispered. And when she met his gaze, this time there was something bright and hopeful in her eyes.

He nodded.

"You're a good man."

Even though I was a criminal? He looked down at his boots before she could see the question in his eyes. He could see that, for now, he would have to be content with earning her trust and affection one tiny step at a time.

Emma stood in the middle of the bedroom, staring at the door. She'd wanted Patrick to invite her to the tower, but after their brief interaction while she was cleaning the cellar, he'd gone up to light the lantern and hadn't returned. Now darkness swirled around her. The light from the oil lamp on the bedside table illuminated a bare spot on the wall above the dresser, as if showing her exactly where she should hang the cross.

Patrick was sweet to give her the wooden cross and beautiful tale of the couple in love. She clutched the cross as the haunting passion of their story spoke to her. She wondered what had happened to Isabelle and Henry. Had he returned for her? Were any doctors able to help the young woman?

Whatever Isabelle's hardships, and whatever she had to face in her future, she'd been brave enough to cling to hope. If Isabelle could find reason to go on living even when her life had seemed so bleak, couldn't she, Emma, learn to hope again, especially now that she had a place to live?

Emma walked over to the dresser and eyed the blank wall above it. She'd hang the cross there and maybe she could use it as a reminder to pray, just as Henry Cole had.

She leaned it against the wall and stood back. Contentment washed over her. She was finally home, and she never wanted to leave.

Chapter 17

"No more paint, Josiah." Emma leveled a stern look at the boy.

He held his dripping brush above the nearly empty paint can and stared back at her. Then he began to lower the brush, his eyes sparked with a stubbornness she'd come to dread.

She now regretted letting him help her with painting at all. Her intuition had told her to wait on painting the hen house until some night after he was in bed, when he wouldn't be able to do exactly what he'd done that afternoon.

He'd splattered paint all over what remained of the grass in the coop. He'd covered himself with it from head to toe, and somehow he'd even managed to get paint on the hens themselves, so that they stalked around squawking through beaks drizzled with white.

Now the paint was almost gone and she still had one side of the hen house to cover.

"Little love," she said as his brush went deeper into the can, "Mamma said no more paint."

"Me paint," he insisted.

She'd selfishly wanted to finish the painting during the day so she would be free to visit the tower if Patrick asked her to join him. He'd invited her up several more times over the past week. She had to admit, going up there at night, talking with him, sometimes holding hands was becoming her favorite part of the day.

She didn't want to appear too busy at night after Josiah was in bed for fear Patrick would decide not to interrupt her. He was polite like that. She wondered if she should paint a sign on the side of the hen house that said *Interrupt me, please.*

With a sigh, she perched her brush on a flat stone, then pushed herself up and started toward Josiah. "If you disobey Mamma, you'll have to repent on your bed."

He hesitated for an instant, but then plunged the brush down into the can in one fell swoop.

She reached his hand before he could lift out the brush and spray more paint everywhere. She pried his fingers loose. By the time she scooped him up and struggled back toward the house, he cried in protest. But it was a weak cry, as if he knew he'd lost the battle.

Though his tantrums had grown less frequent, he still tested her on occasion, especially on days when Patrick was gone all day—like today. Today was one of those days when Patrick hadn't gone fishing, but had taken his mysterious trip instead.

Those were the worst days, not only for Josiah but for her as well. She couldn't keep Bertie's warnings from swarming her mind like pesky gnats. While she told herself the Patrick she was getting to know and admire wouldn't visit another woman, the thought wouldn't go away. More than once, her attention strayed to his desk in the sitting room, and she had to fight the urge to rummage through its drawers.

After Josiah spent time on his bed and repented, she bathed him. He'd grown to enjoy the warm sudsy water, the scrubbing of his hair and face, and the extra time to play in the water.

"There you are," Patrick said from behind them.

From her spot kneeling on the kitchen floor beside the tub, she glanced over her shoulder and found herself looking up at Patrick's handsome face. He'd swept off his hat, revealing his dark tousled hair. The strength of his presence filled the room and seemed to envelop her.

"I can see you were painting today," he said with a laugh.

"Me paint," Josiah said, a serious look on his face.

"Did you misplace your paintbrush," Patrick asked, "or did you use the chickens as paintbrushes instead?"

Josiah nodded.

Emma tried to hide her smile but couldn't.

The second Josiah saw her humor, he grinned, as if knowing he'd done something funny yet not quite knowing what.

She shook her head and then realized her hair and face were splattered with paint too. Wishing she could hide herself and clean up, she focused on Josiah's head and ran the comb through his hair again. Patrick started across the kitchen, and when he stopped in front of her, her stomach quivered at his nearness.

"I found this for you today." He held out his hand, and there in his palm was a rock swirled in pink and red and brown. If she didn't know better, she'd almost believe it was in the shape of a heart.

"It's beautiful."

"For your collection." He cocked his head toward the windowsill, where she'd lined up an assortment of her favorite rocks.

Her chest swelled with tenderness for this man before her.

He was always so thoughtful and noticed the little things she needed or liked. "Thank you." She took the rock, relishing the roughness of his skin brushing against hers.

He shifted shyly and focused on the puddles of water around the tin tub. "Looks like you had a hard day. I'll watch Josiah when you're done here."

"We're okay." She thought back to the first time she'd had to deal with one of Josiah's fits. She'd been a wreck. She certainly had come a long way in a few weeks' time in learning to handle him. While she was far from perfect, she was getting better at parenting, and she was also getting better at cooking.

"I'm sure you're tired," she said. "Why don't you lie down for a bit? We'll be fine."

He nodded. And that was when she noticed the sadness in his eyes and the weariness crinkling the corners. "Promise me you'll come to the tower later?" he asked with a hopefulness that made her middle flutter.

"I promise." He needn't have made her promise. She wanted to come. She longed for it more than anything else.

The time moved too slowly until darkness settled. Then with her heartbeat thrumming in anticipation, she ascended the dark stairway. The tower was always cool and damp. Her footsteps echoed with each stair she climbed.

When she reached the top, she paused in the hatch. He was busy cleaning the window glass, as she saw him frequently do. He must have heard her approach because he glanced over his shoulder, and his somber expression broke into a welcoming smile.

She returned his smile. "I'm not too early, am I?"

"Never." In the humid warmth of the night, he'd tossed aside his coat and wore only his white linen shirt with several buttons undone. His eyes glowed green against his tanned face. "I like it when you're here."

That was all the invitation she needed. She hoisted herself into the room, joining him behind the lantern.

For a few minutes, he asked her about her day, and they shared laughter over Josiah's painting efforts and his other antics. A gust of wind rattled the windows and whistled down the vent above the lantern.

Patrick peered out the west window and then studied the barometer hanging near the door. "The wind is shifting, and the barometric pressure is dropping." His eyes narrowed on the lake. "The lake's starting to kick up."

"What does that mean?"

"We're in for another storm."

"But it was so peaceful when I came up."

"You know the saying here on the Great Lakes—if you don't like the weather, wait five minutes and it will change."

She stood beside him and looked out the window over the tossing-and-turning waves. "With this storm, please don't get knocked unconscious."

He grinned. "I'll try not to."

"I'd appreciate it," she teased. "If something needs fixing, make sure you call me instead of attempting it yourself."

He chuckled.

They watched the long beam of light rotate over the dark waters that were whipping higher with each passing minute.

"So, how was your day?" She wished she could ask him what he'd done and where he'd gone, but she didn't want to probe too much. Somehow she knew that too many questions would put up a wall, the same way Ryan's had when he'd tried to learn more about Patrick and his family.

He was silent for a long moment, and she began to regret she asked anything when finally he spoke. "I had family affairs to deal with. And that's never easy."

Even though the room was cramped and hot, she didn't complain. The narrow space between the windows and the lantern had a way of pushing them together into close proximity.

He stared outside. The muscles in his jaw flexed.

"I'm sorry." She didn't know what else to say or do, so she patted his arm.

At the brief contact, his arm tightened. She was certainly not endearing herself to him tonight. Maybe she should head back to the house.

But before she could move, he swung toward her, and his fingers slipped around her upper arm. "Don't go yet." His eyes had turned murky and pleaded with her to stay.

"Okay," she whispered. She knew she should say something more, maybe direct the conversation to a new topic, but she didn't want to break his hold on her arm. She liked the gentle pressure of his hand on her.

He searched her face. "You have paint . . ." He lifted his hand to her forehead, then hesitated.

"Oh. I thought I'd gotten it all." She was about to wipe at whatever leftover smudge she'd missed when he beat her to it. Tenderly he rubbed at a tiny spot at the edge of her scalp.

Her heart gave a hop at the nearness of his chin hovering just inches from her mouth.

"There," he said. But he didn't pull back. Instead, his fingertips skimmed over her hair.

She'd gotten into the habit of letting her hair down and brushing it before she ascended the tower. She'd rationalized that she needed to do it before going to bed. The truth was she wanted to look pretty for him. Bertie had told her that men couldn't resist a pretty woman.

So far, Patrick had resisted her just fine.

His touch was gentle as he brushed back a wisp of her hair, just as he'd done before. He trailed his hand down the length of her hair, ending at her arm. She was surprised when he brought his other hand up and combed back a strand on the opposite side.

She was eye level with his throat and saw his Adam's apple move up and down. Then he plunged deeper into her hair, letting it cascade through his fingers like a waterfall. Pleasure rippled through her.

He delved into her hair again, but this time slower as he drew her closer, until his scruffy chin grazed her forehead.

Her body sizzled at his nearness. The sparks between them were like nothing she'd ever experienced before.

His warm breath fanned against her, followed by the pressure of his lips, as if he wanted more than a kiss against her forehead but wasn't allowing himself. What was holding him back?

She knew there could be so much more between them. Something had been growing within her. Every day she was with him, she liked him more and only wanted to be closer to him in a relationship that had no barriers, no closed doors, no secrets. Just free and open loving.

That was what she wanted—to love him.

Aye. She was falling in love with him.

Somehow she had to let him know that, before he ended the moment of intimacy as he usually did.

With a burst of courage, she slipped her arms around his waist and leaned into him, resting her cheek against his shirt.

He pulled her tighter. She closed her eyes and breathed out a shaky breath. She'd done it. Beneath her ear she could hear his heartbeat. His body felt warm, but he held himself straight, as if he couldn't give himself to her fully.

She didn't let go. She snuggled her nose into his chest and tried to still the wild, nervous thumping of her pulse.

His fingers intertwined in her hair, and the motion sent tingles up her back. But then he gave a deep sigh and released his hold on her. He was letting her go, and she wasn't ready for the moment to come to an end. She slid her hands upward, letting her fingers skim his back.

He stiffened.

Embarrassed, she pressed her lips against his chest anyway. If that kiss didn't send him a message, she didn't know what else would.

He didn't move.

What was she doing? She was throwing herself at him when he obviously didn't want her in that way. She let her hands fall away and wanted to slink down the stairway, back into the house where she could bury her hot face into her pillow.

He gave a soft groan then, and his hands returned to her hair. He dug in and gently tugged her head back just far enough to see her face, her lips.

Before she realized what was happening, he brought his mouth down upon hers, his lips touching and then crushing hers. The power of his kiss took her captive. She was helpless to do anything but let him have her. She didn't want to resist, didn't want to be free from him.

She was his.

His grip in her hair bound her to him, and he tilted her head so that their mouths fit together perfectly. And even though she knew almost nothing about kissing, she found herself responding, molding her lips to his the same way he was to hers, until she was breathless.

He broke the kiss and moved to her cheek. His breath came in heavy spurts as he kissed her jaw, her neck. She gasped and dug her fingers into his back. She was on fire. She couldn't think, couldn't breathe, couldn't move. If this was what married love was like, she didn't want it to end.

A gust of wind blasted down the vent above with a shrillness that made her jump back. Patrick started too. Before either of them could catch their breath, another gust swept in across the lantern. It blew at the flame, extinguishing it and plunging them into darkness.

Through the blackness and amidst the howling wind, Patrick scrambled forward, bumping and clattering until finally he lit a small lantern. He set about adjusting the wind vent and relighting the Fresnel lens. He worked in silent urgency. She had the feeling he was angry with himself, that she'd been a distraction to him. If she hadn't been there tempting him, he would have been paying better attention to the light and it wouldn't have gone out.

Within minutes he had the beam rotating again, but from the crinkles in his forehead as he peered out the windows, she knew he was worried that even those few moments without the light could have been disastrous for a passing ship.

She didn't know what to say or even if he really knew she was still there.

"Good night, Patrick," she finally said, pressing a hand against the ache that was forming in her chest as she watched their beautiful moment together slip away and vanish. Except for the swollenness of her lips from his kiss, she would have believed it only a dream.

She lowered herself through the hatch.

"Wait."

His call stopped her.

He stepped away from the window and rounded the lantern. He towered above her, strength exuding from him. His features gentled. "Are you . . . ?" He hesitated. "Did I upset you?"

"Not in the least."

"You're not angry with me?" He studied her, his eyes wide and vulnerable.

"Nay. Of course not." Why would he think his holding and kissing her would make her angry?

His shoulders loosened, and the lines in his face eased.

"I was worried I bothered you," she admitted. "I took you away from your duties. You weren't concentrating because of me—"

"Emma, lass," he interrupted, his lips curving into a half grin, "you don't need to worry."

Next to his experience and knowledge about the intimacies of marriage, she did indeed feel like a lass.

"Then you'll come again tomorrow night?" he asked.

Did she hear a hint of longing in his voice, along with the promise of more of what they'd shared tonight?

"Aye," she said. With a smile on her face, she scrambled down the ladder.

Chapter 18

*P*atrick scanned the horizon, gazing out at the emerging sunrise. The storm had rolled through and left in its wake a cloudless sky. While the summer solstice had come and gone, the hours of daylight in northern Michigan were still fairly long. Those extended hours helped save on oil for the lighthouse lantern, something Mr. Yates, the superintendent, would expect when he came to inspect the logbook.

He couldn't complain about Mr. Yates. He was a kind man, albeit overworked and underpaid. The Lighthouse Board appointed a superintendent for each district who was responsible for helping maintain the lights and equipment, as well as buying the necessary supplies. Mr. Yates oversaw the lighthouses along Lake Superior, Lake Huron, and Lake Michigan—an area much too vast for one man. Since the lakes had thawed, he hadn't had the chance to visit yet, though he was due any day now. When he arrived, perhaps he would see for himself the wretched condition of Patrick's tower and send a repair crew.

Patrick looked back at the house, to the closed curtain of the bedroom window. Emma was still asleep. He learned that she usually awoke shortly after he came into the house and started frying fish from his catch the day before.

He tried to be as silent as possible, also keeping Josiah's noise to a minimum, but without exception she stumbled into the kitchen with a yawn and a sleepy smile to join him and the boy. She said good morning, then moved straight to the stove and started making coffee.

What would she say if he went down to the house early, tiptoed into the bedroom, and kissed her again? The morning was bright enough that he could safely turn off the lantern, sneak in the front door so as not to wake Josiah, and then share a few minutes alone with Emma before their day began.

He ached to hold her in his arms again, to kiss her. He'd thought about little else all night long. It still amazed him to think that she'd hugged him, that she'd been the one to seek his comfort.

He'd been afraid to hold her for too long, terrified to kiss her for fear of repulsing her. He didn't want her to think he'd only invited her to the tower in order to force himself on her, because that wasn't the case. More than anything, he wanted to get to know her better.

He hadn't meant to kiss her and had fought against the urge. But when she'd pressed a kiss to his chest, the simple gesture had ignited him. She might not have meant anything by it, yet it had broken his last resistance.

She'd melted into him. She hadn't hesitated to kiss him back, which was so different from Delia, who'd never welcomed his affection. Rather, Emma wanted to be held and kissed by him. How could that be?

Wonder wrapped around him, warming his heart and stirring his blood. Now that he'd kissed her, he wasn't sure how he could keep from kissing her again.

He stared at the bedroom window and swallowed hard. If he kissed her again, he didn't know if he'd be able to stop. He drew a deep breath and exhaled loudly. "Get ahold of yourself," he whispered.

Just because he was her husband didn't mean he had the right to demand anything from her. If she wasn't willing to give herself freely to him, then he had no right to force her.

Of course, there were men who claimed that husbands had certain rights when it came to the bedroom, that a wife should submit and meet her husband's needs no matter what.

But Patrick didn't want that kind of relationship. He'd come to this conclusion with Delia when she'd been cold and unresponsive. He decided that if he couldn't win her affection outside the bedroom, then he didn't deserve it inside.

Shaking his head, he turned away from the window, away from Emma.

She was a sweet lass, and he didn't want to hurt her. He wanted to court her and win her love that way. He wanted her to see that he was truly a changed man, that he could be good to her despite who he'd once been. Until then, he needed to take things slow, maybe share more about his past.

He focused again on the lake. Something along the north shore caught his attention. He pressed his face to the glass. Had a small boat wrecked among the rocks?

Grabbing his binoculars, he looked again. Through the faintness of dawn, sure enough, the stern of a boat and a number of broken boards were strewn over the rocks, with pieces rolling on the waves.

His body tightened as he strained to see through the binoculars, searching for survivors. Other than the pounding waves, nothing moved. He would have to go check. If the boat capsized during the storm, the passengers might have drowned. Their bodies could have washed ashore anywhere.

Quickly, Patrick extinguished the lantern and descended the tower. He didn't want to wake Emma, but he wanted her to be prepared to help should he return with any survivors.

Soundlessly he slipped into the house, then into the bedroom. At the sight of her curled up on one side of the bed and the other side empty, his body ached with renewed longing. *Someday,* he chided himself. Maybe someday he would lie next to her.

He crossed to the bed and crouched beside it, near enough that he could hear her breathing. She'd plaited her long hair, but as usual some silky wisps had come loose. As gently as he could, he moved them off her cheek.

She stirred and released a soft sigh. In the darkness that still hung over the room, her features were shadowed, though he could still see the slope of her chin and neck.

He touched her shoulder. "Emma . . ."

Her eyes fluttered, and at the sight of him hovering over her, they flew open.

He half expected her to recoil, to scramble to the other side of the bed or to yank the sheet up to her chin to cover her nightdress. Instead, she lay very still and studied his face. Was she thinking about their kiss? Had she felt the passion of their encounter too?

He didn't realize he was holding his breath until she smiled. "For a second I thought I was still dreaming."

"You were dreaming about me then?" he teased softly.

Her lashes fell, and she tilted her head away from him. But her smile remained. "I was having very sweet dreams."

"Then you were definitely dreaming about me." Her neck and cheek taunted him. It would be so easy to bend down and let his lips linger there, to breathe her in and bury his face in her hair.

"I admit, you were in my dreams somewhere," she whispered, and when she looked up, her eyes fixed on his lips and he knew she was remembering their kiss.

He fought the urge to bend closer. He couldn't. He needed to show her that he really cared before he could share intimacies with her, and he had to earn her trust and love first. Besides, he had to hurry to the site of the wreck.

"I have to go," he said, brushing his finger across her cheek.

"Where?" She pushed herself up onto her elbows.

"A boat has wrecked near the shore north of here. I need to go see if there are any survivors."

"Do you want me to help?"

"I wanted you to be prepared. Just in case."

She nodded, her innocent eyes staring at him. She was so beautiful. And now after stepping into the bedroom, he needed to plunge himself into the lake to cool off. He stood and left the room before he got himself into a situation where he wouldn't be able to tear himself away.

As he hiked along the shore, he splashed his face with cold water and prayed for the strength to be patient.

Before long he came upon the wreckage of a rowboat. He sorted through the flotsam, tossing boards onto the shore so they wouldn't wash away before he had time to investigate them.

He wound his way farther north and was about to turn back when he stumbled over a body facedown in an area of tall sea grass. Dropping to his knees beside the unmoving form, he braced himself for the worst. He rolled the body over. The man gave a groan, and Patrick felt a small measure of relief. The man was alive.

But at the sight of the pale, bruised face, the relief evaporated and Patrick pulled back as if he'd been bitten by a snake. He sprang to his feet and retreated several steps.

It couldn't be. Yet the black curly hair and beard belonged to only one man. Mitch Schwartz.

He stared at the man's wide back and the oilskin coat that was twisted and ripped at one sleeve. He was tempted to sprint back to the lighthouse and slam the door behind him. No one would have to know there had been any survivors of the wreck. He could pretend he hadn't found anyone.

He could leave Mitch to die, for that was what Mitch had done to him. He'd left Patrick bleeding and gasping for breath in a puddle of vomit in an alley after he'd been tossed out the back door of a warehouse into a pile of garbage.

He could admit he'd been about as worthless as trash. But he hadn't expected his friend and partner to desert him quite so easily. At the very least, he'd thought Mitch would have a couple of the crew carry him back to the ship.

Mitch moaned again.

Patrick took another step back. It wasn't that he was angry with Mitch. In fact, in hindsight he could see now that the loss of the match and the abandonment had been the best thing that had ever happened to him. He ought to thank Mitch for leaving him. If he hadn't, Holy Bill might never have rescued him.

No, he was grateful to Mitch.

Even so, he didn't want to see the man again. He was a part of his past that he'd tried to run from. And now that he'd built a new life for himself out here in the remote wilderness, he didn't want to jeopardize anything.

Patrick crossed his arms over his heaving chest and stared out over the choppy waves and the debris left in the wake of the storm.

If Mitch knew he was alive, there was no telling what the man would do. And Patrick couldn't afford to have anyone in the Presque Isle community learn the true nature of his past. The people in the area wouldn't want him there anymore. They'd ask him to leave the only job he'd ever loved. They'd toss him out into the lake as far as they could throw him.

That was why Holy Bill and even Delia's father had all agreed to bury his history.

And what about Emma? Even if she'd accepted him so far with all his flaws, he'd wanted to wait longer before revealing more about himself.

He wiped a hand across his eyes and groaned. Oh, Lord, help him. He didn't want to lose Emma. But he'd told her she could leave if she wasn't happy with their arrangement. And there was the very real possibility that once she learned the truth about him and his past crimes, she'd catch the first steamer out of Burnham's Landing.

"No!" he cried into the damp morning air laden with the scent of fish and wet grass. He couldn't lose her now. The thought of Emma leaving him was too painful to bear. "What should I do, God?" But even as he lifted his thoughts to heaven, his entire being resisted God's answer. He didn't want to hear what God had to say, because he knew he wouldn't like it.

He glanced again at Mitch's body. After the recent mooncussing incident, he'd hoped Mitch would be long gone from the area by now. "Why are you still here?" he shouted at the prostrate form. "Why didn't you just die?"

As the words slipped out, the whisper of God's presence

admonished him. God had rescued him from the pit of hell, had given him a new life, and had blessed him beyond anything he deserved. If God could do that for him, why couldn't He do it for Mitch too?

Patrick fell to his knees and buried his face in his hands. "Why now, when everything's going so well?"

He pressed his fingers against his eyes, trying to block out the images that haunted him—images of the loot collected after a night of pillaging crops, timber, and liquor. They'd crept into ports in the dead of night and loaded their steamer with anything of value. They'd poached deer and delivered the venison to a company controlled by Chicago's criminal bosses.

For a time, they'd even turned a profit running a gambling and prostitution operation from their ship. That was when he'd done the most shameful of things, when in a drunken stupor he'd taken advantage of a woman.

His shoulders slumped, and the will to go on seeped out of him. He'd been the worst of sinners. It was only by God's grace that he was alive at all. God had given him a second chance, and he had to do the right thing now.

He had to give Mitch a chance, no matter the consequences. Even if, in the end, he lost everything.

Chapter 19

At the stomp of Patrick's boots and the loud knock on the door, Emma was there, swinging it open. She'd been waiting and pacing while also trying to keep Josiah occupied.

Patrick barreled into the front hallway, a body slung across his shoulder and hanging down his back. He was breathing heavily and sweating under the exertion of carrying what she presumed was one of the survivors from the wreck.

Without a word, he brushed past her and headed directly to the bedroom. She hurried after him and watched with surprise as he dropped the man onto the bed. When Patrick backed away, she sucked in a breath as she found herself gazing upon the face of the man who'd come to visit the night of the storm when Patrick was injured.

"Is this the pirate?" she asked.

Patrick nodded but didn't say anything. His expression was a stormy mask, his shoulders rigid. He set to work yanking off the man's boots.

She approached the bed to help Patrick, but he spun toward her with fury in his eyes. "Don't come near him."

She took a rapid step back.

"I'll be the one to help him," he said. "You stay away."

Josiah poked his head around the door.

"And keep Josiah away too," Patrick said.

She reached for Josiah's hand and held him by her side. The situation was serious if Patrick was this upset. She'd never seen him so distraught, almost angry.

"When he regains his senses, I don't want you talking to him. Do you understand?"

"Aye," Emma replied. She wasn't sure which frightened her more, Patrick's tempestuous mood or that they had a dangerous pirate in their house. She tugged Josiah. "Come, little love. We'll have breakfast."

They ate a cold breakfast of leftover biscuits with wild strawberries she'd picked yesterday. Later, when she was heating a kettle of water for laundry, she sensed Patrick's presence in the doorway.

She turned to find him watching her, his expression serious and drooping with weariness. "Would you like some breakfast?" she asked, giving him a tentative smile.

He didn't smile in return.

Josiah came out from under the blanket she'd draped across the two chairs to form a fort. She'd learned that the fort was a perfect way to occupy the boy when she needed him to play quietly. "Bad pirate, Daddy?"

At Josiah's question, Patrick's face blanched. "He's just a man, lad," he said in a strained voice. "A man in need of the Savior."

"Do you think we should report him to the authorities?" she asked. "Maybe he's a part of the group of pirates that's been

226

robbing ships in the area. Maybe if we turn him in, no one else will get hurt or lose their property."

At Patrick's headshake, she fell silent.

Something was wrong, she could sense it, something that went beyond the danger of harboring a pirate in their home. If only she could reassure him.

She poured Patrick a mug of coffee. More than anything, she wanted him to look at her again the way he had that morning he came into the bedroom and woke her with his gentle touch.

He stared at the blanket under which Josiah had crawled again, hiding himself within the makeshift shelter as he pretended to stay away from the pirate in the bedroom.

She pressed the cup of steaming coffee into Patrick's hands. When he took a sip, she waited for his usual compliment about her coffee, but it never came. Instead, he continued to stare at the fort.

"You're a good mother," he finally said.

"Nay. I've made a lot of mistakes and still have so much to learn."

"You love Josiah." His voice was low and insistent. "You're what he needs."

"I do love him," she admitted, smiling at the sound of his chatter coming from beneath the blanket. Even with his temper tantrums, the boy had captured her heart.

Patrick set his mug on the sideboard and reached for her arm with a swiftness that took her by surprise. He tugged her toward him, his grip tight. He brought her against him so that she could smell the coffee on his breath and see the desire in his eyes.

It wasn't the same look as earlier or even last night, but it radiated his wanting her nonetheless and sent a flood of warmth through her.

"Promise me one thing," he said, pressing his mouth against her ear.

"Anything."

His lips slid to the base of her neck, and she sagged into him. How did his merest kiss hold such power over her?

His mouth returned to her ear, grazed her lobe. "Promise me you'll take Josiah . . . when you leave."

Leave? She stiffened. And before he could make her forget herself with another of his kisses, she pulled back. "I'm not going anywhere."

"Not yet. But you will." His tone was ominous.

"Please don't speak that way—"

"Promise you'll take Josiah," he said again, louder this time. "You can give him a better life than me."

"But you're his father—"

"Promise me." Patrick's expression was as anguished as his voice.

How could she make such a promise? She'd never take Josiah away from him, not when he loved the boy so much. Besides, she wasn't about to leave. She loved being married. She loved her home and her new life here.

"Please, Emma."

She'd never leave. Therefore it wouldn't hurt to promise him—not when she'd never have to carry through with it. "Okay," she whispered. "I promise."

He nodded, released his grip on her, and retreated down the hall before she could say anything more.

The pirate was unconscious all day. Patrick stayed home from fishing and even slept in the chair beside the bed. When he finally left the bedroom to turn on the lantern, he insisted that Emma sleep on the floor in Josiah's room and barricade the door.

Throughout the night she'd heard Patrick return to the house to check on them. When morning came, he returned to his place of vigil next to the bed.

It wasn't until midday when she heard voices in the bedroom. The pirate had obviously awoken, and she had no doubt he would be hungry.

She put together a plate of leftovers from their lunch. After arranging the bowl of fish chowder, biscuits, and strawberries on a plate, she stood back and admired her handiwork. She hadn't burned anything in the past few days. In fact, she was baking the biscuits so well they were becoming a staple for almost every meal.

With Josiah playing happily in his fort again, she started down the hallway and paused outside the bedroom. The pirate was laughing and joking, almost as if he knew Patrick. She hesitated. Patrick had said he didn't want her near the man, but surely he hadn't meant she couldn't feed him.

"I've brought our patient some lunch," she said, forcing her feet forward before she changed her mind and retreated to the kitchen.

At her appearance, Patrick bolted up from his chair with a scowl on his face. He took her by the arm and steered her back toward the door.

But the pirate had already sat up and was straining to see her. "And you're married! If that don't beat all!"

"I told you to stay away," Patrick hissed under his breath.

"I thought he might be hungry," she said.

"You got yerself a pretty little thing," the pirate said. "Then again you always did get the pretty ones."

A chill swept over Emma, and she looked at Patrick. Did he know this pirate? How?

As if hearing her unspoken question, he whispered, "I'll explain everything later."

"You gonna introduce me to yer wife, Hook?" asked the pirate.

"Hook?" She glanced at the weatherworn face of the man lying in their bed. His beard hung over his chest and was as bushy as his thick wiry hair.

The pirate grinned. "He hasn't told you about his nickname?"

"Not now, Mitch," Patrick said, shaking his head.

"He had the most powerful hook east of the Mississippi," the man continued, despite Patrick's words. "He could take out his opponent with one good punch."

Emma found herself staring at the men in bewilderment. Patrick had admitted to Ryan that he'd been hurt in a fight, but she'd assumed he fought only on occasion, not that he'd had a career fighting others.

"Don't say any more, Mitch," Patrick warned.

"I bet you could still swing a perfect hook," Mitch said. "Even if you are a few years older, I bet you're stronger than ever. What do you say? Want to take on one of my crew for practice? I've got someone I want you to fight."

"That's enough!" Patrick's voice rose a notch.

"Oh, that's right." Mitch's grin turned derisive. "You got religion now. You're Saint Patrick."

Patrick took the plate of food from Emma. "Go on now," he said.

"Saint Pat," Mitch said with a barking laugh, his body shaking against the thin mattress. "Who would have guessed you'd turn into a holier-than-thou?"

"I'm far from perfect," Patrick said. "I'm simply a sinner who's been rescued."

"Should have known you got yerself cleaned up when I saw that." Mitch nodded to the driftwood cross hanging on the wall.

Emma couldn't move. Her shock seemed to fasten her feet to the floor.

"I suppose this means you won't be willing to help me out," Mitch said, his crooked grin slipping back into place. "I was hoping we could form a partnership now that I know you're here at the lighthouse."

"Don't even think about it," Patrick shot back, his expression tight.

"Aw, come on. We made a great team once. And now that you control the light, we could work together to fool unsuspecting ships. We could split the profits. What do you say?"

"No!" Patrick thundered. "I'm done with that life."

Had Patrick been a pirate at one time? Emma looked at him and pressed a shaking hand to her chest, not knowing what to say or think.

Mitch shrugged. "I guess you really are Saint Pat—"

"As soon as you can stand," Patrick said, cutting him off, "I want you to leave. Take your ship and go. And don't come back."

"What if I don't go?" Mitch said, his dark eyes glittering.

"You're lucky I don't tie you up and turn you in."

"Why don't you?" Mitch held out his hands. "Go ahead. I dare you."

Patrick paused and wiped a hand across his weary face.

Emma was tempted to find a rope in the shed for him. If Patrick let Mitch go, the man would only continue to steal from others and damage their ships and cause more deaths. They needed to stop him. Now.

"If you threaten me," Mitch said, "then maybe I'll threaten to tell your wife more of your dirty secrets. Like the time you woke up with that battered woman in your bed—"

"Stop!" Patrick's fists clenched, and the veins pulsed in his neck.

Emma gasped. *A battered woman in his bed? What did he mean?*

"You know you can't hand me over to the authorities, Hook. We were like brothers, you and I."

"We weren't brothers! You left me to die."

"I thought you *were* dead." Mitch's expression turned serious for the first time. "If I'd known you were alive, I wouldn't have left you."

Emma took a silent step backward. Who was this dangerous man she'd married? She obviously didn't know the first thing about him.

"It doesn't matter anymore," Patrick said. "I've forgiven you."

Mitch started to say something when his eyes brimmed with confusion and he stopped.

"I know I should hand you over to the authorities down in Fremont," Patrick went on, "but I've been given a second chance, and now I'm giving you one."

Mitch studied Patrick's face.

"Stop your thieving, Mitch, and get your life right with God."

A slow grin spread over Mitch's face. "Sophie was right. You're full of surprises, Hook."

Emma didn't wait for Patrick's answer. She turned into the hallway and returned to the kitchen. Patrick *was* full of surprises. Aye, he'd warned her that he didn't have a clean past. But a fighter? And a pirate? How was it possible that Patrick had ever been either one of those?

And who was Sophie?

She leaned against the sideboard, her legs weak, her heart racing.

"Emma?" Patrick's soft voice came from behind her.

She didn't turn around. She wasn't ready to face him yet. How would she ever be able to look at him again?

"I'm sorry. I didn't want you to find out."

She nodded, her eyes on the wall in front of her.

"I didn't think it was important to drag *all* the garbage out of the closet."

Her fingers shook. None of the revelations made sense. None matched the man she knew—or thought she'd known. She wanted to pretend she hadn't heard anything Mitch had said. But how could she? Not when they had a pirate in the next room, not when Patrick had once been a pirate just like his friend. What other things had Patrick done that Mitch hadn't revealed? She shuddered just thinking about Patrick's crimes. Maybe he'd even boarded steamers, stolen from helpless passengers, and left them to die in fires just as the pirates had done to her and Ryan.

"I was planning to tell you more about my past," Patrick said. "Eventually."

"You should have told me everything right away."

Josiah banged a stick he was playing with against the floor. The sound of it pierced Emma. Poor Josiah. Did he know his daddy was once a pirate?

Patrick moved closer and stood behind her. "Can you accept me anyway, now that you know?"

She hesitated.

His fingers grazed her arm, but she jerked away from his touch.

He stepped back, taking the warmth of his presence with him.

"Please give me some time," she whispered through a tight throat. She had to think, had to make sense of everything first.

He stood silently for a moment. "Remember your promise," he whispered. "You promised you'd take Josiah when you go. He deserves a better life than I can give him."

He walked away then, his heavy steps sounding in the hallway.

She closed her eyes against the flood of tears that threatened to spill over. Now she understood his insistence earlier when he'd forced her to promise to take Josiah.

His life was tarnished with a multitude of sins, and he didn't want Josiah to be influenced or hurt by any of it. If Mitch could show up once and badger Patrick, what would happen the next time? The man was obviously dangerous. There was no telling what he'd do.

And what if Patrick decided to aid him? What if Patrick still had a dangerous side to him? She hugged her arms across her chest to ward off the chills.

The rumbling of wagon wheels outside in the yard drew Emma's attention to the open window, to the sight of Bertie Burnham perched stiffly atop the bench of her wagon as she slowed the team of horses to a halt.

Emma wiped her eyes and fanned her face with her apron, hoping to clear away any evidence of her distress. "Come, Josiah," Emma called, trying to keep her voice from wavering. "We have company."

She couldn't let Bertie inside the house and discover Mitch there. She had to keep the woman out somehow. Even if the news of Patrick's past life and crimes was shocking, she couldn't expose him to Bertie's prying.

No matter what Patrick had done in his past, no matter the

crimes he might still be committing, she wouldn't betray him to Bertie. Not now. Not under these circumstances.

Emma slipped through the door with Josiah in tow.

At the sight of the thin woman with her tight braids and severe features, Josiah's footsteps slowed.

"Patrick's inside and doesn't wish to be disturbed," Emma said once Bertie had descended from the wagon. "But perhaps you'd care to sit with me in the shade and have coffee and biscuits."

Bertie grumbled about the arrangement, but eventually Emma persuaded her to join her on a blanket in the shade of one of the towering pines away from the house. She served Bertie coffee and biscuits and took careful notes on how to prepare a pound cake, along with instructions for stuffed trout.

"If you want me to tell you how to do the strawberry preserves," said Bertie, "then I'd best come on in and show you." The woman's attention strayed to the house again, as if she knew something was wrong and was trying to figure it out.

"Maybe next time." Emma was glad the bedroom curtain was closed.

"Some are saying there was a boat that wrecked up here along the shore a couple nights ago."

Emma nodded.

Bertie narrowed her eyes on Emma, clearly waiting for her to share any information she had about the wreck.

Emma shifted her interest to Josiah, who was picking up pinecones and throwing them into the woods. Thankfully he was far enough away that he hadn't heard Bertie. What would happen if Josiah heard Bertie's prying and blurted out the news that they were harboring a pirate in their house?

Emma squirmed and took a sip of her coffee. Maybe it hadn't been such a good idea to invite Bertie to stay.

"Something ain't right," Bertie said, setting down her half-eaten biscuit. "You been acting jumpy since I got here. Spill it out, young lady."

Emma stared down at her coffee. What could she say?

"You know that's what friends are for." Bertie's tone softened. "To listen."

How could Patrick ever have been close to Mitch? It was unthinkable. And yet at one time they'd been as close as brothers. Emma's stomach crushed with the weight of all she'd learned, like a heavy stone was pressing upon it. The burden felt too heavy to bear on her own. Maybe she didn't have to tell Bertie *everything*, but it wouldn't hurt to share a little, would it?

"It's just that I've learned some things about Patrick I didn't know."

"What things?"

Emma swallowed her reservation. "Things about his past. And they just came as a shock to me, that's all. Did you know he was a boxer or fighter or something like that? And that he once hurt another woman?"

Bertie's lips pursed. "Not surprised in the least. In fact, I wouldn't be surprised to find out he was once a pirate."

Emma froze and stared at Bertie.

Bertie watched Emma's face as if gauging her reaction. "Ah, I can see that I've hit on something close to the truth."

Emma looked away as she took another sip of her coffee.

"Don't worry, young lady. I already had my suspicions. Delia hinted at his unsavory past. But she was always too embarrassed to say much."

Emma shook her head and wanted to deny Bertie, but the woman harrumphed and continued before Emma could speak. "If you ask me, that's what caused their problems. Then of course if he was a fighter and already had a history of abusing women, that would explain Delia's fall. Maybe he hit her and pushed her down the stairs."

"Nay!" Emma scrambled to her knees. "Please don't say such things. I could never believe that about Patrick. He's much too kind."

But even as she said the words, doubts clouded her mind. If he could hurt a woman once, what was to prevent him from doing it again? As she struggled to her feet, her coffee spilled and trailed across the blanket toward Bertie, who clambered up too.

"How about his secret lover?" Bertie asked. "Do you have any more reasons to suspect he's seeing another woman?"

Emma hesitated, but again it was enough for Bertie to see the truth.

"Young lady," she said, lowering her voice and glancing toward the house, "as your closest friend, I suggest you get out of here before you get hurt."

"I won't get hurt." She'd never believed Patrick capable of hurting anyone, no matter his past. But now . . .

Bertie's eyebrow quirked as if she sensed Emma's doubts. "If you need to run, you know the way to the fisheries?"

Emma shook her head and prayed she wouldn't need to know.

"Take the road along the harbor." Bertie pointed toward the ruts her wagon had made in the grass. "It ain't far. You could walk it. Just make sure the harbor is always in sight."

Emma now wished she'd stayed silent. "You won't say anything about this to anyone, will you?"

"'Course not," Bertie said, starting back toward her wagon. "You know me. I'm not one to gossip."

Even with the woman's words ringing in her ears, Emma

couldn't keep a surge of guilt from crashing over her. She shouldn't have said anything at all about Patrick, about his past or about the troubles in their relationship. Even if Bertie was her friend, this matter with Patrick was private. She needed to work it out with him first before she talked about it with anyone else.

Aye. That was what she'd do. Talk with him and get everything straightened out. She needed to find out what really happened with Delia's death. And she had to ask him if there was another woman.

She needed to know everything, regardless of how painful or embarrassing the truth might be.

Patrick let the curtain fall back into place and resumed his pacing across the bedroom. A breath of relief pushed for release amidst the stuffiness of the room and the sour stench of sweat that surrounded the bed.

That tongue-waggling Bertie Burnham was finally leaving. Somehow Emma had managed to keep her outside. He was grateful to her for making an effort to keep Mitch and his secrets hidden.

Now the woman would be gone, and hopefully his past would remain buried. He didn't want to think about what could have happened if Bertie had come into the house and found Mitch in their bed. Like Emma, she would have easily connected him to the pirate. But unlike Emma, she would have run back to town and shared the news with everyone.

Most recently he'd heard some of the fishermen whispering that Delia's fall hadn't been an accident, that he'd pushed her down the tower stairs. He figured Bertie was the one who'd started the rumor. The woman had always sensed Delia's unhappiness and had blamed him for it. And maybe she was right. Maybe he hadn't made Delia happy.

Nevertheless, the rumors stung. He kept praying people would see the love of God pouring out of him, and that he'd live in such a way that they wouldn't be able to believe anything Bertie said.

"Hey, Saint Pat, take it easy." Mitch was sitting up against a couple of pillows. His hair stuck to his forehead in the dankness of the room. "You're wearing me out just watching you."

"Then go back to sleep."

Mitch chortled. "Sophie told me not to expect any help from you, but I was hoping she was wrong."

"She shouldn't have told you I was here."

"Why? You afraid once they know the whole truth, they'll send you packing?"

Patrick shifted his attention to his boots. He didn't want Mitch to see how close he'd come to the truth. He didn't want his neighbors and friends to know about the life he'd once lived. If they found out, they'd be appalled, just like Emma.

His body ached every time he pictured her hunched over in the kitchen, tears streaking her cheeks, dismayed by who he really was. He hated that he'd hurt her, and now he wished he'd had the courage to tell her much earlier, to share the truth with her.

She probably wouldn't have married him, and he would have missed out on the past beautiful month with her as his wife. Even so, he should have been honest with her from the start. That way he could have spared her the pain today.

Holy Bill had assured him that his past didn't matter anymore, not after Patrick had spent two full years working hard to repay the debts he owed to those he'd robbed. After those two years living with Holy Bill, being mentored by him, and doing all he could to make up for his past mistakes, the reverend told him he was ready to move on.

Holy Bill was the one who told him about the assistant keeper position with Delia's father down at Fort Gratiot. Patrick's sea-faring knowledge, his familiarity with shipping, the lake, and the weather had all worked to his advantage in getting the position. And the district superintendent respected Holy Bill.

"If Holy Bill tells me you're the man for the job," Mr. Yates had said, *"then I know there's no better person I could hire."*

Holy Bill had insisted they tell Mr. Yates the details about his wayward past. Even so, Mr. Yates had been willing to give him a trial period as assistant keeper. After a year of Patrick working hard to prove himself, Mr. Yates was open to Holy Bill's suggestion that Patrick be given the full keeper position at the Presque Isle Light, and Holy Bill would continue to hold Patrick accountable.

What would Mr. Yates say now if he learned he'd been in contact with Mitch, that he'd saved the man and given him refuge in his home? What would he say if he learned about the moon-cussing incident and resulting shipwreck from a couple of weeks ago?

He'd likely think Patrick had returned to his pirating ways. He'd fire him from his job as keeper and never let him step foot in another lighthouse as long as he lived.

Mitch grinned, a wicked gleam in his eyes as if he'd read Patrick's thoughts. "I'm sure people won't be so eager to have you keeping this here light once they learn the truth about your past."

Patrick's shoulders sagged. Sweat plastered his shirt to his back. He knew he ought to open the window again now that Bertie was gone, but there would be no relief from the heat inside when the heat outside was just as oppressive.

"Maybe we can work out a deal." Mitch rubbed a hand over his scraggly beard, which Patrick thought only made him look meaner and older than the fun-loving man he'd once been.

They'd been close as young boys, after Mitch's father had run off and completely deserted him, leaving him alone in the world. Even before the days of drinking and thieving, they'd looked out for each other. At the time, Patrick was closer to Mitch than most of his family.

He supposed that was why it had hurt so much when Mitch abandoned him after the last fight. He'd figured Mitch thought he was worthless, that after being beaten nearly to death, he wouldn't be any good in the ring—that he'd gotten too old and wouldn't be able to win and bring in money anymore.

He'd always believed that Mitch hadn't wanted him and had left him to die. Alone.

Even though Mitch denied it now, Patrick still couldn't shrug off the feeling of abandonment. He may have forgiven Mitch, but the pain of the betrayal still lingered within him.

"I'm not working out any deals with you," Patrick said. "Except that you're sailing away from here and never coming back."

"Or else?"

Patrick didn't say anything in response.

"That's what I thought," Mitch said. "You can't do anything to me. In fact, I think you should start asking yerself what you can do *for* me."

"Or else?" Now it was Patrick's turn to ask the question.

"Or else I'll make sure everyone knows exactly who you are."

"You mean who I *was*."

"Doesn't matter. Once a crook, always a crook."

"I'm done with thieving," Patrick said. "You can go down

to Burnham's Landing and tell everybody there whatever you want. But it won't change my mind, Mitch."

He knew he'd already ruined his chances with Emma. No doubt she would leave him. He didn't deserve her anyway. So long as she took Josiah, he'd let her go. Hopefully, Ryan would look after them, make sure they had a decent place to live.

Once Emma and Josiah were gone, he'd head south and maybe find work in one of the lumber camps or sawmills of the Saginaw Valley. He loathed the idea of giving up his lightkeeper job, but as much as it pained him, he had to do the right thing.

He'd spend the rest of his life doing the right thing. Perhaps someday, somehow, he would eventually make up for all his wrongs.

Chapter 20

mma ran the brush through her hair one last time. Then she set the brush on top of the dresser and lifted her eyes to the cross. She wanted to say a prayer for wisdom and courage . . . and hope. But the words wouldn't come. She made quick work of parting her hair into three strands of a braid. She wasn't leaving her hair down tonight. Nay, she wasn't going to the lantern room for pleasure and companionship. Tonight she was aiming to discover the truth—the whole truth—about Patrick.

She wouldn't let embarrassment or propriety or fear stop her from asking him the hard questions. It was past time for her to know everything. Whether Patrick welcomed her to the tower or pushed her away, she couldn't let anything distract her from what she needed to do.

She looked out the slit of the curtain into the darkness of night. The tower door had squeaked a few moments ago, signaling Patrick's return from the dock where he'd been saying good-bye to Mitch. Apparently the pirate's crew had come after him in a rowboat, and Patrick had gone down to see him off.

Steeling herself, she slipped through the house, past Josiah sleeping in his bed. She opened the back door and let the breeze from the lake soothe her overheated face.

She forced herself across the yard to the tower, silently entering through the open door and climbing the steps, the stones cool beneath her bare feet.

Aye. She would ask him to share all that he'd been hiding. Who was the woman he'd hurt? What had caused Delia's death? Was he seeing another woman now? She tried not to think about the fact that he'd hurt people in his past, that he could hurt again if provoked enough. She didn't want to be scared of him, but how could she stop herself?

Her heart pounded against her rib cage when she reached the top of the stairway. She wanted to believe her legs trembled from the exertion of the climb rather than from nerves, but her dry mouth and throat betrayed her.

One fleeting look around the lantern room told her Patrick wasn't inside making notes in his logbook or cleaning the glass.

"Patrick?" she croaked, stepping out onto the catwalk. A quick walk around the gallery revealed he wasn't there either.

Back inside, she paused. Perhaps he hadn't returned yet from the dock like she thought he had. Maybe she'd only imagined the squeak of the tower door.

The lighthouse beam was rotating and flashing in its unique pattern. She stepped to the south window, the side of the tower that overlooked Presque Isle Harbor and the dock. For a moment she couldn't make out anything in the darkness.

She pressed her face closer to the window, and when the beam swept over the harbor, it illuminated the dock briefly, enough for her to see Patrick's strong frame and broad shoulders.

Emma's heart nearly stopped beating.

He was standing there with someone else. A woman. The light revealed her hair, which tumbled down her shoulders, and her long elegant gown. Then the beam moved on and darkness descended again.

He's with a woman.

She peered in the direction of the dock. She could make out a tiny light from the lantern Patrick had carried with him. It now sat near his feet and cast a faint glow over him and the woman.

He was holding her arms, and she stood only a short distance from him. If she leaned in any closer, he could kiss her.

Jealousy cut into Emma. She'd wanted to deny the possibility of another woman in Patrick's life, to ignore all the symptoms—the day-long trips away, the perfume on his coat, and his disinterest in her physically. But how could she disregard the facts any longer?

Not when Bertie had reason to believe he was seeing someone else. Not when he'd been with other women in the past. Not when he'd already withheld so much information from her about his crimes. This was simply one more thing he hadn't been honest with her about.

Emma leaned into the glass, not caring that her breath was steaming the window or that she was leaving hot smudges where Patrick had cleaned so meticulously earlier. She stared as the beam rounded the harbor again.

This time she caught a glimpse of the bodice of the woman's gown, the way it dipped low and revealed her creamy skin. It was much too tight and seductive for a moral woman. The lace and the fancy puffs were more like something a loose woman would wear.

Was she a prostitute? The thought made Emma's stomach churn.

The light of another lantern bobbed in a boat nearby. Had the woman come ashore with the pirates? Perhaps she was someone Patrick had loved in his past life. After all, Mitch had insinuated that Patrick had always attracted lots of women.

He was handsome enough to have hordes of women falling over him, women more beautiful than she was. If he had himself a pretty woman already, why would he be interested in her?

Bertie had been right. Patrick didn't really need her. She'd had to practically throw herself upon him to gain his attention.

Her face burned with shame at the thought of their kiss. He'd been about to release her, but she clung to him. He probably only kissed her because he'd felt sorry for her desperate attempts to attract him.

"Heaven have mercy," she whispered. She'd made a complete fool of herself.

She knew she should tear herself away from the window and run back to the house, yet she couldn't make herself move. Riveted to her spot, she watched as Patrick drew the strange woman into a tight hug.

With a cry, Emma pushed away from the window and almost fell to her knees. "What have I done?"

But she knew what she'd done. She'd allowed herself to fall in love with a man who didn't feel the same way.

With a hand pressed against her aching chest and with tears clouding her eyes, she stumbled down the ladder. She slipped and tripped her way to the bottom of the stairway and couldn't keep from wondering if this was how Delia had fallen.

Had she been watching out the tower too? Had she witnessed her husband's unfaithfulness and been so distraught that she fell in her race to descend?

Blindly, Emma sped back to the house. All she could think

about was leaving before Patrick returned from the dock. She had to get away.

A sob caught in her throat as she stuffed her few belongings into her grain sack. She tried to ignore the driftwood cross on the wall, but it seemed to watch her every move, pleading with her to take it and not give up hope.

But what hope did she have? Even if she waited to talk with Patrick when he returned, even if she tried to discover who the woman was, there was no changing the fact that he'd deceived her, that he hadn't been honest about who he was and what he'd done. He'd practically invited her to leave him. If she stayed, she'd only humiliate herself more than she already had.

She glanced again at the cross above the dresser. Patrick had given it to her. She had every right to do with it what she wished. Wiping the tears from her cheeks, she reached up and grabbed the cross from the wall and stuffed the gift into her bag.

She looked around the room one last time, an ache tightening her chest. Why had she thought she was finally home? When hope of a real home had eluded her for so many years, why had she believed it was within her grasp?

"Mamma?" Josiah stood in the doorway in his pajamas. His red hair was sticking up, and his thumb was half in his mouth.

"Go back to bed, wee one." She hid her face and wiped once more at her cheeks, trying to erase all traces of her sorrow.

"Trip, Mamma?" He plodded over to the bed and touched her bag.

She hesitated. How could she leave this little boy? He'd captured her heart, and the thought of saying good-bye to him was unbearable.

"You should be asleep, little love." She couldn't take Josiah. He wasn't hers. Patrick loved the boy, and it didn't matter that he'd told her he wanted her to give the boy a better life than he could. Josiah belonged with his daddy.

"Me go too," Josiah said.

More tears spilled down her cheeks. This was going to be harder than she'd imagined. She dried her face against her shoulders and kneeled down next to him. He stared at her with heavy-lidded eyes.

"Mamma has to leave." She squeezed the words past her constricting throat.

He reached his hand to her cheek and touched a stray tear she'd missed.

She couldn't do this. She couldn't leave him behind. With a sob, she wrapped her arms around him and drew him into a fierce embrace.

Why had Patrick done this to them? Why couldn't he have been a normal man with a normal past? Anger coursed into her blood.

"Me go with Mamma," Josiah said again, struggling to free himself from her.

The anger slipped deeper, flooding her broken heart. She should take Josiah. It would serve Patrick right. It would hurt him, but maybe he deserved to feel some pain—some of the terrible pain that was tearing at her insides.

"Aye," she whispered, smoothing a hand across the boy's unruly locks. "You can come with me."

As she hurriedly stuffed Josiah's few belongings and clothes into her bag, she tried to ward off the guilt. Patrick had made her promise to take Josiah. He'd been adamant about it. She wasn't doing anything he hadn't already asked her to do.

Even so, when she darted across the yard, dragging Josiah with her, the guilt rose up to taunt her as surely as the shifting shadows of the night. As much as she loved Josiah and considered him her son, he needed Patrick.

Josiah would throw a temper tantrum once he learned they weren't going back. She supposed after all the turmoil of losing his mother and the upheaval in his life, he coped the only way a toddler knew how—by clinging to his daddy and feeling insecure whenever he wasn't with the rock of his life.

The full moon lit the path Bertie had driven on with her wagon, the one she said led to the fisheries. Even with the moonlight to guide them, Emma couldn't keep from stumbling over the many rocks that dotted the path. In spite of her effort to stay calm for Josiah's sake, each step away from the lighthouse squeezed her chest more painfully, until she wasn't sure she could keep going.

She wanted to fall to her knees, pound her fists against the ground, and scream.

If she'd thought losing her mam and childhood home had been hard, she knew now that losing the man she'd fallen in love with was even harder. His betrayal stabbed her like nothing else ever had.

Chapter 21

atrick plodded up the winding stairway. The chirping of crickets and katydids became fainter as he ascended, and the humidity of the night fell away for just a moment within the thick-walled tower. A mixture of sadness and relief weighted him down, making each step feel heavier than the last. He'd never been more relieved to see someone go than Mitch. The man had been a thorn in the flesh since the moment he'd regained consciousness.

But Patrick was sad that Mitch was so lost, not caring to change his ways, and sad that Sophie felt the same as Mitch. He agreed with her, though, that she was safer now that she was with Mitch, for it was better than what she'd been doing before.

Still, he'd begged her to stay with him, to let him take care of her and allow him to help her build a decent life for herself. As usual, her response was to laugh her seductive laugh, telling him she wanted her freedom. She didn't want to be tied down with a child.

"Ah, Sophie, lass," he whispered as he reached the top of the stairs. The heat of the lantern room was stifling, and he propped open the door to allow in the cool night breeze, along with the familiar scents of the lake—the unique mixture of sea grass and fish.

He sucked in a deep breath. He would miss it. And he would miss the lighthouse, the beauty of the solitude and silence. After years of revelry and fighting, his soul had found healing in the solitary life that came with a lightkeeper job. He knew the isolation drove many men crazy, but he loved it.

More than that, he'd loved sharing it with Emma. Her presence here had brought joy that he now realized had been missing from his life.

He peered out of the tower to the darkened bedroom window and guessed she'd be in bed by now. He couldn't keep from yearning for her to come up to visit him. His muscles tightened with the overpowering desire to wrap his arms around her. His gut stiffened at the memory of the last time she'd been with him in the tower a couple of nights ago, of how he'd held her, how they'd passionately kissed.

He clenched his fists, the need for her rising swiftly again. The only problem was that he had no right to a good and kind woman like her.

"Oh, God," he whispered, doing the only thing he knew how to do in moments of agony. All he could do was pray—pray that God would help him endure the burdens he'd brought upon himself from his past.

Was there anything he could do to keep Emma from spurning him? Could he fall on his knees and beg her to live with him anyway, in spite of all she'd learned about him? He didn't want to lose her. As selfish as it was, he didn't want her to leave.

With a heavy sigh, he stared out over the harbor. If only Mitch hadn't decided to show up again.

But even as the thought sifted through him, he knew he would have had to tell her eventually. And he knew he had to tell her the truth about Josiah too. She needed to know everything.

At the sight of a smudge on the window, he frowned and turned to find the cloth he used to clean the glass before he'd left the tower to go down to the dock with Mitch. He lifted the cloth to wipe away the handprint, then stopped.

His heartbeat hitched. He studied the handprints, two of them, and the place where lips had hovered near enough to the glass to leave a mark. He raised one of his hands and held it over the print. Through the flashing of the light, he could see that the handprint belonged to someone other than himself. It was smaller, more delicate.

Was it Emma's?

He studied the prints. She must have come when he'd been at the dock saying good-bye to Mitch and Sophie. He didn't want to think about the possibility that maybe she'd come to say good-bye to him.

He lifted his other hand over the print so that he could imagine he was holding both of her hands. At that moment the beam fell upon the dock like a spotlight. His pulse chugged to a standstill.

What had Emma seen? What if she'd witnessed his interaction on the dock with Sophie?

He fell back with a groan. A sickening in the pit of his stomach told him that was exactly what had happened. Emma had seen him with Sophie. She'd probably watched them and drawn her own conclusions. Conclusions that had likely added to the hurt he already caused with his revelations earlier in the day.

He rushed down the tower ladder and descended the stairway two steps at a time. He didn't care that the bedroom window was dark and that she was already in bed, he had to talk to her, had to reassure her that . . .

That what?

At the bottom of the tower he stopped, his breath coming in gasps. His chest ached, but not for lack of air. It ached because he loved her. The emotion swelled until he was light-headed with the knowledge of it.

"I love her," he said into the night, letting amazement drift over him. As much as he'd liked various women over the years, he'd never really loved any one of them. Not even Delia.

He'd tried to love her. Every night he'd prayed for God to help him cherish his wife and treat her with the kind of love she needed. But never in all the days they shared together did he feel anything quite like what he felt with Emma.

He stared at the bedroom window, and his heart yearned to see her, to tell her his true feelings. Even if she rejected him, even if she couldn't forgive him for deceiving her, he had to tell her of his love for her. He couldn't hold it back any longer. She had every right to leave, but he'd beg her to stay and give him a second chance, to let him prove himself.

Determined, he entered the house and went directly to the bedroom and stepped inside. "Emma?" he whispered.

She didn't respond.

"Emma," he said again, louder this time. He knelt down beside the bed. He put out a hand to touch her, but all that met his fingers was the smoothness of the bed.

He surged to his feet, crossed to the window, and yanked the curtains open. Moonlight and the glow from the tower lantern poured into the room, revealing an empty bed.

She'd made the bed since Mitch had left, but why wasn't she in it? Was she sleeping with Josiah again, afraid that perhaps

Mitch would return? He spun around and started to cross the room again when his eyes fell on the wall above the dresser. He stumbled to a halt.

Her cross was gone.

With a burst of panic, he rushed through the house until he charged into Josiah's room. One glance at the empty bed told him the worst.

She'd left him. And she'd fulfilled her promise. She'd taken Josiah.

"No!" His knees weakened, and he sagged to the edge of the bed. For a moment, pain washed over him, sucking him down and drowning him.

Of course, he never wanted to lose Josiah. He loved the boy more than he ever thought possible. But the idea of life without Emma? The thought was unbearable. Unthinkable.

"I *won't* lose her," he said to himself, pushing up from the bed. He fought off a wave of despair and a voice telling him he didn't deserve her, that he should just let her go.

All he wanted was to go after her, to fall on his knees before her and plead with her to come home. To their home. To him.

But hadn't he promised he'd let her go if she was unhappy?

Reluctantly he returned to the tower. He had to do the right thing by Emma, and the right thing was to let her go and give her the chance to find happiness with someone else more worthy.

Emma leaned into Ryan and sobbed quietly against his shoulder. He didn't say anything, just cradled her and let her cry.

She was hot from her hike around the harbor after leaving the lighthouse, the humidity of the night enveloping her. If only she could go up into the tower and stand on the gallery. The breeze coming off the lake would comfort her.

At the thought, her tears flowed only faster. She'd never visit the lighthouse again. Never climb to the top. Never peer at the dark expanse of sky filled with its multitude of stars.

And worst of all, she'd never see Patrick again.

"Oh, Ryan," she said, brushing the wetness from her cheeks, "I didn't want to believe he was capable of loving someone else. I wanted to believe he was a good man."

Ryan patted her back.

She'd easily found Burnham's Landing when she'd reached the cleared part of the harbor. When she'd rapped on the Burnhams' door, Bertie had answered it almost immediately, as if she'd been waiting for Emma, her lips pursed and her eyes radiating with I-told-you-so.

Josiah had tired of the hike not long after they started, so Emma had carried him most of the way. Thankfully he'd fallen asleep in her arms and hadn't woken when she placed him on a mat next to Bertie's sons who were asleep on the floor.

Bertie had peppered her with whispered questions, and after the woman had gone back to bed, Emma had sought out Ryan. She hadn't been able to wait until morning to talk to him. Yawning and half asleep, he'd led her a safe distance away from the shack where he bunked with the fishermen.

The darkness shadowed his face, even more now that they sat at the edge of the forest on a bench made from a log.

"Maybe he's still a good man, Em," Ryan said softly.

She'd finally had to tell Ryan the truth about Patrick's past, and she'd been surprised he wasn't angrier at Patrick or even concerned for her safety.

She sniffled. "I think he wants to be a godly man, but he's trapped in the sins of his past."

Ryan pulled a wrinkled handkerchief out of his pocket and handed it to her.

"Maybe it just takes time to stop doing some things." She dabbed her nose with the cloth. "And maybe some people can't change no matter how hard they try. Like Dad."

Ryan leaned his back against the maple that towered behind them. "Dad could've changed if he'd really wanted to."

"He tried to quit drinking several times—"

"He was still hanging on to his guilt too tightly," Ryan said, a thread of bitterness edging his voice. "If he'd repented before God, if he'd let go of the past, and if he'd moved forward in the confidence of God's forgiveness, then maybe he could have put his drinking behind him."

"But don't you think it's hard for some people to change, I mean really change, if they've developed bad habits?"

"It might be hard." Ryan crossed his arms, giving her his undivided attention, making her feel as though everything she had to say was important, just as he always did. "But I'd like to think that no one can sin too much or stray too far from God that He can't bring them back, heal them, and give them a new life."

The distant howl of a wolf mingled with the insects buzzing around them. She shivered, even though the night was muggy. "Then you don't think it's hopeless for Patrick?"

Ryan swatted at his neck. And Emma slapped at the mosquito hovering near her ear. "It's not hopeless," Ryan said. "I may not know Patrick well, but I know a godly man when I see one. And Patrick Garraty is a godly man."

Emma wanted so much to believe Ryan. "Then why is he unfaithful to our marriage?"

"We don't know for sure what's going on. Maybe we should talk to him first and see what he has to say for himself."

"But I've noticed other things. Long, unexplained absences, the scent of women's perfume on his coat." And his lack of interest in the consummation of their marriage, only she couldn't admit that to Ryan.

Ryan started to shake his head.

"And Bertie said that another woman came between Patrick and Delia."

"Bertha Burnham is nothing but a gossip."

"She's my friend, and she's been concerned about me."

Ryan snorted.

"She tried to warn me about Patrick's past. She suspected that he wasn't telling everything."

"Listen, Em. I like Patrick a whole lot more than I do Bertie. And if I had to bet money on whose word I trusted more, I'd choose Patrick."

But Patrick had withheld information from her about his past. How could she trust him to tell her the truth in other things? She lowered her head, letting the misery of her situation swamp her. "I guess this means you won't take me with you, that you want me to stay here with him?"

Ryan reached for her hand. "Of course I'll take you with me. We made an agreement with Patrick that if you didn't like it here, you could leave." His hands surrounded hers, strong and solid.

She could always count on Ryan. He'd provide for her. She'd be all right. Except that she'd be homeless again . . .

A deep sigh pressed for release.

"You know I want you to be happy," Ryan said. A shaft of moonlight came through the branches and glinted off his blond hair. "I haven't liked the idea of leaving you here."

"I know." She squeezed his hand, grateful for his presence in her life. She tried to ignore the voice that told her he needed his freedom, that she wasn't his responsibility anymore, and that she couldn't burden him. That was one of the reasons she'd married Patrick in the first place, so that Ryan could move on with his life and figure out what God had planned for him.

"I've earned enough for passage. We can leave on the next steamboat if that's what you really want," Ryan continued. "But I want you to do one thing first."

"What?"

"I want you to talk with Patrick."

She stared at the long willowy grass that grew in patches here and there among the moss. She reached for a piece and plucked it, letting her fingers caress the soft, seedy end. She wanted to protest Ryan's suggestion. Just thinking again about how Patrick had embraced that other woman renewed the painful throb in her chest.

Of all the things that had hurt her during the past day, seeing him with the strange woman had pained her the most. She didn't want to have to face him again. She wanted to hide behind Ryan, slip silently onto the next passing steamboat, and go lick her wounds in private.

"It's the right thing to do," Ryan said.

Even though she wanted to leave, she knew Ryan was right. She had to talk to Patrick first, because she couldn't leave with Josiah. She had to return the boy to his daddy.

"Okay." Tears pressed the back of her eyes again. "I'll talk to him as long as you're there with me."

For a long moment they sat quietly, and she realized just how exhausted she was. She started to rise, ready to stumble back to the Burnham cabin and let herself collapse onto the mat

Bertie had offered her, when Ryan yanked her down and lifted a finger to his lips.

He was peering through the darkness toward the lake.

"What is it—?" she said, but Ryan clamped a hand over her mouth, cutting off her words.

He nodded toward the docks. Several dark shapes were making their way toward the enormous pile of cordwood stacked in a grassy area along the shore. With his hand covering her mouth, she could feel Ryan's muscles tense.

Emma tried to make sense of what appeared to be three or four men who'd come ashore from a small rowboat. Now they were in the process of loading their arms with the chopped wood.

When one of the men moved back to the docks, his arms loaded with the wood, Ryan let out a gasp of indignation. "Those men are stealing my wood."

She knew the wood wasn't really Ryan's. But it *was* the result of his weeks of labor, chopping and stacking for the Burnhams.

"I bet they're a bunch of pirates coming ashore," Ryan whispered harshly, "thinking they can steal the wood rather than paying a fair price for it."

Two more of the men with loaded arms moved away from the stacks and headed toward the dock.

"Hey!" Ryan released her, stood and stepped away from the edge of the forest into the moonlight.

"Hush, Ryan." Emma reached for him, but she grabbed a handful of air instead.

"Hey!" he shouted again. "You better be planning to pay for that wood."

The men halted. Their hats were pulled low and hid their faces. But in the cleared span of the beach, the moonlight spilled over them, clearly illuminating their crime and the waiting boat that bobbed next to one of the docks.

For a moment the men didn't move. They glanced at each other as if trying to decide what to do next.

"Put it down and be on your way," Ryan called.

Finally one of them shrugged and let his armful of wood drop to the ground. He turned and took a step toward the boat—a limping step.

It was Mitch.

Emma sucked in a breath. "Be careful, Ryan."

Her warning came a second too late. Instead of continuing back to the boat, Mitch spun around, a pistol in his hand, its silver barrel gleaming.

"Get down!" she called, but a loud bang drowned out her voice.

An instant later, Ryan jerked back, cried out in pain, and fell to the ground next to her.

Chapter 22

At the echo of gunfire, Patrick shifted his oars and directed his cutter into the shadows of the shoreline. Hopefully the dark swaying shapes from the thick evergreens would conceal his boat from anyone who might be keeping a lookout.

He didn't know what was happening at Burnham's Landing, but it sounded ominous. His heart pounded with the sudden need to get there and make sure Emma and Josiah were safe. That was all that mattered.

The scrape of rocks and sand against the hull made it more difficult to navigate in the shallow water. He plunged the oars into the gravelly mixture, using the lake bottom to propel him closer to shore.

Finally, in his impatience, he leaped over the side into the water. He strode forward, tugging the boat with him, not caring that the water was level to his knees and that a splash of a wave soaked his trousers to his thighs and seeped down into his boots.

Another bang filled the night air. He had no doubt Emma had run to Burnham's Landing, to Bertie or to Ryan. Even though he'd told himself he had to let her go, that he didn't deserve her and would never be good enough to be her husband or Josiah's father, he'd spent the last hour driving himself crazy with the need to see her again, to talk to her.

He'd paced around the tower gallery, praying and crying out to God. He raged into the night air. He shouted at the stars, pretending they were his family, his mother and father who'd never been there for him, who'd been too busy to train him in what was right, who'd been too interested in drinking and fighting and surviving to care.

Then, after he'd poured out his sorrows and regrets, he dropped to his knees and buried his face in his hands. He knew he couldn't blame his parents for the man he'd become. He'd had a mind of his own. He'd made his own bad choices. And now he had to live with the consequences of his mistakes.

Still, couldn't he be a better father to Josiah and a godly husband for Emma? Couldn't he love and lead his own family in a way he'd never been loved or led?

"I don't know what to do, God," he prayed as he heaved the boat onto the bank. He'd told himself he was only going after her so he could give her all the money he'd saved. She'd need it to start a new life somewhere else with Josiah. It wasn't much, since he'd been giving as much as he could to Sophie every month. He'd hoped the extra cash would keep Sophie out of the brothel, would help her get by until she could find proper work.

He certainly wasn't headed to Burnham's Landing in the middle of the night to try to stop Emma or to persuade her to stay. He was only going now because he was afraid that if he waited until morning, she'd already be gone, that maybe she'd catch an early passage out of Presque Isle.

But deep inside, he knew that he wasn't fooling anybody, least of all himself. The truth was that he wouldn't be able to live with himself unless he saw her one more time and said good-bye.

He shoved the little boat into the underbrush and then pushed his way through the tangle of windfall and bushes until he stumbled onto the path that connected Burnham's Landing to the lighthouse.

Cautiously he made his way forward until he reached the clearing. He peered across the length of open beach and took stock of the situation. On the shore side, a band of men hunkered down behind a mountain of cordwood. They were firing in the direction of one of the log shacks that stood closest to the forest.

He guessed that these pirates had stopped to pilfer cordwood and had gotten caught in the act. He didn't imagine the fishermen would be able to do much to stop them from getting away. Maybe they'd save most of the wood, but the pirates were tough men and wouldn't be easily beaten, even if the fishermen had a gun or two and could fight back.

Nevertheless, Patrick crept through the woods. He wove soundlessly through the thicket until he was near the fishery. He crouched low and through the darkness could make out several forms pressed against the bunkhouse.

He moved slowly forward, stopping at the snap of a branch. It took a moment for his eyes to adjust and find the source of the sound. When a sliver of moonlight touched upon a golden head, his body jolted with dread.

"Emma?" he whispered.

The head spun toward the sound of his voice, and the faint light fell across Emma's face, illuminating her fright. She was lying on the ground behind a log, with Ryan sprawled beside her.

"What are you doing out here?" Anger made his whisper harsher and louder than he'd intended.

"Ryan's hurt," she said. "He was shot in the arm. And when he fell, he knocked his head on a rock."

Patrick crawled toward her regardless of the crackling and crunching he made in the leaves and fallen branches. When he reached the log, his chest burned with the danger of her position. "You need to get farther back into the woods," he said, unable to stop himself from reaching out and touching her face.

"I can't leave Ryan." The young man was on his back. Even in the darkness, Patrick could see the blood staining Ryan's shirtsleeve and dribbling down the side of his head.

"Can you help him?" Emma asked, kneeling down only inches away from both Patrick and Ryan.

Another bullet whizzed above their heads. Emma gasped while Patrick peeked over the log in the direction of the cordwood. "How long's this been going on?"

"Too long," Emma said. "It's Mitch."

"It can't be," Patrick replied. But even as he denied that Mitch would ever engage in a shooting battle, nausea clutched his gut at the truth of Emma's statement. After leaving the lighthouse and rowing back to his steamer, Mitch and his friends had probably discovered their boat was low on fuel and decided to stock up by helping themselves to the cordwood piled near the harbor.

"I saw him," Emma said.

She didn't have to say anything more. Regret was already pummeling him. He should have tied Mitch up and taken him down to Fremont to the authorities. He'd only wanted to give his old friend a second chance. And after talking with him again on the dock as he was leaving, Patrick had prayed Mitch would decide to give up his thievish ways.

But apparently Mitch was determined to do what he wanted regardless of how it hurt others. Patrick lowered his head, and the shame of his association with the man stole over him.

"Come with me. I'm taking you to safety," Patrick said, holding out his hand.

She shrank back. "Nay. I'm not leaving Ryan."

"Come, lass." His fingers wound around her arm.

She yanked and struggled against his hold.

He slipped one arm under her legs and the other under her back, intending to carry her if need be. "Please, Emma," he whispered against her ear. The silkiness of her hair brushed his lips, and the softness of her cheek grazed his chin.

She ceased struggling, rested against him, and wrapped her arms around his neck. For a fleeting second he could almost believe she'd forgiven him for all that had happened and for who he was.

But the ping of more gunfire, this time hitting the nearby shack, urged him into action. Hunkering over Emma and protecting her with his body, he stumbled into the cover of trees, moving deeper into the woods. He tensed and waited for the bite of a bullet to puncture his back, but nothing came.

In the black shelter of the forest, he knelt and lowered her to the ground. He was surprised when she clung to him. Her breath came in bursts against his neck.

Darkness enveloped them, as the canopy of leaves and branches blocked out the moonlight. The scents of pine and damp moss were as thick as the foliage. She was so soft and warm in his arms, and his heart ached to think he might never get to hold her again.

The least he could do for her was save Ryan.

He pressed his lips against the top of her head and held her fiercely for one last moment. Then he let her go, wrenching her arms off his neck and setting her gently on the ground. "Stay here. I'm going back for Ryan."

Without waiting for her reaction, he threaded his way through the thicket, not caring that the twigs scratched him or the thorns tore at him. It was the least of what he deserved. If he hadn't been so trusting and careless, Mitch wouldn't have had the opportunity to sneak into this community and harm them.

When he reached the forest edge, he crawled on his belly toward Ryan and, as gently as he could, carried the man back into the cover of the trees. Once he reached Emma, Patrick was breathing hard from the exertion. But he lowered Ryan down next to her and then spun and started walking away.

"Where are you going?" Emma called.

"I'll be back for you both soon," he said. "Don't move until I come for you."

Another of her questions trailed him as he hiked away from her. He didn't stop to answer. The best way to make up for his mistake in letting Mitch go was to put an end to the stealing and fighting. He didn't care that he was without a gun. He still had the best weapons God had given him—his fists. And even though he'd told himself he'd never fight again, he was going to break his vow and break it badly.

With his jaw set and his shoulders squared, he circled the shore until he reached the edge of the lake a short distance away from the docks. He stripped down to his trousers and then plunged underwater.

He swam toward the pirates' rowboat, the same one he'd watched drift away only a little while ago with Mitch and Sophie inside.

There was one man in it. And from what he'd been able to

tell, there were three others by the stack of cordwood for a total of four pirates.

He swam with the deftness that came from his years of working near the water. Unlike many sailors, he'd been determined to learn to swim and had taught himself. Over the years he'd saved many lives, including his own, because of the skill.

When he reached the boat, he surfaced silently, wiped the dripping water from his eyes, and slipped one of the back oars out of the boat. He then glided as close to the pirate as he could, raised the oar behind the man, and whacked him across the back of the head.

The man didn't have time to turn around. He grunted, then slumped over the front bench, his fingers losing hold of his rifle. The weapon dropped to the floor of the boat with a clatter.

Patrick hefted himself over the side of the boat. Cold lake water dribbled down his face and arms, and the breeze coming off the lake hit his bare back. He shuddered but picked up the rifle anyway. He didn't relish using it. He didn't want to kill anyone, but he had to protect this little community, the people and place he'd come to love.

Quietly he wrapped the bowline around the man's hands so that he'd be immobile when he regained consciousness. He took stock of the other men. Thankfully the pirates hadn't noticed him in the boat knocking out their comrade. He studied them for a moment, his mind racing to formulate a plan.

How could one man take on three? Especially when one of them was Mitch?

He frowned. Mitch had been shot in the leg during one of the last raids they'd made to a small village like Presque Isle. Usually their thieving had amounted to nothing more than a few barrels of venison at a time or lumber stacked on the docks awaiting transport to the mills. They'd been more interested in the profit they could make from prizefighting.

Even though Mitch had a limp, he was stronger than most men. He was the one who'd taught Patrick to fight.

Patrick eyed the shore. He could row the boat closer to the men and lure them away. Even if Mitch and his men overpowered him, at least the fishermen who were trying to defend the village would be safe. And so would Emma and Ryan.

He slipped the shirt off the unconscious pirate and put it on. It was tight against his wet skin, but it would suffice. Then he donned the man's hat, tipped the hat low, and started rowing closer toward the cordwood.

As he glided to the shore behind the cordwood, he whistled through his teeth. The three men turned at the same time. One was squatting on the edge of the stack. Another had climbed the woodpile and was shooting over the top. The third man with the outline of a bushy beard was pointing his gun at the woods.

At the sight of the rowboat, the one who'd been squatting rose and began running toward the shore. Several shots rang out from the bunkhouse. When he reached the water's edge, he was panting. Without hesitating, he jumped into the water and made his way toward the boat. Patrick held out a hand as if to help the man. But the instant the pirate reached for him, Patrick brought his fist up into a punch that connected squarely with the man's face.

The man reeled back, gave a shout, but Patrick sent another jab to his jaw and this time knocked him out. He had to set the gun down and use all his strength to drag the man over the side of the boat.

He retrieved his gun and glanced at the other two pirates, who were too focused on the gunshots to pay any attention to

Patrick's punches. He hoped they assumed he'd merely helped the man into the boat and directed him to stay out of the line of fire.

Patrick gave another whistle. This time both of the men turned from the cordwood and began to race to the boat. With his limp, Mitch lagged behind the other.

As they drew nearer, Patrick's fingers slid into position against the trigger. But even as he started to raise the gun, he knew he couldn't shoot. He never had been able to threaten anyone with a gun. And he couldn't start now. He would have to continue the battle with his fists or die trying.

Patrick stood but kept his hat tilted down until the third pirate jumped into the lake and splashed his way to the boat. Patrick averted his face until he'd helped the man over the side.

The man started at the sight of the two bodies lying next to each other in a puddle of water on the floor. "What's going on here?"

The second he lifted his head, Patrick was ready. He swung a powerful hook, yet the man didn't fall as easily as his companions. He cursed and then took a swing at Patrick. The fist came at Patrick's face, and he quickly ducked to avoid the hit while at the same time leveling a hard punch to the man's abdomen.

The pirate lunged at him, both fists swinging, with a speed that took Patrick by surprise. He danced around the dangerously rocking boat, over the legs of the unconscious men, ducking and swaying to avoid the punches. The man hit him several times before Patrick could find an opening for another punch.

Out of the corner of his eye he could see that Mitch had stopped on the bank. He'd lowered his gun, crossed his arms, and was watching the boxing match with apparent interest.

"You know who you're fighting, Steel?" Mitch called in a voice drenched with excitement. "You're face-to-face with Hook. The one and only Hook."

The young pirate didn't respond except to grunt and try to send an uppercut to Patrick's chin. So this was the man Mitch had wanted him to fight. He was probably Mitch's new well-trained prizefighter, his biggest money-maker.

For a moment, the surrounding lake faded as the swaying boat turned into a fighting ring and Patrick was back in a crowded warehouse amidst cigar smoke and the shouts of those placing bets on the fight. His body glistened with perspiration, and he reacted without thought.

All he knew was that he had to knock out his opponent. He swung back his arm, then looped it forward in a semicircle, putting all his weight behind it. His fist connected against Steel's jaw, throwing him off-balance. Then Patrick delivered a stinging blow straight to the man's nose.

His opponent crumpled and started to fall over the edge of the boat. Patrick grabbed a fistful of the man's shirt and maneuvered him to the floor next to the other two. His stomach lurched at the sight of blood on Steel's face, and he wanted to curse himself for hurting the man.

But one look at the bloody pulp left of his knuckles told him where the blood had come from. Only then did the agony in his hands taunt him. He'd fought with his fists and knocked out three men, and he'd done it without hesitation.

He took a step back from the carnage, guilt pummeling him as surely as Steel's fists.

"Just as I thought, Hook," Mitch called from the bank, his arms crossed in satisfaction, as if they were at a boxing match instead of in the middle of a gun battle over stolen wood. "You haven't lost your touch. You're still as good as you used to be, maybe better. All that rowing and fishing you've been doing has made you even stronger."

Patrick stared at the men he'd knocked out, the moon shining on their upturned faces. It had been all too easy to fall back into his old self, to hit and to hurt others. Was it always going to be a battle to force his past to stay behind him, to keep it from catching up and attempting to take over?

"I could turn you back into a big name," Mitch said, staring across the water to the boat. "With your strength and size we could make bucketfuls of cash every night."

Patrick yanked off the hat and shrugged out of the filthy shirt. He wouldn't take on that lifestyle ever again.

"Beautiful women, endless parties." Mitch was relentless. "It could all be yours again, Hook."

Behind Mitch, Patrick could make out the forms of several of the fishermen zigzagging stealthily toward the cordwood, their guns aimed at the last standing pirate.

"I don't want it, Mitch," he said, bending and wrapping a rope around Steel's hands, hoping to distract Mitch from the approaching men. He certainly didn't want to end up in a boxing match with Mitch. He wasn't sure he could hit the man, even if he came at him with both fists flying.

Besides, Mitch was armed. He didn't think Mitch would shoot him, but he didn't want to find out. He'd have a much better chance of surviving if he had help from the fishermen.

"This fight tonight," Patrick said, winding the rope around his captive's ankles, "is the last time I plan to use my fists."

"Oh, that's right," Mitch said with a bitter laugh. "Yer Saint Patrick, aren't you? Too good for the likes of me now that you got religion."

"I'm not too good. I'm the worst of sinners." Patrick pulled the rope into a tight knot, then took the remainder of the rope to the other man he'd knocked out. There was just enough left to bind him too.

"If you're such a sinner," Mitch said, "then you'll fit right in with the lot of us."

"Thanks to God's love, I'm a sinner who's been set free from my past." Patrick tossed Mitch what he hoped was a casual glance, noting that Fred Burnham was almost upon him, his gun leveled and ready.

"Set free? Set free from a good time and plenty of money?" Mitch laughed again, but the sound was hollow. "Free so that now you can go to church and follow all kinds of rules?"

Patrick shrugged. He couldn't explain it, but in the process of giving up his old life, it was as if a breeze had blown through him, cleaned him, and given him hope that he'd never had on his own. He didn't feel in bondage to rules. He also didn't feel as if he'd lost any pleasure in life. In fact, it was just the opposite. And since he married Emma, he'd felt more pleasure being with her than with all the other women he'd known in the past.

"You're telling me you're happy here?" Mitch asked.

"I've never been happier," Patrick said. He knew it was the truth. He loved Emma. His short time with her had been the best time of his life. The thought of losing her ripped at his heart again.

Fred Burnham and two other fishermen approached Mitch's back. One of them shoved the barrel of a gun into Mitch, and he stiffened. Before he could move, the other men had grabbed his arms and wrenched them behind his back.

Surprise arched Mitch's brow. Then as he stared at Patrick, his eyes filled with the pain of betrayal.

Patrick didn't say anything. He simply watched, aching at the sight of his old friend, shut off to the ways of God. Patrick had given him a chance to turn his life around and do the right thing. Mitch had only spurned his offer by robbing and hurting the people he'd come to care about.

It was time for Mitch to face the consequences of his actions. But even knowing that Mitch's arrest was the right thing, Patrick couldn't watch as the men hauled him away and locked him into the supply shed, along with his three accomplices who were finally starting to stir.

Fred posted a guard in front of the shack and sent a couple of men down to Fremont to fetch the sheriff. In the meantime, Ryan had regained consciousness, and Emma helped him into the Burnhams' log cabin. Widow Burnham was tending to his bullet wound.

Dawn started to break, and Patrick knew he needed to return to the lighthouse and turn off the lantern, along with the other duties he'd put off during the night. Even so, he lingered there, chatting with the other men about the shooting, receiving their good-natured congratulations on almost single-handedly defeating the thieves.

He didn't care about any of that. All he wanted was to see Emma and his boy Josiah and wrap them both in a fierce hug before saying good-bye. From where he leaned against the side of a fish shanty, his attention kept straying to the doorway of the Burnham cabin.

Faint sunlight streaked the lake when Bertie finally strode outside. "We fished the bullet out of Ryan's shoulder and got him stitched up real good."

The men nodded, one after the other. During the shooting, Ryan had been the only one injured. They were grateful to him for alerting them to the thieves and being willing to help them fight, even though he wasn't one of them.

Bertie scanned the men until she saw Patrick. Her lips pinched with obvious displeasure. "You better arrest Patrick Garraty too," she said, pointing at him.

His heartbeat took a dive, but he didn't move.

The men standing around him grew silent. They were sipping coffee and readying their nets and sails for their day of fishing.

"He's a pirate, just like the rest of the lot." Bertie's accusation rang out in the morning air. She stood on the grassy bank outside the cabin, the lamplight from the interior illuminating her, making her loom larger than life.

The men murmured their disbelief.

"It's true," Bertie said louder to make herself heard, her sharp gaze fixed on him. "I've got plenty of proof, so there's no sense in denying it, Patrick."

Patrick could feel all eyes upon him, burning into him with suspicion and mistrust where only minutes ago had been warmth and acceptance. He knew he had to say something to defend himself, but what could he say now that the truth was out?

"I won't deny I was once a pirate," Patrick said. "But I gave up my sinful ways. I'm done with that life."

Bertie took a step toward him, her thin body stiff. "I suppose that's why you gave shelter to their ringleader, Mitch Schwartz, this past week? From what I hear, he's an old friend."

"I found him in a wreck north of the light. I could have left him there to die, but I didn't. I brought him home and bandaged him up."

"Or maybe you concocted this here whole thieving business." Bertie spat the words. "Bet he was planning to give you a cut of profit if you helped him. You're probably in cahoots with him to rob the all the ships passing through here."

"That don't make sense," said one of the older fishermen. "Why would Garraty knock out the pirates and stop them from the thieving if he was aiming to help them?"

"'Cause they didn't expect anyone to see them doing the stealing," Bertie replied. "Once Ryan caught them at their dark deeds, then Patrick had to cover up his part in it."

The men muttered among themselves again, and Patrick didn't know what to say. Now that Mitch had taken his revenge by revealing his past, he'd have an uphill battle ahead of him to prove his innocence.

Deep down, he'd known the moment he found Mitch washed up onshore that saving the man would ruin the good life he'd tried so hard to build over the last few years. He just hadn't expected it to come crumbling down so quickly.

Emma stepped outside the cabin and went to stand next to Bertie. Her face was ashen, and her hair hung in disarray. She was obviously shaken by Ryan's injury. Regardless, she'd never looked lovelier.

She scanned the crowd, coming to an abrupt halt on him. Relief softened her features, making her even more beautiful. Was she glad to see him? Had she been worried about him?

He wanted to give her a reassuring smile and let her know how happy he was to see her. He wanted to pull her away from the crowd and have the chance to say good-bye in private.

"Well," Fred Burnham said, pushing back his hat and watching Patrick, his eyes pleading with him to deny Bertie's accusations. "What do you have to say for yourself, Garraty?"

Emma's attention swung back and forth between him and the tall weather-worn man.

"I've already told you," Patrick said. "I gave up that life—"

"I suppose that's why your wife caught you in the arms of another woman last night." At Bertie's words, silence fell over the gathering, leaving only the sound of the waves as they lapped against the shore.

The noise in Patrick's head tapered to a deadly calm, the lull before the storm. The only way Bertie could know that information was if Emma had shared it. But surely Emma wouldn't have told the woman anything without first talking with him, would she?

Emma shrank back, half hiding her face behind Bertie. Apparently she had.

"If you're so high-and-mighty," Bertie continued, "then why are you throwing yourself into the arms of loose women instead of taking your own wife to bed?"

The low whistles from some of the men sent a rolling surge about his stomach. "What I do with my wife is none of your concern," he finally said.

"It is my concern," Bertie said. "Delia was my cousin. I know how unhappy she was with you. And it's no wonder. You being a pirate and an adulterer and all."

Each of Bertie's cruel words stabbed him. Not because he cared a whit what Bertie thought about him but because he knew that was how Emma felt. She despised him and she'd run straight to Bertie and told the woman all that had happened. Maybe Emma had been the one to tell Bertie about his harboring of Mitch. Maybe Mitch hadn't said anything to the townsfolk after all.

Emma refused to look at him, but instead cowered at Bertie's side.

The knife sank deeper into his chest. What hurt him most was knowing that Emma hadn't trusted him. She'd believed the worst about him. She'd rushed to judge him. Just like Bertie.

The faces surrounding him were shrouded with shock. Obviously they found him wanting. In their eyes, the sins of his past outweighed the new man he'd become.

Patrick's shoulders slumped. What more could he expect? If he stood in their shoes, he'd probably feel the same revulsion.

"Patrick Garraty's a dangerous man," Bertie called. "We don't need the likes of him around here." The men began talking among themselves when Bertie shouted above the commotion, "Besides, you can't let a man like this run the lighthouse. He ain't fit for the job. No telling what kind of mischief he'll make. I say we arrest him."

Emma grasped Bertie's arm. "Surely he doesn't deserve to be arrested. He's committed no crimes—at least not tonight."

"'Course he's going to deny he was involved in stealing our wood." Bertie shook off Emma's hold on her. "But until we talk to the sheriff, he has to be locked up with the others."

Patrick bowed his head. He wouldn't convince Bertie or the others here that he was innocent. If he couldn't convince Emma after the weeks of living with him, after getting to know him, how would he ever convince the rest of the townspeople?

Fred Burnham stepped forward. "Who's gonna tend the light while he's locked up?"

"Emma will," Bertie answered. "She told me she knows how to light the lantern and that she's handy with that sort of thing. She won't have any trouble."

Emma uttered a protest while Patrick forced himself not to look at her again.

"If you don't arrest him now," Bertie said, "he's gonna get away and cause more trouble. We need to put a stop to it right here and now."

Patrick had no energy left to argue with them. Even if he had repaid in full all those he'd hurt or robbed, maybe his finally going to jail for his crimes was inevitable.

When Fred Burnham snaked a rope around his wrists to bind him, Patrick didn't resist. And when the man muttered an apology under his breath, Patrick simply nodded.

Chapter 23

I'm fine, Em. Stop fussing over me." Ryan leaned against the headboard of the only bed in the two-room log cabin. After the noon meal, Bertie had applied fresh bandages on his head and upper arm, then bustled out of the room, leaving Emma alone with her injured brother.

Emma sat back in the chair she'd dragged next to the bed. Exhaustion fell upon her like a heavy blanket. "What should we do?" she whispered, glancing at the open door, which hardly afforded a breath of air in the heat and humidity that permeated the room. "Patrick didn't deserve to be arrested."

The bedroom's only window was covered with a dingy curtain that blocked out the daylight. The room was only big enough for the bed, two chests pushed against one wall, and her chair. Clothes were strewn over the end of the bed, heaped on the floor, and draped across the chests, all of it making the place feel even smaller.

"Tell me what to do, Ryan." The panic had been growing with each passing hour.

"We can't do anything right now. But once I'm stronger, I'll head over there and do what I can to free him."

"That might be too late." She'd overheard Bertie talking with her husband. The sheriff was on his way, and the superintendent of lighthouses had been at Thunder Bay Island, inspecting the lighthouse there. His next stop was to be Presque Isle, but now because of Patrick's arrest, he was coming here with the sheriff. Both would arrive before the day's end.

Ryan shifted his legs toward the edge of the bed and moved as if to sit up, but he fell back with a grimace and pressed his hand to the bandage on his head.

He was right. He couldn't do anything right now. Not when he could hardly move from the pain and blood loss.

"Maybe I can go over and free him," she said. She doubted Patrick would want to see her, not after the way he'd looked at her that morning when he learned she'd shared the intimate details of their relationship with Bertie.

She hadn't meant to say so much, hadn't even told Bertie everything, but somehow the woman had a way of reading her and figuring things out.

Ryan shook his head. "How will you free him?"

"How will *you*?"

"I'll figure out something."

"So will I."

"No. It's too dangerous."

She pressed her lips together to hold back her response. It was no use arguing with Ryan. She would have to come up with a plan to free Patrick on her own.

No matter what Bertie said, Emma couldn't believe Patrick would have partnered with Mitch. All the while he'd doctored Mitch, she sensed his disapproval of Mitch's pirating ways. Yet none of her protests to Bertie or the men had made any difference in stopping Patrick's arrest.

Bertie's word was like the law around Burnham's Landing. The woman's sharp voice drifted into the bedroom from the other room. Disappointment and hurt came wafting back to pierce Emma once again. When she'd arrived last night distraught and confused, Bertie had acted so concerned. She'd listened and patted her back while she poured out her soul. In fact, for the first time, Emma had felt like she had a friend—besides Ryan—someone to listen to her and understand what she was going through.

If Bertie considered her a friend, why had she told everyone the things she'd shared with her privately? Emma didn't want to accept the fact that Bertie had betrayed her, that perhaps Bertie had never been interested in friendship.

Everything she'd thought she had—a husband, a son, a home, and a friend—it had all been a passing dream. None of it had been real.

"I guess I'm destined to remain homeless," she said, breathing out an anguished breath.

Ryan closed his eyes, his features tight with pain. "You really want a home, don't you, Em?"

"I thought I finally had one."

"Don't give up yet."

She dropped her face into her hands. "I think it's time I let go of my wanting a home like the one we used to have."

"I've always missed our home and Mam too," Ryan said quietly. "But over the years, even though we didn't have anything permanent, I never felt homeless."

"I wish I could have felt the same."

"Of course, you were older and had been with Mam more

years than me," he continued. "I guess I figured that as long as I was with the people I loved, I was home. It didn't matter where we were or what kind of place we lived in. We had each other and that was enough."

She nodded. "You're right, Ryan. I should count my blessings—"

"But since you got married, with all the important people gone in my life, I started to feel lost," he admitted. "Then when Holy Bill was here last time, he said if I'm putting my hope in people, I'll eventually end up disappointed. First and foremost I have to put my hope in the Giver of Life. He's the only one who will always be there."

Emma studied Ryan's face and the seriousness that radiated from his eyes. Had she been putting her hope in people and places too?

"Speaking of Holy Bill," Ryan said, sitting up. "Has anyone sent word to him about Patrick's arrest?"

"Is he nearby?"

"I think he's north in Rogers City this weekend," Ryan said. "Then here next weekend, and south in Fremont the following."

She knew Holy Bill didn't stay in one place for very long, not longer than a few days before visiting what he called "the other souls needing God's Word." He helped do the work right alongside his parishioners, whether it was plowing, fishing, or chopping trees. They housed and fed him, and then he moved on to help someone else.

"Can you write a note for Holy Bill?" Ryan asked.

"But how can he help?" She didn't know how long it would take to ride to Rogers City, the next small town north of Burnham's Landing. She didn't know if there was even a road that led there. "Even if I write a note, who will deliver it? Everyone around here thinks Patrick is guilty."

"Not everyone." Ryan sank back into the pillows and closed his eyes with a weary sigh. "I'm sure there are still some men who've gotten to know Patrick and don't believe he could have done the things he's been accused of."

"Why didn't they stand up for him when he needed them?"

"Nobody has proof that he's innocent. Not even Patrick denied his involvement."

"You don't believe he was capable of helping Mitch steal the wood, do you?"

"He's innocent, all right. I've known him less than most of the men and even I can tell he's a godly man. He wasn't a part of stealing the cordwood."

"Aye." She had to agree with Ryan on that. In spite of his other crimes, he wasn't guilty of stealing the wood.

The sound of Josiah's voice from the other room pushed Emma to her feet. She had other duties awaiting her. She'd already been back to the lighthouse to turn off the lantern, and now Josiah needed her care. It was only midday and she felt as tired as if she'd been up for several days straight.

She didn't know how she could last the day without getting any sleep. And then hike back to the tower again at dusk to relight the lantern? She didn't want to even think about that.

At a shout, Emma's eyes flew open, and she sat forward with a start. The late afternoon sunlight slanted through the branches and leaves overhead and blinded her.

She blinked, trying to clear the drowsy haze from her eyes. The grassy area that bordered the forest spread out before her, along with the mound of a recent grave.

Delia's grave.

A few straggly weeds had sprung up among the dry soil. The wooden cross that marked the grave had a newly carved look that made it stand out among the weathered markers of the neighboring graves.

If she couldn't accuse Patrick of assisting Mitch in stealing the cordwood, how could she blame him for pushing Delia? That was the question plaguing her as she'd rested in the shade.

Patrick was too godly, too sincere, too caring to lead a double life. Deep inside, she knew he was no more capable of hurting Delia than he was of helping Mitch steal. Did that mean he was also incapable of involving himself with loose women? Should she believe in him, no matter what she'd witnessed?

Emma sat forward, her eyes focusing on the Burnhams' log cabin, the fishermen shacks beyond, the supply shed where the prisoners were locked up, the waterfront and the harbor.

Two rowboats had docked, and men were stepping out of them. The waves lapped gently against the boats, and sunlight poured down on half a dozen black hats. Sea gulls circled above and made their grating calls as if expecting the men to toss unwanted fish overboard.

But these were no fishermen returning from their catch of the day. The sheriff had arrived, along with a posse of men. Most wore casual attire, but one taller man stood apart in a crisp navy waistcoat and matching trousers, polished black boots, and a flat-topped cap, similar to the one Patrick wore. She guessed he was the lighthouse superintendent Patrick had spoken of from time to time: Mr. Yates, who was overdue for a visit.

And now the man was finally here, though Patrick wouldn't get to petition him for repairs on his beloved light. Instead, he'd earn the man's displeasure. Even if by some miracle Patrick managed to get out of the arrest, the superintendent would likely still fire Patrick once he learned about his unsavory connection to Mitch Schwartz.

She swallowed the lump that had lodged in her throat and pushed herself up from the grassy area in the shade. She untangled her skirt from her legs. The humidity she'd come to expect from Michigan summers had plastered her skirt and bodice to her body. If only she'd had time to freshen herself before meeting the sheriff and superintendent.

Then she remembered she had a son and that he'd been playing nearby while she rested. "Josiah?" she called. "Come to Mamma, little love." She glanced at the shoreline, the gill nets being repaired, and bags of salt near the drying racks. She swiveled toward the thick woods that stretched for miles and miles to the west.

There wasn't a sign of his fiery red head anywhere. Even the long origami snake she'd folded for him was gone. Panic rose inside her as she frantically searched the clearing again. What had she been thinking to doze off and let Josiah out of her sight, even for the slightest moment? There was no telling what kind of trouble he could have gotten into.

Fred Burnham strode around the cabin, wiping his sweating forehead.

"Have you seen Josiah?" she asked.

He gave her a curt nod. "Last I saw, he was inside with the wife."

Emma raced toward the half-open door of the cabin. Just as she reached it, Bertie barged outside. Her eyes sparkled with anticipation. She was learning the woman thrived whenever anything exciting happened around Burnham's Landing. Certainly Bertie was on a mission to avenge her cousin's death, but Emma couldn't help but wonder if the lack of female companionship and the remoteness of the wilderness home intensified Bertie's need to create drama.

"Is Josiah inside?" she asked as Bertie slipped past her, heading toward the men who were now striding up the dock.

"He was with your brother," Bertie said over her shoulder.

Emma peeked inside the cabin. Widow Burnham was knitting in her usual spot by the window. The table was covered with the remains of the noon meal, and the odor of fried fish permeated the stale air. The door to the bedroom was open, but the room was dark, and she couldn't see inside. She turned and saw Bertie walking with her short but choppy steps toward the sheriff, no doubt aiming to share her version of the story before anyone else could give the facts of what happened.

Emma ran from the cabin and went after the woman. She wouldn't let Bertie be the only one to speak her piece. She'd talk to the sheriff too. As Patrick's wife, surely the sheriff would want to hear her side of the story.

"Sheriff!" Bertie waved a hand at the man. Thankfully he was talking with Fred Burnham and didn't stop to acknowledge Bertie.

Instead, the sheriff followed Fred to the shed where they'd locked up Patrick, along with Mitch and his accomplices. One of the older fishermen who usually worked at the flakes was sitting on a stump against the door, his rifle across his lap. He sat with his head laid back, his mouth open, snoring.

Emma stopped next to Bertie. Her muscles tightened with the need to speak first. She needed to make sure Bertie didn't color the sheriff's opinion of Patrick before she could defend him.

But as the sheriff talked with Fred, Emma got the sinking feeling the lawman had already made up his mind to haul all of the pirates, including Patrick, down to Fremont and toss them in jail. The sheriff claimed he'd been trying to capture the elusive Mitch Schwartz over the past year.

When the sheriff and his men pulled the pirates out of the dark hovel, the men blinked against the sunlight. Only Mitch remained unscathed. The other three men had bruised faces, black-and-blue puffy eyes, and crusty blood on their noses.

Emma couldn't keep from staring and shuddering at the effects of Patrick's punches. Even though she hadn't witnessed his fighting, she'd heard it recounted several times from the fishermen who'd seen the battle.

When the sheriff came out a moment later with Patrick, Emma's heart pinched painfully. His shoulders were still as slumped as they'd been when they took him away hours earlier. He'd wrapped his knuckles with a strip of linen he'd torn from his shirt. But the blood had seeped through the linen, had dried, and was now rusty brown.

She took a step forward, hoping he'd look her way, wanting him to see the apology in her eyes. She shouldn't have said anything to Bertie, and she wanted him to know she was sorry she hadn't been more discreet.

But he squinted in the sunlight and then nodded at the superintendent of lighthouses, who stood next to the sheriff. "Mr. Yates."

"Patrick," the man said, "I hear you've been involved with pirates again."

Patrick's face was unshaven, his hair mussed, and he had dark circles under his eyes. He opened his mouth to respond, but Emma spoke first.

"He didn't want to give Mitch shelter. He was only trying to show him God's love, like the Good Samaritan."

Mr. Yates spun toward her, his spectacles sliding down his sweaty nose. "And who are you?"

"I'm Patrick's wife, Mrs. Garraty." The name came off her tongue as smoothly as butter cream.

She knew then she didn't want to give up on being his wife. Not so easily. Patrick had shown Mitch grace, had given him the chance to repent and change his ways. She needed to do the same for her husband.

Patrick stared at his boots.

"You're just the person I wanted to see, Mrs. Garraty," the superintended said with a forced smile.

"You have to know that my husband is innocent."

"How can you be so sure?" Mr. Yates asked.

She didn't know for sure the extent of his crimes, but she did know he was a good man. "Because he's a man of God and he wouldn't intentionally do anything to displease Him."

Only then did Patrick look at her. She expected tenderness in his eyes like she'd seen there in the past or at the very least a measure of gratefulness that she was defending him. But his eyes were filled with hurt. She almost got the feeling he was letting her go, that he'd resigned himself to his fate and wasn't planning to change it.

She silently pleaded with him to forgive her, to see that she hadn't meant to betray him. She'd been hurt and had reacted in fear and foolishness. Yet he looked away without acknowledging her unspoken request.

His aloofness sent a chill over her.

"Unfortunately, Mrs. Garraty," said Mr. Yates, "I need more evidence before I can release your husband."

"Then perhaps you need to have more evidence than one woman's gossip before arresting him." Once the words were out, she clamped a hand over her mouth, surprised at her audacity.

Next to her, Bertie sniffed.

This time the superintendent smiled a real smile. "Don't you worry. I plan to get to the bottom of things, including the moon cussing and shipwreck that happened a few weeks ago."

But how long would Patrick have to languish in jail before he was justified? And who would take care of the Presque Isle Light in his stead?

"In the meantime, I need someone to take care of the lighthouse," Mr. Yates said as if reading her mind. "How would you like to be the one? I understand you have a working knowledge of the lantern and the care of it."

She nodded. "Aye, but—"

"Good. I'll promote you to the title of assistant keeper until I can find a suitable replacement for your husband."

Did that mean Patrick would lose his job regardless of what happened? She'd feared the worst, but now that he was faced with it, she ached for him.

"I'll pay you a fair wage for your work," Mr. Yates added. "In fact, I'll row you out there in a short while, inspect the light, and train you in some of the other responsibilities. The steamship with supplies and the tender crew won't be far behind."

She shook her head. She didn't care about wages or lighthouses or saving ships. All she wanted to do was find a way to help Patrick. "Maybe you should let my husband continue his responsibilities until you complete your investigation."

"I can't do that, Mrs. Garraty."

"Please. He wasn't stealing the wood. And he hasn't been involved with Mitch." She didn't care that she was pleading. She glanced around at the gathering, at the few men who hadn't gone out fishing for the day, the ones who'd been laying out and drying and salting the fish. And of course there were Fred Burnham and Bertie.

Bertie stood back with her arms crossed, frowning at Emma, and not speaking because her husband had taken hold of her arm and was squeezing it every time she opened her mouth.

"Please tell Mr. Yates that Patrick is innocent," she said to the men. "You know as well as I do that he's a good man, that no matter what he might have done in his past, he's proven himself to be hardworking and God-fearing."

"Have to agree with her," said the old fisherman who'd been sleeping against the shed door when they'd arrived. "Can't find a better man than Patrick Garraty."

She smiled gratefully at the man before trying to get Mitch's attention. He stood nearby, flanked by the sheriff's posse. "Tell them, Mitch," she demanded. "Please tell them the truth about Patrick. You know he's innocent."

Mitch shook his head. His dark eyes glittered with anger as he gave Patrick a sideways glance. "Hook knows he's guilty."

"Don't forget," Bertie chimed in, regardless of her husband's grip, "Patrick's been an unfaithful husband. He's been fooling around with other women when he was supposed to be on duty."

The superintendent's eyebrows rose, which caused his glasses to slide to the end of his nose again.

"He's been a good father and a good husband," Emma countered. No matter what had happened up until now, Patrick had treated her kindly. He'd been tender and sweet and considerate. And he was a wonderful father to Josiah.

Bertie yanked away from her husband's grasp. "I have grounds to believe that Patrick may have pushed my cousin, his late wife, down the lighthouse stairway and caused her death."

At Bertie's declaration, silence once again descended over the waterfront, broken only by the cries of the sea gulls.

"That's a strong accusation," Mr. Yates said. "What proof do you have to level such a serious charge?"

"Mrs. Garraty herself told me Patrick has a history of abusing women."

Emma gasped. "I never said such a thing, only that I heard Mitch accusing Patrick of beating up a woman." Patrick's shoulders sank even further, and Emma regretted saying anything at all.

"Everyone knows that my cousin Delia wasn't happy with Patrick," Bertie said. "My guess is that she caught him in an affair, that he got angry, and then decided to silence her."

Mr. Yates gave Emma an apologetic look. "It looks to me like we're better off holding Patrick until we can find out for sure what's been going on here."

The sheriff nodded at the superintendent. "Ready then?"

"You're free to go, Sheriff," Mr. Yates said. "I need to make sure the situation is in hand. I'll stay a couple of days to train Mrs. Garraty before moving north to Lighthouse Point up in Duncan Bay with the rest of my crew."

She wanted to protest his assumption that she'd take over the care of the light. But Patrick would want her to stay and keep the light burning. He'd loved his job and taken pride in keeping the passing ships safe. She could show him she cared by staying and taking over his duties.

Still, she couldn't let the sheriff take Patrick away without one last effort. If she brought out Josiah, and the superintendent saw the little boy, maybe he'd have compassion on them. Maybe he'd realize how difficult it would be for her to run the light and take care of the boy at the same time. If Patrick hadn't been able to do it, then what made the superintendent think she could take care of the child while also running the light?

As the sheriff herded the pirates and Patrick toward the waiting rowboats, Emma raced across the clearing toward the cabin.

"Josiah!" she called breathlessly, rushing through the door and into the front room.

Widow Burnham didn't pause in her knitting. Emma moved past the woman on her way to the bedroom.

Ryan was asleep, his arm draped gingerly across his body, the tightness of his features attesting to his pain even while resting.

"Josiah," she whispered. "Come with Mamma, little love."

She half expected him to crawl out from underneath the bed. But the room was silent. Ryan remained still. Only the stale heat of the afternoon wafted around her, suffocating her with its mustiness.

Where had the boy run off to now?

"Widow Burnham," she said, returning to the main room, "did you see where Josiah went?"

Maybe he'd gone down to the landing to see Patrick. The boy had been asking about his daddy with increasing frequentness.

"He's long gone," widow Burnham said without missing a stitch.

"What do you mean 'long gone'?" The bubble of panic Emma had felt earlier began to rise again.

"He came in a while ago, but then said something about going to find his daddy."

"Do you know which direction he went?"

"It's not my job to keep track of your child, Mrs. Garraty."

Frantic, Emma left the cabin. Once outside, she scanned the harbor and the waterfront, where the sheriff and his posse were prodding the pirates into the boats with their rifles.

She didn't glimpse Josiah anywhere. She ran among the shacks, circling them, peeking into doorways, her fear increasing with each step she took. "Oh, God," she cried, "help me find him."

Patrick had trusted her to care for the boy. And now she'd lost him.

What if the boy had fallen into the lake? What if he'd wandered into the forest? She wanted to sink to the ground and weep at the thought of Josiah out there somewhere. Such a wee boy. He would be frightened, maybe hurt and crying, but with no one to hear or comfort him.

Fear propelled her toward the one person she needed the most. She stumbled along the rocky shore. She hoped Patrick would see her running and realize something was wrong. But he was already in one of the boats, his back bent, his head down, his hat tilted low as if he wanted to block out everything.

"Patrick!" she shouted.

He didn't move, not even to flinch.

"Patrick!" she cried again.

This time he lifted his head slowly and glanced over his shoulder. His eyes were shadowed within the brim of his hat, but the sadness there was visible in every line of his handsome face.

A sob pushed into her throat and came halfway out with her words. "Josiah's missing!"

Chapter 24

Josiah's gone!" Emma repeated, fighting back tears. "I can't find him anywhere."

Patrick stood so quickly that he rocked the boat.

"Whoa, steady!" The sheriff jumped up and grabbed Patrick's arm.

Even though Patrick's bloodied hands were bound, he yanked them upward and easily freed himself from the sheriff's grip. If he'd been angry with her before, she could only imagine how much he'd despise her now and regret he'd ever married her or asked her to care for Josiah.

"Let me find my son," Patrick demanded. "I won't go with you until I find him."

The sheriff whipped his pistol out of the holster at his hip and had the barrel shoved into Patrick's ribs before anyone could move. "You're not going anywhere, Garraty, unless it's with me to the Fremont jail."

Patrick eyed the gun. Emma was close enough to see the muscles in his jaw twitch. She didn't want him to do anything foolish and get himself hurt in the process.

297

"Please, Sheriff," she called. "I think Josiah was missing his daddy and is out there somewhere trying to find him."

The sheriff kept his gun on Patrick. The others in the boats stared. And the few of the sheriff's men left on shore had their rifles raised, ready to shoot if necessary.

"We need to hurry," Emma pleaded. "There's no telling where he's gone. And he's just a wee boy, only two years old."

The sheriff studied her face, obviously testing the sincerity of her words.

"Let me go, Sheriff, please," Patrick said, desperation in his voice. "Once I find my son, I give you my word that I'll return."

The sheriff turned to the superintendent, who was standing on the dock next to Fred Burnham. "What do you think, Mr. Yates?"

Mr. Yates pushed up his glasses. In his crisp navy coat and matching cap, the superintendent had an air of authority that set him apart.

For a long moment, no one spoke.

"For the love of Moses," Fred Burnham said, swiping at the perspiration on his forehead. "Let the man look for his boy. There ain't anywhere Garraty can go 'round here to run from the law. Besides, Garraty's a man of his word. If he says he'll return, then he'll return."

Emma nodded her agreement, relieved Fred was finally making an effort to support Patrick.

"These parts ain't safe for a little boy, not after nightfall," Fred continued with a glance overhead at the position of the sun. The afternoon was rapidly fading. "We've got to form search parties and get looking for him right away."

Fred was right. They couldn't waste any more time. But Emma feared if she said too much, they would think she was setting a ploy to free her husband.

"Let him go look for his son, Sheriff," Mr. Yates said with a nod at Patrick. "I've known Patrick for the past couple of years. And Fred Burnham is right—Patrick's a man of his word."

Emma released a sigh of relief as the sheriff unbound Patrick. They divided into several search parties. She joined Patrick and the sheriff, who had decided to stay with his prisoner and keep an eye on him while they were searching. One of the groups headed south, the other west, while she and Patrick started north.

"Josiah!" she called as she trailed behind Patrick.

Patrick had already searched the beach for footprints. Having found none, he now swept his hand over the tall grass that dotted the shore between the rocks. He stopped and looked at the sheriff. "There's no sign of him in the grass either."

She didn't ask how Patrick could tell. He hadn't spoken to her or looked her way since they'd started searching in earnest. She didn't expect him to, and yet his avoiding her hurt all the same.

She wanted to tell him that she hadn't meant to fall asleep or let Josiah out of her sight. She wanted to tell him it was killing her that she'd failed him when he'd trusted her with his son, the one thing in the world that mattered to him.

But she didn't try to make conversation with him, for she was too ashamed. With tears pricking her eyes, she went on scanning the edge of the woods and calling out Josiah's name.

She'd known from the start of her marriage that she wasn't talented at much of anything, that she wasn't anything special to look at, and that she was inadequate when it came to mothering skills. She thought, though, she'd gotten better and was earning Josiah's trust.

But she'd never be enough for him. What would she do now that Patrick had been arrested? How would she ever be able to console the boy once Patrick left for good?

She wiped her eyes and took a deep breath, willing herself to focus. Now wasn't the time to worry about Josiah's reaction to Patrick being taken away and put in jail. In fact, Josiah wouldn't have any reaction if they didn't find him soon. There was no possible way for a boy his age to survive in the wilderness after dark.

"Lord . . ." she whispered, then hesitated. What had Patrick said? God didn't have to answer any of their prayers. He didn't have to save any of them. But He always heard them. He always cared. And in His wisdom, He sometimes answered yes. "Please help us find Josiah," she said softly. "Please keep the boy safe and bring him back to us."

As she spoke, somehow she felt as if her petition had been lifted and placed into the presence of God. She had a gentle assurance that He'd listened, that He cared, and now it was her turn to trust Him for the outcome.

Maybe it was time to start trusting that He loved her no matter what He allowed to happen.

"Any idea where the boy might have gone?" the sheriff asked as he headed toward the woods, walking away from the shore. "Would he have tried to go back to the lighthouse?"

"He wouldn't know how," Patrick said, "except to follow the shore. And there's no sign of him going that way."

"Maybe he tried to find the woodland trail," Emma said.

"He wouldn't be able to find it." Patrick spoke to her for the first time.

It had been dark when she'd run away from the lighthouse, and Josiah was asleep during most of their trek into town. But he was a smart boy . . .

She knew then where Josiah had gone. He'd tried to find the path that led to the peninsula, thinking that if he found the lighthouse, he'd find his daddy.

Without waiting for Patrick or the sheriff, she raced toward the woods, searching for the wagon wheel ruts that indicated the start of the trail. She shoved aside the overgrown weeds until the path came into view.

Something white lay in the dirt several feet ahead. Once she reached it, she gave a cry of excitement. "This way! He's gone this way!"

Carefully she picked up the paper snake she'd made for him. It was wrinkled and damp, but it was definitely Josiah's and a sign that he'd been here.

Patrick caught up to her, his breath coming fast. He looked at the crumpled mass of paper. "What is it?"

"I made it for him this morning."

Patrick assessed the length of the trail that disappeared into the woods. "Do you think he went home?"

"Aye." *Home.* The word taunted her, reminding her of all that she'd lost.

Patrick took off at a sprint down the path, leaping over ruts and rocks. He didn't stop, not even when the sheriff shouted at him.

Emma started after Patrick, but couldn't run nearly as fast. By the time she reached the peninsula, she was out of breath, her side aching. Her hair had come loose and stuck to her neck. She kept moving and didn't stop until she came upon Josiah's cap in the middle of the yard, not far from the tower. She scooped it up, squeezed it against her chest, and pressed a kiss to it. He'd made it back; he hadn't wandered off the path and gotten helplessly lost.

"Thank you, Lord," she whispered past the tightness in her throat. Somehow she knew that this time God had answered yes to her prayer. Maybe He wouldn't always, but this time He had, and she was beyond grateful.

Clutching the little cap, she rounded the tower and stopped short at the sight that greeted her.

Patrick was kneeling in the grass next to Josiah, who was curled up, asleep in a ball in front of the tower door. The boy's dirty face was streaked with dried tears.

Patrick's chest heaved in and out as he bent down and kissed the boy's forehead, brushing back the red hair with his fingers, his battered knuckles still bandaged in the same bloodstained strips from before.

Josiah's eyes fluttered open. He gave a shuddering breath, the tail end of the many sobs he'd likely shed as he tried unsuccessfully to open the heavy door before crying himself to sleep.

"Daddy?" Then, opening his eyes wider, he smiled. "Daddy!"

"It's me, lad." Patrick's voice wavered, and he dropped another kiss on the boy's head. He seized the boy into a hug and clung to him tightly, his face buried in Josiah's hair.

Tears sprang to Emma's eyes, and her heart overflowed with love for both of them. She couldn't imagine life without either one. But she knew she had no right to them or to this home. Not after today. Not after speaking ill of Patrick to Bertie and then losing his son.

The sheriff stumbled to a halt behind her, coughing and wheezing from his pursuit. Sweat trailed down his forehead, and he took off his hat to wipe his face with his sleeve.

"Me go home," Josiah said, wrapping his arms around Patrick's neck and looking up at him. "With Daddy and Mamma."

Emma was at a loss for words. What could she tell the boy to help him understand the situation when she herself didn't know how to make sense of all that was happening?

Patrick didn't answer right away. He swallowed hard, kissed

302

the boy again before pulling back to look him in the eyes. "Daddy has to go on a long trip."

"Me go with Daddy." Josiah reached up to Patrick's cheek and laid his hand there.

"No, lad . . ." Patrick's voice broke. "You have to stay with your mamma."

Emma wanted to shake her head. She couldn't take care of Josiah. She'd allowed the boy to wander off and get lost.

Josiah turned to her, his eyes big and trusting. "Mamma go with."

"Mamma can't go. She has to stay and take care of the lighthouse. And you have to help her."

Josiah looked back at Patrick. She could tell he was digesting the truth of his daddy's words. After several seconds, his lip quivered and he shook his head. "Me go with Daddy."

Patrick glanced at her over Josiah's head. He silently pleaded for help. The pain etched on his face told her that talking with Josiah was torture for him, that it would have been easier to leave for the Fremont jail without having to say good-bye to his son.

She quickly wiped her tears away. "How will I manage without you, Josiah?" She knelt in the grass facing the boy. "I need a man to help me with the chickens and the garden and the cleaning and all the other things."

Josiah's bottom lip protruded further.

She ran her fingers through his hair. "We'll have to work together to keep the lighthouse in good shape until your daddy returns."

Patrick nodded at her, his gratefulness only sending more guilt ripping through her.

She wasn't good enough to be Josiah's mamma, but she knew

what she had to do. She had to stay and take care of Josiah and the light. She could do this one last thing for Patrick. Until he came back.

And he *would* come back. She refused to think about the possibility that a judge might find him guilty and lock him away for a long time. Maybe he wouldn't have his keeper job, but he'd have Josiah again.

Patrick hoisted Josiah up until they were face-to-face. "I need you to be a good boy for your mamma while I'm gone."

"Okay, Daddy."

"And you can't go off by yourself again." Patrick's expression was stern. "You must always stay where your mamma can see you, do you understand?"

"Me will," Josiah said in almost a whisper.

Patrick nodded, lowering Josiah to the ground again. "Now, it's time for me to leave."

The sheriff shifted behind them and gave a little cough. He wiped his sleeve across his face again, although Emma couldn't be sure if he was wiping away tears or sweat.

"Don't go yet, Daddy."

"I have to, lad." Patrick started to walk away.

"Maybe we can go with you back to the harbor and say good-bye there," Emma suggested with a nod toward the forest path. In the growing shadows, the thick green was dark and uninviting. With all her being she wished they didn't have to return to the harbor.

Patrick shook his head, but Josiah rushed forward and clung to him and wouldn't let go.

Patrick didn't say anything for a moment, and then he released a weary sigh. "Okay. As long as you promise you'll stay with your mamma."

Josiah smiled. "Me promise."

Emma couldn't smile, not when her heart was breaking into a million pieces. If only she'd never said anything to Bertie.

All of this was her fault. And as much as she wanted to make everything right, she had no idea how.

Chapter 25

*P*atrick stood on the dock next to the sheriff, who had begun to fidget with his badge. Evening was upon them now. While the sun was still visible in the western sky, the woodland shadows were lengthening along the shore. They needed to put out if they hoped to reach Fremont before nightfall.

He was thankful the sheriff had been decent enough to allow him to search for his missing son. Now the little boy hopped up and down between him and Emma, holding each of their hands.

"One, two, three, Mamma," Josiah said with a grin.

Emma smiled down at the boy, though the smile didn't reach her eyes. "One, two, three," she said, and then she lifted him and swung him back and forth in a game she'd played with him since they'd walked back to the harbor.

The shore was crowded with the fishermen who'd returned in their rigs from their day's catch. They were busy unloading wooden crates of fish and laying out their nets and sails. The usual good-natured teasing and laughter that accompanied their return was absent. Instead, the shore was eerily quiet, except for Josiah's happy chatter.

Farther up the beach, Fred Burnham stood near his sons and wife. Even Ryan had managed to drag himself out of bed and was propped against a barrel, his face pinched with pain. Emma's brother had protested loudly to the sheriff, vouching for Patrick's innocence and demanding his release. But it hadn't made any difference.

Patrick nodded at Ryan, grateful for his support. Across the distance they shared a long look. He could read the assurance in Ryan's eyes, the message that he would do all he could to take care of Emma and Josiah.

That was all Patrick needed to know.

The sheriff cleared his throat. They'd just finished reloading Mitch and his men into the boats, having allowed them to rest on shore during the search for Josiah.

He could feel Mitch's eyes on him, glaring at him. Patrick figured the only thing keeping the man from killing him had been the rope binding his hands behind his back. He wasn't sure what bothered Mitch more, that Patrick allowed the fishermen to catch him or that he'd turned down the offer of fame and fortune. Either way, Mitch wasn't likely to ever forgive him.

Patrick crouched down next to Josiah. He dreaded having to say good-bye to his son and Emma. Even if she'd hurt him, he still hated the idea that this might be the last time he'd see her. He had no idea what awaited him once he reached Fremont. Of course, he'd have to sit in a jail cell for a while. Beyond that, he didn't know what the judge would rule once his case was heard. If the judge set him free, he couldn't return to the Presque Isle Lighthouse. He'd have to disappear someplace where no one knew about his previous life. He'd have to start over. Again.

"This is it, lad." Patrick placed a quick kiss on the boy's forehead. "Time for me to go."

Patrick was unprepared for the speed and force with which Josiah threw himself against him. The boy's tiny arms wound tightly around his daddy's neck.

Patrick wrapped the boy into a hug. "Good-bye, Josiah. I love you. Don't ever forget that."

Emma laid a loving hand on Josiah's head.

Patrick kissed the boy one last time, knowing he had to break away and leave now, even though it was tearing his heart in two. He started to rise, but Josiah's grip around his neck tightened.

"Don't leave me, Daddy!"

"I told you, I've got to go now," Patrick said gently. He began prying the boy loose.

Josiah's fingers dug into his shoulder, and he pressed his trembling body against Patrick. "Don't go!" he cried.

Patrick glanced at Emma, hoping she'd see his plea for help, that she'd take the boy and comfort him before Patrick lost all self-control and started sobbing.

Emma's cheeks were already wet. She nodded at Patrick with understanding mixing with sadness in her beautiful brown eyes. He'd seen an apology there earlier, but it wasn't enough to ease the ache inside.

"Come to Mamma, little love." She reached for the boy, grasping him and attempting to pry him loose. But his cries turned into screams.

Patrick was helpless to do anything but peel Josiah from his body and go with the sheriff. He got one arm loose and then the other and handed him to Emma.

"Don't leave me, Daddy! Don't leave me!"

He jumped into the boat, needing to put as much distance between himself and Josiah as he could.

"Daddy!" Josiah struggled against Emma, craning his neck, squirming in her arms to get down.

Emma couldn't hold the boy. His desperation was too great. He scrambled down from her hold and stood at the edge of the dock, teetering too near the water. Tears rolled down his cheeks as he held out his arms toward Patrick. Emma hurried forward and gripped the back of Josiah's shirt to keep him from falling into the lake.

"I love you, Daddy!"

"Stop!" shouted Mitch, who was sitting behind Patrick in the boat. "I can't stand any more of this. Just stop."

The shout startled Josiah enough that Emma was able to kneel down next to him and draw him into her embrace, away from the edge of the dock.

Patrick hung his head. He couldn't bear to look at his wife and child a moment longer. He wanted the sheriff to get in so they could be on their way, so he could put an end to this ongoing torment.

The boat swayed as Mitch rose to his feet. Before Mitch could steady himself, the sheriff pulled out his pistol.

"Take it easy now, Sheriff," Mitch said. "I ain't gonna try anything funny. I've got my hands and feet chained together. If I try to jump, I'll get a one-way ticket to the bottom of the lake."

"Then sit back down, son. Nice and easy."

"First I gotta come clean." Mitch stared at Josiah, who had his face buried into Emma's shoulder and was sobbing inconsolably. "I might be a terrible man, but I can't sit here and let that little boy be ripped away from the only dad he's ever known."

"You don't have a say in the matter," the sheriff said. "So sit down and be quiet."

"That's where you're wrong," Mitch said. "I may have been partners with Patrick Garraty at one time, but I ain't seen him or talked to him in all these years."

The sheriff straightened. Mr. Yates, who'd been standing near the Burnhams, pushed his hat up.

"You can ask every single one of my mates," Mitch continued, raising his voice. "We didn't even know Garraty was in these parts until a few weeks ago."

"Then why did he give you shelter?" the sheriff asked.

"'Cause he's a good man. He could have left me on the beach to die. Probably what he should have done. But Garraty saved my life and tried to get me to change my ways."

"That's the honest truth, Sheriff," Emma said over Josiah's muffled sobs.

"Don't listen to her," Bertie cut in. "She's unreliable. Lost her own child today. She's not fit to raise the boy."

Emma's expression was stricken, as though Bertie had run up and stabbed her in the back.

Anger pummeled Patrick's gut. He wouldn't let Bertie talk about Emma that way. He needed to put an end to Bertie's hurtful words once and for all. But before he could say anything, Mitch spoke again.

"Patrick Garraty didn't have anything to do with the thieving here last night. He was trying to stop us, even if it meant he got himself killed in the fight."

Patrick sat up in surprise. Why was Mitch telling the truth about what had happened?

"He didn't want nothin' to do with his old ways," Mitch said, "even though I tried my hardest to get him to come along with us."

"Why you sharing all this now?" the sheriff asked, lowering his pistol. "Why didn't you tell us the truth earlier when we were questioning you?"

Mitch shrugged. "Guess I wanted to make Garraty suffer for letting me get caught, thought he deserved it for turning his back on me." He looked back at Josiah. "But when I saw his boy crying out like that, it broke me down. I realized there's no reason the boy should lose his father, not when too many other boys already have."

Patrick knew that Mitch was referring to his own childhood, to the day he'd awoken alone, not knowing where his dad had gone. The man hadn't even said good-bye, probably figuring that Mitch was old enough to fend for himself. But if not for Patrick's family and their friendship, Mitch might have died.

"Let him go, Sheriff," Mitch said. "Let him stay with his boy and wife."

The sheriff stared hard at Mitch, as though attempting to decide on the truth. And for the first time since Patrick had been arrested, he allowed himself a sliver of hope.

"What about the murder charge and my dead cousin," Bertie said. "You can't just set a murderer free."

"I may have roughened up a woman once," Patrick said, sick to his stomach at the admission. Yet he couldn't stay silent any longer. If Mitch had spoken up, so could he. "But I never, ever hurt Delia. Never."

"You done it once," said Bertie. "Who's to say you can't do it again."

"Might as well come clean with something else," Mitch said. "Hook—I mean, Garraty—never beat up that woman. He was too good for that kind of thing. Wouldn't even lay a finger on a girl to hurt her. Guess he already had the makings of Saint Patty even back then."

Patrick's head snapped to Mitch. "What?"

"I hit her, took advantage of her," Mitch said, refusing to look at Patrick directly. "I was so ashamed, I thought if I put her in your bed, I'd feel better about myself and what I did."

Relief swept over Patrick, and he sank to his knees. He'd lived with the guilt of that crime for so long and he'd hated himself for it. But he hadn't done it after all. He bowed his head and fought back a wave of emotion. All these years he'd believed himself capable of violating and hurting a woman. Even though he'd been too drunk to remember much of what happened that night, he'd accepted responsibility for his actions. Later, he'd tried to locate the woman so he could apologize and make amends, but her friends told him she'd passed away.

"I'm sorry, Patrick."

He lifted his head in time to see Mitch say the words. For an instant he caught sight of the boy he'd once known, who'd never known a father's love. And he could only pray that maybe one day, Mitch would come to know the Heavenly Father, the one who would never leave or abandon him.

The sheriff looked at Mr. Yates, who nodded. Then the lawman surveyed the fishermen lining the docks and shore, taking in their looks of encouragement and relief. He turned and gave Patrick the briefest of nods.

That was all the permission Patrick needed. He leaped out of the boat and onto the dock. He fell to his knees in front of Emma and Josiah and gathered them into his embrace. They pressed against him. Emma cried silently, her body shuddering.

Josiah's sobs tapered into hiccups, and after a moment the boy pulled back his splotchy face and glanced between Patrick and Emma.

"Daddy, Mamma."

"Aye, little love," Emma whispered, kissing his head.

"Daddy stay?"

Patrick nodded and prayed the sheriff and Mr. Yates were serious about releasing him.

"Mamma stay?" Josiah asked, reaching his chubby hand into Emma's hair. He stuck the thumb of his other hand into his mouth and began sucking noisily.

Emma cupped Josiah's cheek. "I'm here." *For now.* She hadn't spoken the words, but they hung in the air anyway. She probably didn't have the heart to tell Josiah she would be leaving soon, most likely after Ryan regained his strength. But Patrick knew that was what she meant.

Her answer seemed to satisfy Josiah, though it left Patrick feeling hollow inside.

Chapter 26

Emma hugged Josiah against her on the bench of the rowboat. His babble was like a sweet but sad melody. Patrick had rowed silently, occasionally answering one of Josiah's questions. But he had, like her, seemed content to let Josiah do all the talking.

After Patrick's release, Josiah hadn't wanted to let go of either one of them. Even when Patrick had needed to talk with Mr. Yates, Josiah insisted on holding both her and Patrick's hands. Mr. Yates had finally told Patrick to head back to the lighthouse, that he would row out tomorrow so they could talk privately about the future and Mr. Yates could carry out his inspection.

From the nature of the conversation, Emma was fairly certain Mr. Yates was inclined to let Patrick remain head keeper of the Presque Isle Light. But they wouldn't know for sure until Patrick had the chance to talk with him further.

"Me see tower!" Josiah clapped his hands. His eyes were round with excitement, his freckled face smudged with dried tears and dirt. Above the tree line, the tower's windows reflected the oranges and pinks of the setting sun.

"Aye, little love." Emma forced a smile and tried not to think about the first time she'd seen the tower, which was on her wedding day. She'd been filled with such hope then—for the future and the prospect of having a home to call her own, including a husband and a child.

She'd lost everything all too quickly. And the loss was almost unbearable.

As Patrick steered the cutter alongside the dock, her chest ached with the knowledge that this wasn't her home anymore, that this time she was only a guest.

Patrick secured the boat and hopped out. He reached for Josiah, lifting him high in the air and earning a squeal of delight before setting the boy on the dock. Then he turned back to Emma and extended a hand to her.

His expression was unreadable. She was already half out, her grain sack with all her possessions slung over her shoulder. She placed her hand into his, and when his fingers closed around hers, the strength and warmth of his grip made her realize she would miss his touch.

He helped her onto the dock but didn't immediately release her hand.

"Thank you for coming back," he said softly.

Josiah was already skipping toward the shore. She swallowed the lump clogging her throat. "I couldn't leave him. Not tonight."

"I appreciate it."

"I'll stay until Ryan's able to travel," she offered.

He nodded, but didn't say anything more.

As she started after the little boy, she wondered if Patrick would insist on her taking Josiah again, or if he'd realized that Josiah needed him, was in fact hopelessly lost without him.

"Boat, Daddy!" Josiah pointed toward the northeast.

Emma turned and stared into the distance.

Sure enough, a rowboat bobbed up and down to the rhythm of the waves. With each passing second it drew closer. Emma shielded her eyes and squinted and was able to make out a bushy white beard of a skinny man dressed in a dark suit. Next to him sat a woman. Two other men were manning the oars, one in the bow and one in the stern.

"Is it Holy Bill?" Emma asked, moving next to Josiah and grasping his hand.

Patrick nodded. He watched the boat, the muscles in his jaw working up and down.

Holy Bill caught sight of them and raised his hand in a wave.

Patrick waved back, yet he didn't look at all happy to see the reverend.

Or maybe it was the woman?

Emma studied the woman, and when the boat was finally close enough for Emma to make out the woman's features, she gave a soft gasp and took a step back.

It was the same woman she'd seen with Patrick on the dock, the woman he'd been embracing. She wore the same low-cut gown, except by the light of day Emma could see it was even more revealing. Her head was covered with a wide-brimmed cap adorned with ribbons that flapped in the wind.

The woman was beautiful and alluring. The same jealousy Emma felt the previous night came rushing back, and she had to get away. She couldn't watch Patrick with her again.

"Come with Mamma, Josiah," she said, spinning away from the approaching boat.

"Please don't leave, Emma." Patrick's fingers closed about her arm. His voice had a note of desperation to it that halted her.

She took a deep breath in an attempt to calm herself.

"It's time you knew everything about me."

She hesitated.

"Please stay," he pleaded.

She nodded. The right thing to do was talk to Patrick. And she'd promised Ryan she would. Slowly she turned back until she was facing the boat.

"Hello," Holy Bill called across the span of water.

"Hello!" Josiah yelled back.

Emma couldn't move. Patrick was frozen to his spot too, his fingers burning into her arm, as if he were afraid she'd bolt at any second.

When the boat finally pulled alongside the dock, Patrick stepped toward it, reluctantly letting go of her.

"I came as soon as I got the news," said Holy Bill as Patrick assisted him onto the dock. "But it looks as if God got here plenty ahead of me and already worked things out."

"That He did," Patrick replied.

Holy Bill's bushy brows rose, the concern in his eyes touching Patrick's face before moving on to Emma and then Josiah.

Patrick had already turned to the woman, who'd stood and was waiting for him with a smile. "And here I thought this time I'd get to race in and rescue you, just like you've rescued me so many times."

With a strained smile, Patrick lifted the woman out of the boat and placed her gently on the dock. He started to let go of her and back away, but she launched herself toward him so that he had no choice but to catch her in a hug.

"I was so worried!" she cried, wrapping her arms around him. "As much as I like Mitch, I couldn't stand to think that you'd have to be locked up just like him."

Once again, envy gnawed at Emma. If only it had been that easy for her to fling herself into Patrick's arms. Would he have loved her then?

"Sophie was the one to alert me," Holy Bill said, stepping over to Josiah and patting the boy on the head.

"I had Mitch's crew take me over to Rogers City," Sophie said. "I didn't rest until I found Holy Bill. I figured if anyone could vouch for your innocence, Holy Bill could."

Patrick disentangled himself from Sophie and took a step back. He nodded at the two men still in the rowboat. They returned Patrick's nod while glancing around nervously.

"You rowed down from Rogers City?" Patrick asked.

"No, silly!" Sophie punched his arm with a grin that was oddly familiar. "The *Mad Maiden* is out north of the light. Not too far away."

Emma guessed the *Mad Maiden* to be Mitch's steamboat. She had no doubt they were staying well out of the way of Presque Isle Harbor and the sheriff.

"Even if you didn't need me to set things straight around here," Holy Bill said, taking hold of Josiah's hand, "I told Sophie I wanted her to come ashore with me. I think it's time Emma and Sophie meet, don't you?"

Josiah had finally noticed the strange woman. He popped his thumb into his mouth and stared at Sophie, at her shimmering gown that was the color of a sunset.

For the first time, Sophie looked at Josiah, and pain flashed in her eyes. She quickly shifted her attention back to Patrick and smiled—too brightly. "Yes. I want to meet this new wife you've been raving about."

Patrick gave the reverend a pointed look. "Will you take Josiah up to the house, please?"

Emma wanted to shout out that *she* would take Josiah to the house. But while part of her dreaded hearing what Patrick had to say about this woman, another part wanted to know the truth once and for all, no matter how much it hurt.

Holy Bill and Josiah started toward the path that led to the house. "Josiah and I are hungry. We'll go see if we can find something to eat, won't we, sonny?"

Josiah nodded reluctantly, his thumb still in his mouth. It took a moment of convincing before Josiah finally left with Holy Bill down the rocky path. Even then, he kept glancing over his shoulder as if he were afraid his daddy would disappear again.

Once they were gone, Sophie's shoulders relaxed and she let out a sigh. "I hate seeing him."

Patrick didn't say anything. It looked as though he didn't quite know how to respond.

Sophie shrugged, reached over and took Patrick's arm. "Come on, Patrick. I know I embarrass you half to death, but you can't hide me from your wife forever."

Emma's mouth went dry. She tried to smile, but her lips refused to cooperate.

"Emma," Patrick said, "this is Sophie, the woman you saw me with the other night."

Sophie tipped up the brim of her hat, and for the first time Emma saw her eyes—green with a tint of brown. She had a pretty face, thin and delicate, with a smattering of freckles across her nose.

Emma could see why Patrick loved her. She was indeed beautiful.

Sophie studied her face too, her eyes bright and filled with mischief. "No wonder you picked her," she said, punching Patrick in the arm again. "She's absolutely stunning."

Emma glanced around to see who they were talking about. Surely not her. She was far from *stunning*.

Sophie smiled at Emma, a genuine smile, devoid of any jealousy or malice. "Yes, she's perfect for you."

"I agree." Patrick regarded her with such keen longing, it took Emma's breath away.

Sophie giggled. "And you're in love. I can tell."

Patrick's face turned red, which made Emma's heart race. He didn't acknowledge Sophie's statement, but neither did he deny it.

Was it possible that he might care for her? Even after all that had happened? Even after the way she'd hurt him? A thin beam of light broke through the grayness hovering about her soul.

Sophie reached for the enormous bow tied under her chin. She tugged the ribbon loose and lifted the hat from her head.

Emma stared in fascination at the mound of curls the hat had mostly hidden. Bright red curls that flamed the same shade as her gown. Without the cap, the fading sunlight spotlighted the woman. She was exquisitely striking, and Emma couldn't help feeling again that there was something familiar about her.

The red hair, the light-green eyes . . . they were the same as Josiah's. If she didn't know better, she'd almost believe Josiah was related to this woman, that perhaps she was even his mother.

Emma pressed a hand to her chest.

Patrick had been watching her as if gauging her reaction. "Emma," he said in a low voice, "Sophie is Josiah's real mother."

Sophie's smile faded, and she fidgeted with the brim of her hat. "Not anymore."

"I see," Emma managed to say between dry lips.

"I won't ever be his mother. I can't." Sophie's eyes glistened. "I refuse to drag him around in the kind of life I have."

Emma couldn't resist looking again at the flesh peeking out of her tight bodice. So she *was* a loose woman.

"I asked Patrick to raise the boy," Sophie said. "I figured if anyone could give Josiah a good life, it would be him."

"You were right," Emma said with a budding admiration for Sophie and the hard choice she'd made. "He's the best daddy in the world."

Sophie smiled sadly and reached for Patrick's hand. "He was a good daddy to me too."

Patrick squeezed Sophie's hand. "I could have done so much better."

"You did the best you could for a little boy." Sophie stretched on her tiptoes and planted a kiss against Patrick's cheek. "A girl couldn't ask for a better brother than you."

"Brother?" Emma glanced at Sophie, then Patrick.

"Yes, Patrick's my brother," Sophie said. "Didn't he tell you?"

Emma shook her head. "I thought Patrick was Josiah's real daddy."

Sophie socked Patrick in the arm hard enough to make him flinch. "You didn't tell her that you're Josiah's uncle?"

Patrick's expression was tight. "And how was I supposed to tell her that?"

"I know it's embarrassing to admit you have a whore for a sister," Sophie said.

Patrick flinched, and Emma ducked her head in mortification.

"And I know you don't want anyone to know about me. But you can't hide me away forever."

"You know I don't want you living like you do," Patrick said. "I beg you every time I see you to give it up and come live with me. If God can give me a new start in life, I know He can do the same for you too."

Emma scrambled to put all the pieces of the puzzle together. Was this the woman Patrick went to visit on occasion? Had it been Sophie's perfume she'd smelled on Patrick's coat? She wasn't sure whether to feel relief for this explanation of the other woman in Patrick's life or whether to feel stupid for thinking the worst of him.

"After Sophie brought me Josiah," he continued to explain, "we both agreed it would be better for the boy to think I'm his real dad."

"I don't want Josiah to know who I am," Sophie said, her voice strained. "It's much too hard to see him."

Emma could hear what Sophie *wasn't* saying. She loved the boy too much to drag him into her life. And it was too painful to see the boy and know she couldn't have him.

Sophie grabbed Emma's hands. Her fingers were cold and her grip desperate. "Please be a good mother to him." Tears brimmed in her pretty eyes, fell over and splashed down her cheeks.

Emma's throat squeezed. What could she say when she would soon be leaving? She certainly couldn't lie to Sophie. She looked at Patrick, silently begging for his help.

He nodded his understanding and said, "Emma is a wonderful mamma." He reached for Sophie, extricating her from Emma and pulling her into an embrace. "Josiah loves her very much."

Patrick met her gaze above Sophie's head, and the sincerity Emma saw in his eyes surprised her. He couldn't really mean she was a wonderful mamma, not after her failures over the past month, and not after today with her falling asleep and letting Josiah wander off.

Sophie pulled back from Patrick. She wiped her cheeks and straightened her shoulders.

Nay, Patrick would be better off finding a more qualified woman to be Josiah's mamma.

"We better get going, Soph," said one of the pirates waiting at the oars of the rowboat.

Sophie forced a smile. "The crew's decided to get out of the area. They're sailing the horseshoe to Lake Michigan, maybe to Chicago. And I'm going with."

Patrick held out a hand to her, but she stepped back toward the waiting boat. "Please stay, Sophie."

"The men are kind to me," she assured him.

"I'll take care of you."

"I'm not your baby anymore," she said with a sad tone to her voice. "I don't need you to watch over me."

"Please, Sophie . . ."

But she turned her back on him, bunched her skirt, and hopped down into the boat.

Patrick's shoulders slumped, and weariness settled over his face.

"Good-bye, Patrick," Sophie called before settling on the bench and arranging her hat back on her head.

"I'll always be here for you," Patrick said.

"I know." Sophie smiled as she tied the hat ribbon under her chin.

Watching the boat row away, Patrick didn't say anything more. Emma could tell from his silence and the expression on his face that he'd already said everything a hundred times in the past and that he had nothing new to say that would convince Sophie to stay.

Sophie was determined to leave and to live her life the way she wanted. Perhaps she felt she was too sinful, too far beyond the reach of God's love to ever come back.

Whatever the case, Sophie was breaking Patrick's heart, perhaps broke it every time he saw her. That would explain why he'd been so weary and sad those days when he returned after visiting her.

As he stood on the dock and watched the boat move farther out into the lake, Emma started up the path to the house. She wanted to comfort him, but she knew he didn't want her comfort tonight, not after all that had happened.

Patrick stood on the gallery of the tower and let the darkness and the canopy of stars overhead soothe his hurting soul.

Though he'd only been gone one night, it felt like forever. He was grateful to be back and to have his job still, for at least one more night. Mr. Yates hadn't seemed too concerned about allowing him to return to the light. In fact, he'd almost looked relieved. Patrick knew it wasn't easy to find men who were willing to travel to the remote lights and live in isolation and sometimes deprivation—especially given the low wages the board paid keepers.

"Beautiful night," Holy Bill said, leaning on the rail next to him and staring out over the lake.

"It is," Patrick agreed.

"And you have a beautiful wife down there." Holy Bill dragged a hand down his shaggy beard. "I think she's waiting to talk to you."

Patrick sighed.

"I can stay up here for a while," Holy Bill said. "Keep an eye on things while you . . . well, you know."

If Patrick had ever thought he was making progress courting Emma and getting her to fall in love with him, he'd been sorely mistaken. He hadn't made her fall in love; he'd driven her away.

"She's only staying until Ryan's healed enough to travel," he admitted to Holy Bill. "After learning everything about me, she doesn't want to have me. Not that I can blame her."

"Emma doesn't strike me as the kind of girl who lets the past stand in the way of the future."

Patrick thought again about Emma's reaction to Sophie, first shock and then sorrow dancing across her face. Now she knew everything. He'd laid out all the filth of his family and his sins before her. "Why would she stay? I haven't given her much reason to stay before. She has even less now."

"You've been a good husband to her. And if you've made mistakes, you can ask her to forgive you."

"I don't deserve it."

Holy Bill didn't say anything for several minutes. The July night was thick with the buzzing of insects, the humming of the lantern, and the crashing of the waves below. Finally, Holy Bill clapped him on the back. "You're a good man, Patrick, and you love God, but there's one thing you're missing."

Patrick shifted so that he was looking the reverend in the eyes.

Holy Bill smiled. "You're following the Lord wholeheartedly, yet you're missing out on the forgiveness part. God's not just in the business of saving us from our sins. He's also in the business of forgiving those sins and putting them as far as the east is from the west."

Holy Bill made a point of looking first toward the lake in the east and then toward the expanse of forest in the west. Neither ever came together. They were as far apart as anything could ever get.

"God's already let go of your past, Patrick. He doesn't remember it. He doesn't count it against you. Now it's time for you to let go too."

Holy Bill squeezed his shoulder.

Patrick's throat tightened and he couldn't speak.

"Forgiveness in marriage works about the same way," said Holy Bill gently. "You're willing to forgive Emma for not trusting you, aren't you?"

He nodded. He'd already forgiven her. He didn't know when, but at some point he'd let go of the hurt she'd caused him when she told Bertie their private matters. It didn't seem so important anymore. And in hindsight he blamed himself. If he hadn't been so afraid of sharing the truth with Emma about himself and his family, then she wouldn't have been tempted to listen to Bertie's gossip.

"Then give her the chance to forgive *you* for *your* mistakes," Holy Bill said.

"Do you really think she will?"

"All you can do is ask her."

After a few more minutes, Holy Bill left Patrick by himself.

He didn't mind. He had a long night of praying ahead of him, and he might as well get started by asking God to help him accept His forgiveness for his past.

Chapter 27

*E*mma clamped two wooden clothespins between her lips and draped Patrick's damp shirt over the line. The linen was ripped in several places where he'd formed bandages for his battered knuckles. But at least she'd been able to scrub out the bloodstains. She'd find a way to salvage the rest of the shirt somehow.

She took a pin out of her mouth and secured the shirt on one side before doing the same to the other. Then she bent to retrieve another damp shirt—this one Josiah's—along with two more clothespins.

A quick glance to the sky told her it wouldn't be long before Patrick started the lantern. The clothes likely wouldn't dry much during the night. While she'd washed them earlier in the day, she hadn't had time to hang them, not until after Josiah was tucked in bed for the night.

She couldn't blame Josiah's busyness for distracting her from her tasks. Her own excitement had been the culprit. When Patrick had taken Holy Bill into town in the morning, he'd brought Ryan out to the house to recuperate.

She hadn't asked Patrick to do it, but somehow he'd known how much it would mean to her to have her brother close at hand and to be able to care for him. So she'd spent the major part of the day tending to Ryan and doctoring his wounds.

In fact, she hadn't even had the chance to thank Patrick. Shortly after he'd returned with Ryan, Mr. Yates had arrived, and Patrick had spent the rest of the day with the superintendent. They'd closeted themselves in the sitting room and talked for hours.

Mr. Yates had stayed for dinner. She'd attempted fried fish cakes, and they'd been slightly overcooked and dry. But thankfully her biscuits had baked to perfection. Mr. Yates had been gracious enough to compliment her on the meal, unlike Ryan who'd teased her when she took him a plate later.

The day had been nearly perfect. In some ways she felt as if she'd never left the lighthouse, that everything was the way it should be and this was still her home.

Emma stuck more clothespins in her mouth and draped Josiah's shirt over the line. A cool breeze swept off the lake and whipped the shirt, moving it high enough that she caught sight of Patrick standing in the tall grass by the tower, staring at her.

His expression was intense and serious and filled with something that made her insides flutter.

He pushed away from the stone wall and started toward her with long purposeful strides. She focused her attention on pinning Josiah's shirt, until soon Patrick was standing on the opposite side of the line from her. She couldn't concentrate on anything but his thick arms and torso.

"Emma." His tone begged her to look at him.

She lifted her eyes and caught her breath at the nearness of his face above the line.

His brows formed a line above his troubled eyes, and yet his tanned face with its dark whiskers had never looked more handsome.

"I've been waiting for the chance to talk with you alone all day," he said.

Her pulse sped up. "You have?"

"Until now I haven't had the chance to tell you. I'm sorry . . ."

"It's all right. I'm the one who should be apologizing to you—"

His fingers touched her lips, and the gentle pressure cut off her words, her breath, even her thoughts. She found herself staring into his green eyes, helplessly lost.

"Let me finish," he said.

She nodded. When he dropped his hand away from her mouth, she wanted to grab it and put it back.

"I should have been honest with you from the start about my past—about Sophie, about Josiah, about everything. But I was ashamed and wanted to hide it all from you, and from everyone else around here."

"None of that matters—"

He lifted his hand and silenced her again. She didn't protest.

"I prayed last night, and I realized that when God saved me, He also forgave me. I don't have to live with the burden of my sins anymore."

She let her lips linger against his fingers, savoring the softness of his touch.

"He's forgiven me. And now I want to ask you—will you forgive me too?"

She nodded as something warm flooded her heart. "Does this mean you don't hate me for my mistakes?"

"Ah, lass." His voice dipped low, and he brushed his thumb across her cheek. "I could never hate you."

"Then you'll forgive me for saying things to Bertie I shouldn't have said?"

"Done."

She smiled. His one word was everything she'd been waiting to hear, everything she'd needed. "Thank you," she whispered.

He didn't smile in return. Instead, his brow wrinkled again with worry. "There's one more thing about my past you should know." He dropped his hand from her face.

"It doesn't matter," she said. "I don't need to know any more."

"But I want you to know." He glanced at the tower. "I want you to know the truth about Delia."

"You already said you didn't hurt her. That's enough for me."

"I want you to know everything. I don't want any more secrets between us." He took a deep breath. "Delia married me because that's what her father wanted. She didn't love me. I didn't tell her much about my past, but she knew I'd been a criminal. And she was embarrassed by it. I thought if I was a good enough husband, that she'd learn to love me. But each time I came to her—touched her—I repulsed her more."

Emma's face flushed at his insinuation. He looked away, clearly embarrassed too.

"When Sophie brought me Josiah, Delia didn't want me to take him in. She didn't want the baby of a prostitute. She fought against it. But she gave in when her father told her to be a good mother."

Emma reached for Patrick's hand and wound her fingers through his. All she could think about was how difficult his life had been, how little happiness he'd had. And it made her want to cry.

At her touch, Patrick responded by grasping her hand tightly. "When we moved here to Presque Isle, when Delia learned that

Sophie was in Rogers City, she begged me to return Josiah." He paused for a brief moment. "I couldn't do it, Emma. I loved him too much already. I couldn't throw him back into that life. I wanted more for him than either Sophie or I ever got from our parents."

"I understand," she whispered.

"The night Delia fell down the stairs," he continued, "we'd been fighting again. She said I had to give Josiah back or she'd return to her father."

He swallowed hard.

She squeezed his hand.

"I told her Josiah was here to stay. She yelled at me and then ran down the steps. I called after her, telling her to slow down. To stop. To come back so we could talk more. But . . ." Patrick stared blankly at the tower door. "She fell."

Emma's heart cracked open and filled with his pain. Without thinking, she slipped her arms around his waist and pulled him into a hug.

To her surprise, he didn't resist. Instead, his strong arms surrounded her, and he clung to her, pressing his face into her hair and breathing heavily as if trying to steady himself.

"I was afraid if I told you the truth about Josiah and Sophie, that you'd be like Delia, that you wouldn't love Josiah anymore. I didn't want you to reject him."

"I wouldn't have." She breathed in Patrick's scent, mingled with the wind and lake. "It's not Josiah's fault that Sophie chose to live an immoral life. In fact, he needs love and stability even more."

"Maybe I should have found another family to take Josiah."

"Nay," she said against his chest. "You did the right thing. You're his daddy. He needs you more than he needs anyone."

For a long moment, they just held each other, the wind blowing the damp shirts on the line against them, a distant sea gull echoing the cries of their hearts.

Finally, Patrick pulled back so that he could see her face. "He needs you too." She started to shake her head, but he pressed on. "Josiah needs both of us. Together." He brought a hand up and gently touched her cheek.

She closed her eyes and tilted her head back. She needed him, wanting more from him than a hug.

But instead of kissing her or running his fingers through her hair, he let go, took a step back, and retrieved something he'd dropped in the grass. He held it out to her. "I carved this for you."

She accepted the gift. It was a roughhewn carving of dark wood in the shape of a lighthouse tower, the Presque Isle Light, with a cross at its center.

"It's not much," he said, "but I thought maybe you could find a place to hang it in the house . . . our house."

Joy swelled deep within her as she traced the little cross with her finger, a smaller version of the driftwood cross he'd given her. "Oh, Patrick, I love it."

"Please don't leave, lass."

She smiled and hugged the lighthouse gift. "I'm sure I can find a nice place for it. In our house."

His eyes lit up, and he looked as though he was going to pull her into his arms and give her that kiss she wanted. Instead, he held himself back and smiled in return, a smile that turned the green of his eyes into a lush forest, a forest where she wouldn't mind losing herself.

As if hearing her thoughts, his grin quirked higher on one side. "It's about time for me to light the lantern."

"Aye. It's that time." She glanced at the pink streaks in the sky and tried to keep the disappointment out of her voice. She wasn't ready for their time together to be over, not when it had only just begun.

He ducked under the clothesline, and her heart followed after him. He retreated several steps before stopping and peering at her over his shoulder. "Would you come visit me in the tower later?" The invitation in his eyes was filled with hope.

All she could manage was a nod.

Emma leaned back and studied the wall above the dresser. The dark wood of the carved lighthouse glimmered in the light of the bedside table lantern.

"What do you think?" She tossed the question over her shoulder at Ryan, who was reclining in the bed.

"I think it spells L-O-V-E," he teased. "Patrick is madly in love with you."

She couldn't contain the smile that she'd worn ever since she finished hanging the laundry. "I don't know about love, but at least he's willing to give me and our marriage a second chance."

Ryan sat at the head of the bed enthroned in all the pillows they had in the house. The color had begun to return to his face, and his grin was as mischievous as always. She was relieved he was getting better.

"So I suppose this means you're not leaving with me after all?" he asked.

Emma dug through what was left in her sack. She'd already unpacked most of it into her drawer. Her fingers found what she was looking for. She pulled it out and handed it to Ryan. "I want you to have this."

"What is it?" He took the wooden cross and turned it over in his hands.

She lowered herself onto the end of the bed. "It's a beautiful story. One I'm now passing on to you."

She read him the letter and told him the tale that went with the cross. When she finished, she knew somehow she'd finally been able to give up her own hopes and plans and had trusted in the Giver of Hope himself. She'd made a wreck of things, but thankfully God could take the wreckage and turn it into something beautiful.

"I've always dreamed of having the kind of home we used to have," she said. "I kept waiting for that. I didn't think I'd ever be happy until I had a home like that again. But now, after all that's happened, I realize I can't put all my hopes and dreams in a home or a husband. I have to put my hope in Him above everything else."

Ryan smiled.

She handed him the folded letter that had once belonged to Isabelle Thornton. "Hang on to it. Maybe God will teach you something about hope too. And when He does, then you'll be ready to pass along the cross to someone else."

"I have all the hope I need."

"I have a feeling you'll need more someday," she said. "Besides, I figure without me around, you'll need some way to remember me."

"I won't forget you, Em."

"And I'll always be here for you, if you ever need someone."

"Don't worry about me. I'll get along just fine."

She turned away from him to hide the sudden ache that came at the thought of their parting ways. It was only a matter of days before he'd be back on his feet and well enough to travel.

"What are you still doing here?" Ryan's voice was thick with emotion. "Go on now. Your man is waiting for you."

Heat rushed into her cheeks. She shouldn't have told Ryan that Patrick had invited her up to the tower. She should have known he'd tease her mercilessly about it.

"You need to put on your prettiest nightgown," he continued, "take up some blankets, and spend the night with him. I'll stay here with Josiah."

"Ryan!" She squeaked his name, mortified at what he was implying, but at the same time surprised with herself for even briefly considering the possibility.

After what Patrick had shared regarding his marriage to Delia, she could understand now why he'd been so hesitant with her. He probably thought she'd be embarrassed by him too, maybe even repulsed by his touch as Delia had been.

Maybe at first she'd been timid. After all, they were strangers then. And maybe she'd been taken aback when she learned more details about his former crimes.

But now . . .

She loved him. She loved him more than anyone she'd ever known. She didn't despise him for his past because she knew the man he'd once been had helped shape him into who he was now, a God-fearing man.

She longed to be with him, to be wrapped in his arms, to have him hold her and never let go.

She wasn't like Delia in the least. Maybe it was finally time to show him that.

Emma hesitated, pressing a hand to her wildly thumping heart. Was she doing the right thing? "Heaven have mercy," she whispered as she forced her feet up one more of the winding tower steps.

Her nightgown swished around her bare feet. Her hair fell in soft waves down her shoulders. And she carried a blanket under one arm.

"I can't do this." She retreated one stair before stopping herself.

She had to do it. She had to let Patrick know she was his and that she wasn't ashamed of him. He was too kind to ever force himself on her. If anything was going to happen between them, she would have to make the first move.

And the truth was, she was ready to be his wife in the fullest sense. She wanted the rest of the barriers to fall away between them and to be as close to him as possible.

She drew another deep breath and climbed several more steps, her bare feet moving soundlessly. She'd come without a lantern, feeling her way up the dark tower, the light from the top her only guide.

From above came the thud of footsteps. They were rapid for a moment, then halted, then continued again. The glow of a small lantern grew until Patrick stood on the steps above her.

"Emma, what are you doing?"

"I was on my way up to visit you," she said, feeling foolish. "Where are you going?" She wanted to shake out the blanket and wrap it around her nightgown and cover herself before he noticed what she was wearing.

But his gaze was already raking over her. His lantern illuminated the thin linen of her nightgown and the fact that she was wearing almost nothing underneath. His eyes widened and then lifted. He took a quick step back. "I was just on my way to see where you were. I thought maybe you'd changed your mind about coming."

His voice was breathless and echoed against the stone wall. Had he been waiting for her, even anxious to see her? The possibility made her senses reel.

"I didn't change my mind," she said softly.

He stared at her face, but it was clear from the battle raging across his features that he wanted to lower his eyes again.

She took courage from his reaction. "I took a little longer getting ready tonight. That's all."

"I can see that," he said hoarsely.

Slowly she continued up the steps, not stopping until she was standing on the stair directly beneath him. He didn't move back this time. Instead, he waited, his eyes questioning her, probing deeper.

She reached for his free hand, the one not holding the lantern, and brought it to her shoulder, to the bare skin where her nightgown had slid aside. She placed his hand there, sucking in a breath when his fingers skimmed over her shoulder underneath the material to her collarbone.

"I'll never loathe your touch," she whispered. "Never."

He set the lantern aside, lowered himself to the step, and pulled her down onto his lap. His hand slipped to the back of her neck. Then his lips came crashing down upon hers, and his mouth moved hungrily against hers with the rhythm of the waves, ever in motion.

Strangely she didn't want it to end. It stirred in her a longing, and she wanted more. She didn't quite know what that *more* was, but she was ready.

He broke away abruptly. "I'm sorry." He was breathing hard, and she felt the heat of it against her cheek. "I didn't mean to get carried away."

"It's all right," she said.

"I don't want to push you away."

"You won't." Her voice sounded odd to her ears, almost sultry. "I love you. And I want to be your wife."

His fingers wound into her hair, tugging her head back and exposing her neck and the dip of her nightgown but also giving him access to her eyes.

His were filled with desire. Yet they also overflowed with something else—love. It burned there brightly. Even before he could say the words, she knew that somehow over the past month he'd fallen in love with her too.

That knowledge flooded her with joy.

"If you're sure," he whispered.

"I'm sure," she whispered back.

He scooped her into his arms and started back up the winding stairway. His pounding heart and the heat of his lips against her forehead were promises of the love he would give her that night.

His nose nuzzled her hair, and his breath fanned her ear. "I love you, lass. I'll always love you."

Not only was he promising her love that night, but she knew without a doubt that he was promising her a love to last a lifetime.

Author's Note

*D*on't you just love lighthouses? I hope you learned a lot about lighthouses and were swept back in time with *Love Unexpected*.

I wanted to write a series about lighthouses for a number of reasons. First, my state of Michigan is home to the greatest concentration of lights in the U.S. In fact, Michigan is noted as the state where the most lighthouses were built, and now today more than 120 remain compared to 500 total for the rest of the nation.

Second, I was drawn to lighthouses because I'm fascinated by the women keepers who have largely been forgotten by our modern world. During the prime lighthouse era, from the 1800s to the early 1900s, most lightkeepers were men. But occasionally women were appointed to the head keeper or assistant positions.

Michigan has the distinction of having had the most women keepers. During my research, I was thrilled to come across a book that focused on those Michigan women keepers, *Ladies of the Lights: Michigan Women in the U.S. Lighthouse Service* by Patricia Majher. I loved reading about the approximately fifty women who served as principal or assistant keepers to Michigan lights. I highly recommend this book.

I knew I wanted to center my series on the women who worked in Michigan's lighthouses, but as I researched these fascinating women, I had a hard time narrowing down which of them I should bring to life.

Finally I decided on Mary Chambers Garraty, who's known as "Mother to a Lighthouse Dynasty." Though I changed her name to Emma, I pieced together the few facts that are known about Mary Chambers. She was born in County Mayo in Ireland in 1832 and immigrated to America as a teenager. While there's no record that she came as a result of the Irish Potato Famine, I speculated that the bleak, starvation-like conditions in her homeland drove her to America as they did the hordes of other Irish immigrants at that time.

Mary settled on Mackinac Island, where she met and married Patrick Garraty in 1859. Patrick didn't become keeper of the Old Presque Isle Lighthouse until 1860, so I took some license with the dates in my story, having him as keeper a year earlier than he really was. I also took the liberty of having Mary meet Patrick while he was already a lightkeeper at Presque Isle rather than on Mackinac Island.

They lived at the Old Presque Isle Lighthouse until 1871. At that time, the district inspector reported that the keeper's dwelling was in such poor condition, it would need to be rebuilt. Because of the limitations of the lighthouse with its diminutive height, the Lighthouse Board decided to build the taller New Presque Isle Light a mile to the north on Presque Isle.

After they moved to the new lighthouse, Mary became an

assistant to her husband for the next ten years, after which one of her sons took over as assistant. Patrick and Mary had seven children in all. Four of them eventually became keepers, including one of their daughters, Anna. In fact, Mary and Anna have earned the distinction of the only mother-daughter keepers in Michigan.

I've tried to portray the Old Presque Isle Lighthouse as it originally stood. While the keeper's house the Garratys lived in is long gone (replaced by a quaint cottage), the tower remains to this day. I had the privilege of climbing the spiral stone staircase and peering out the windows over beautiful Lake Huron just as the characters in the story did.

Burnham's Landing was also a real place at the Presque Isle Harbor. Starting in the 1850s, the Burnhams acquired large tracts of Presque Isle County's rich timberland. They provided shelter to ships during foul weather, as well as selling cordwood for fuel to passing steamers. In its early days, the harbor consisted of nothing more than a couple of docks, a store, a log barn, and several shanties for fishermen.

Archdeacon William Poyseor, Holy Bill, was also a real person taken from Michigan's history. He was a circuit rider for the Episcopal Church in the small lumber towns in the UP. For the sake of the story, I moved him farther south into northern Michigan. He started as a missionary preacher in 1895 and served his scattered flock wherever he found them, traveling by Indian pony in the summer and by dogsled in the winter. He lived with parishioners and served them however he was needed and earned the beloved nickname Holy Bill because of his zeal and love for the Lord.

You may be wondering if the Great Lakes really had pirate problems as I've portrayed it in *Love Unexpected*. While there isn't as much recorded about freshwater pirates compared to the epic stories of ocean-faring pirates, we do know that pirating was a problem on the Great Lakes. I based Mitch on a real pirate, Dan Seavey, who terrorized the Great Lakes during the late 1800s and early 1900s.

Dan Seavey and his two-masted schooner the *Wanderer* would silently slip into ports in the dead of night and carry off anything of value, including venison, timber, and fish. He would even pluck cargo right off other boats. Sometimes he would extinguish lighthouse lanterns and replace them with fake lights, which caused unsuspecting ships to wreck, allowing the pirates access to their cargo.

Most often Seavey would dispose of his loot in Chicago, where the large criminal underworld didn't ask any questions. Seavey gained a reputation for smuggling liquor, turning his boat into a whorehouse and gambling casino, boat theft, common thievery, poaching, and murder.

Most of all, Seavey loved to fight. At the time, boxing didn't have many rules in place to protect fighters. Like most other northern Michigan fighters, Seavey followed a few simple rules: no knifing and no guns. A fighter could tear apart his opponent, so long as he only used his bare hands. While we have no evidence that Patrick Garraty was a fighter, I thought it added an interesting connection to the villain.

Seavey's life as a pirate was long and dangerous. He's said to have earned millions of dollars as an outlaw, although no one's sure what happened to his treasure because he didn't take it with him to the grave. He died a penniless pauper in a Wisconsin convalescent home.

Unlike Seavey, Mary Garraty earned the highest praise among the captains and sailors of the Great Lakes. When she died, the

Alpena Evening News noted that "Thousands met her when they put in at Presque Isle for shelter from storms. Many a shipwrecked sailor and passenger have known Mrs. Garraty's gentle attentions and kindly hospitality."

As you close the pages of this book, I pray you'll find hope like the heroine, that God is your home. No matter where you've wandered, no matter what you've faced, He is there as steady and constant as a lighthouse to bring you safely into His harbor where you can find rest.

Acknowledgments

*A*s with all my books, I have to start by thanking the staff at Bethany House for their hard work and dedication. I'm blessed to have such a talented publisher that strives to make each of my books the best it can be. Thank you from the bottom of my heart.

A very special thank you to my mom and daughters for going with me to visit Presque Isle Lighthouse on Lake Huron. It was a wonderful research trip, one I'll never forget.

Another huge thank you to my mother for helping provide feedback on my book. You are a saint for your willingness to devote large chunks of time to not only reading my drafts but also brainstorming and helping me think through the spiritual messages.

Thank you to my friend Nancy Willis for loaning me her lighthouse book *Lanterns & Lifeboats: A History of Thunder Bay Island* by Stephen D. Tongue, which proved to be an invaluable resource on the Thunder Bay and Presque Isle areas. And thank you to Steve Tongue for answering additional questions I had about lighthouses. I truly appreciate your willingness to share your expertise with a novice like myself.

I can't forget to thank my husband and family for their continued support of my writing career. It's not always easy to live with a writer, especially one under deadline. So thank you for doing your best to understand and put up with a writer-mom!

I want to thank my Heavenly Father for always being my hope, for making beauty out of the wrecks in my life.

And finally, dear reader, I would like to thank you for taking the time to read this book. I always love hearing from readers, so don't be shy about sending me an email at jodyhedlund@ jodyhedlund.com or visiting with me on Facebook.

Jody Hedlund is the bestselling author of several novels, including *Captured by Love*, *Rebellious Heart*, *A Noble Groom*, and *The Preacher's Bride*. She holds a bachelor's degree from Taylor University and a master's degree from the University of Wisconsin, both in social work. Jody lives in Michigan with her husband and five children. Learn more at JodyHedlund.com.

More From Jody Hedlund

To learn more about Jody and her books, visit jodyhedlund.com.

On British-occupied Michilimackinac Island, voyageur Pierre Durant and his childhood friend Angelique MacKenzie must decide where their loyalties lie and what they will risk for love.

Captured by Love

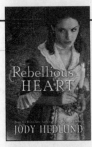

Massachusetts, 1763. When Susanna Smith and Benjamin Ross act to save the life of a runaway indentured servant, they'll risk everything for love and justice in a nation on the brink of revolution.

Rebellious Heart

Annalisa needs a husband to save her farm, but she's given up on love. Desperate, she allows her father to write to Germany for a groom. Then feelings begin to stir between Annalisa and her new farmhand. The trouble is, her husband-to-be could arrive any day.

A Noble Groom

◊ BETHANYHOUSE

Stay up-to-date on your favorite books and authors with our free e-newsletters. Sign up today at bethanyhouse.com.

Find us on Facebook. facebook.com/bethanyhousepublishers

an open book

Free exclusive resources for your book group! bethanyhouse.com/anopenbook

More Fiction You May Enjoy

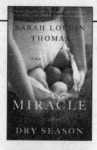

In small-town West Virginia, 1954, one newcomer's special gift with food produces both gratitude and censure. Will she and her daughter find a home in Wise—or leave brokenhearted?

Miracle in a Dry Season by Sarah Loudin Thomas
sarahloudinthomas.com

United in a quest to cure tuberculosis, can physician Trevor McDonough and statistician Kate Livingston overcome past secrets and current threats to find hope for a future together?

With Every Breath by Elizabeth Camden
elizabethcamden.com

To fulfill a soldier's dying wish, nurse Abigail Stuart marries him and promises to look after his sister. But just as the Calhouns learn to accept her, the *real* Jeremiah appears alive—and confused by more than her presence. Can Abigail provide the healing his entire family needs?

A Most Inconvenient Marriage by Regina Jennings
reginajennings.com